"'Never-Marry Margar
"I never credited that man with an ounce of wit, but I must concede him a hit for that. I love it! And it's quite apt."

"It's meant to be an *insult*," Julian protested, still angry on her behalf.

"Oh, pish-tosh. Perhaps if I really did wish to marry, I might be annoyed, but as I have no intention of altering my blessed single state, I'm only amused. I didn't expect I'd have to worry about potential suitors this Season, but can I count on your help to repel any persistent aspirants, if the need arises?"

"Of course. I'll be happy to protect you, as I did last year."

"Then I am content. Or I will be, if you will grant me another dance. Tonight was for enjoyment, but after this, I must get to work. The Season will end all too soon, and I'm determined to see my friends settled. For now—is that our dance?"

Fortunately, Julian could tell from the introductory music that the next number would not be a waltz, with its temptation to hold her too close and dream of forbidden delights. "I believe it is. If it is your pleasure, my lady?" He offered his arm.

"The only pleasure in which I can indulge...at the moment," she murmured, pressing his arm as she took it.

Author Note

Sometimes a character seizes your imagination and just won't let go. That was what happened to me with Lady Margaret D'Aubignon, younger sister of Crispin, hero of *The Railway Countess*. The not-yet-out Maggie announced her determination to escape her controlling father by marrying a wealthy older man who would leave her a rich widow. I knew that at some point I'd have to finish Maggie's story.

After Maggie was exiled for refusing to marry the man her father chose, Crispin's turning an aunt's bequest into a fortune makes Maggie suddenly wealthy and independent—without the need to marry. She sets off for London, determined to persuade her two best friends to adopt her former marriage strategy to becoming wealthy and independent.

She tries to employ the help of Julian Randall, Lord Atherton—a widower who, though he enjoys the outrageous and outspoken Maggie, thoroughly disapproves of her plan. Their friendship is further complicated by a deep attraction that, as neither wishes to marry, they both initially try to deny.

But as Maggie's plans unravel and passion grows, can these dear friends manage the affection and desire that pull them together?

I hope you will enjoy Maggie and Julian's journey.

A Season with Her Forbidden Earl

JULIA JUSTISS

HARLEQUIN®
HISTORICAL™

Recycling programs for this product may not exist in your area.

ISBN-13: 978-1-335-59613-0

A Season with Her Forbidden Earl

Harlequin Enterprises ULC
22 Adelaide St. West, 41st Floor
Toronto, Ontario M5H 4E3, Canada
www.Harlequin.com

Printed in U.S.A.

Julia Justiss wrote her own ideas for Nancy Drew stories in her third-grade notebook and has been writing ever since. After publishing poetry at university, she turned to novels. Her historical Regency romances have won or placed in contests by the Romance Writers of America, *RT Book Reviews*, National Readers' Choice and the Daphne du Maurier Award. She lives with her husband in Texas. For news and contests, visit juliajustiss.com.

Books by Julia Justiss

Harlequin Historical

Least Likely to Wed

A Season of Flirtation
The Wallflower's Last Chance Season

Heirs in Waiting

The Bluestocking Duchess
The Railway Countess
The Explorer Baroness

The Cinderella Spinsters

The Awakening of Miss Henley
The Tempting of the Governess
The Enticing of Miss Standish

Sisters of Scandal

A Most Unsuitable Match
The Earl's Inconvenient Wife

Visit the Author Profile page
at Harlequin.com for more titles.

To my darling grandchildren Anna, Samantha, Bennett, Austin and Casey. Life sometimes truly does save the best for last.

Prologue

April 1836

Pulling on her riding gloves, Lady Margaret d'Aubignon was descending the stairs at Montwell Glen when the butler appeared at the foot. 'Lady Margaret, I was just coming to fetch you,' he called.

'What is it, Viscering?' she asked, her ever-present foreboding deepening as she hastened to meet him.

Had her father given some new order? As she hadn't—recently—done anything to anger him, surely he hadn't banned her from riding. Although as she knew only too well, the Earl of Comeryn didn't need a reason for the arbitrary dictates he issued.

'Nothing alarming, my lady,' the butler reassured her. 'Only there's a courier with a message for you. He's waiting outside.'

A message sent by private courier? Arriving on a Friday morning, when her father was away from Montwell Glen at his weekly meeting with the JP in the village, the letter must be from her brother Crispin—who knew the Earl's routine as well as she did. It also meant the missive must contain something he didn't want their father to intercept.

'Thank you, Viscering. I'll be off on my morning ride

after I collect it.' She increased her pace, trying to restrain her desperate hope. Had Crispin's venture succeeded? Might she be free at last?

Hurrying through the door and down the front steps, she met the rider, who bowed. 'A letter for you, my lady.'

She took it eagerly, noting with a leap of excitement that her name was indeed inscribed in Crispin's hand. 'Are you to wait for a reply?'

'No, my lady. The sender said I might leave once the letter was delivered.'

'Go round by the kitchen first and ask for Anna. She'll see that you get a meal and have your mount tended before you ride back.'

'Thank 'ee, my lady.' The rider doffed his cap again before leading his horse off.

Repressing the desire to break the seal and scan it immediately, she made herself tuck it inside her jacket and walk at a sedate pace towards the stables. Any of her father's spies who might be watching would have noted she'd received a message, but their attention might wane if she didn't seem very eager to read it.

At the stable, she discovered to her relief that Higgins, her secret ally, was available to ride with her. Even supervised, she was not permitted to go farther than the north pasture, but when she was fortunate enough to snag Higgins as her escort, once they were out of sight of the house, the groom lagged behind and gave her some privacy.

Still, not until they reached the copse of trees bordering the pasture's farthest point did she dismount and leave Mahogany to graze.

'I'll keep watch as usual, m'lady,' Higgins said, nodding to her before she walked off.

Once far under the sheltering trees, she pulled out the letter, broke the seal and quickly scanned it.

Her heartbeat accelerated and a wild joy seized her. 'Halleluiah!' she cried, kissing the parchment before reading it again, the rest of the information it contained blurring beneath her tears as she focused on the most important words.

...investment succeeded beyond my fondest hopes... handsome sum deposited in London bank...will come to Montwell Glen next week to escort you to London...

She was indeed free, she and her mother, with the means to escape the Earl's restrictions for ever. As she would inform her father when he returned tonight.

But she had no intention of waiting a week to make her escape. She would gather Mama and a few belongings and steal away tomorrow before first light. Before the Earl of Comeryn could devise a way to prevent her.

Chapter One

A few days later, Maggie was walking along Bond Street in London, a footman carrying the packages from her first shopping expedition, when a voice from behind called out, 'Lady Margaret?'

She looked back, surprise turning to delight as she recognised the speaker. 'Atherton!' she cried as the Earl hastened to meet her. 'What a pleasant surprise.'

'It really is you!' the Earl said, smiling. 'I wasn't sure I could believe my eyes—I thought perhaps I had only conjured you, like a mirage. You are back in London, then? How did you manage it?'

'A long story,' she said drily.

'I can't wait to hear it. You've been shopping, I see. You must need some refreshment. Would you join me at Gunter's for tea and cakes?'

'Tea and cakes sound lovely. Jackson,' she said to the footman, 'please take my purchases back to Portman Square and inform the Countess when she returns that I will be taking tea with Lord Atherton at Gunter's. Have the carriage return for me in—' she looked back to the Earl '—an hour?'

'No need for that. I'll send for my phaeton and drive you home, so it will be quite proper. We can have a good chat and not worry about the time.'

'I accept your offer, then. Jackson, if you'll have Mama informed that Lord Atherton will drive me home?'

After dismissing the footman, she turned back to the Earl. 'What a happy chance to meet you on my very first excursion in London! Which, by the way, is why I was so rude as to not ask you back to Portman Square for tea. We arrived only yesterday, and as the house has been shut up since last year, everything is at sixes and sevens. We came on ahead with just horses, grooms and a maid, so I'm afraid we're not quite ready for company.'

'Your company is all that's required. Shall we?' he said, offering her his arm.

Smiling, Maggie took his arm, surprised at first by the little shock that tingled up her fingers. Though she shouldn't be.

He'd affected her just as strongly during her disastrous Season last year, when she'd briefly considered him as a marriage candidate. Apparently, time hadn't weakened the attraction.

Handsome, witty, charming and older—but not old enough for her purposes—despite that strong physical pull, she'd managed to turn him from potential suitor to friend. Next to her brother Crispin, he'd become her best and dearest male one.

Now that she was back in London, she might have the delight of continuing that friendship. As long as she could keep that pesky sensual attraction under control.

Of course you can, she told herself stoutly. *Just ignore it and enjoy him being handsome, witty and charming.*

'I'm as relieved as I am delighted to discover you back,' the Earl was saying. 'Given the…circumstances of your leaving town so abruptly last year, I've been worried about you.'

'Worried because my father literally dragged me out of

that last ball after he'd announced my engagement to Lord Tolleridge and I emphatically denied it?'

'Did he think you could be cowed into going through with it if he made such a public announcement?' Atherton asked. 'That you would be too afraid of being ostracised for being a jilt?'

'I suppose, though he should have known me better. But then, the Earl of Comeryn often thinks the world should arrange itself as he wishes, despite reason or reality.'

'The episode at the ball was alarming enough, but when I called the next day and found you'd been whisked to the countryside... I was about to manufacture an excuse to visit Montwell Glen and check on you when I received your letter.'

'Thank heavens you did not! With you an eligible widowed gentleman, my father would have engineered some way to get us into what he would have deemed a "compromising situation", then used your sense of honour to force you to marry me.' She grinned. 'Us, married? What a way to spoil a friendship!'

Though there might have been compensations, she thought, another tingle travelling from his arm to her fingertips.

Atherton chuckled. 'I cannot thank you enough for writing and letting me know you were...well.'

Well... Maggie grimaced, remembering the chamber into which she'd been locked for weeks, the Earl's way of expressing his displeasure at her refusal to bend to his will. 'As well as could be expected,' she replied noncommittally. 'Mama was distraught enough on my behalf, she mustered the bravery to send my letters under her seal. Fortunately, her correspondence has always been so vast the Earl never thought to check her letters or their replies for...inclusions.'

'I'm just glad she continued to act as intermediary, so I knew at least something of what was going on. But you never hinted you were returning to London.'

By now they'd reached Berkeley Square. After exchanging greetings with acquaintances taking refreshment in their carriages beneath the plane trees, the Earl led her to a table. 'So, tea and cakes? Or would you prefer ices?'

'Tea, I think.'

After giving the waiter their order and sending a message to summon his phaeton, Atherton said, 'Tell me, then, how did you come to return to town? Did the Earl finally relent?'

Maggie made a scornful noise. 'You should know my father better than that. Now,' she lowered her voice, 'I'll tell *you* the truth, but you must keep it in confidence. Not that I care about Society's opinion of my father, but I do want to protect Mama.'

'Surely you know I would never reveal anything you said to me in confidence!'

She patted his hand, frowning as another spark sizzled through her. Shaking it off, she continued, 'I do know. I just want to emphasise that it's best the real story not get out—at least for the present. After the Earl hauled me back to Montwell Glen, my brother Crispin visited and tried to plead for me. The Earl, still furious at my rejecting his crony, refused to lift his order of banishment, but he did allow Crispin to see me. My brother offered to approach Lady Ulmstead, my mother's aunt—the one, you may remember, who gave Crispin the funds he used for his initial railway investments—and ask if she would advance me the sum she'd intended to leave me as a bequest for him to invest on my behalf. Should the investment prosper, it would create a fund large enough for me to live independently of my father, and as I've just turned one-and-twenty, the Earl would not be able to prevent me. Well, Aunt Ulmstead agreed, Crispin's investment was wildly successful, and so—' she gestured towards herself '—you see before you an independently wealthy woman!'

'Bravo, Lady Margaret! That's excellent news! So the Earl was forced to swallow this? I can't imagine he was very happy.'

The waiter returned then with their refreshments, halting conversation while she poured tea and dispensed cakes.

Maggie smiled grimly as she did so, remembering the confrontation in her father's library the night after Crispin's message arrived. Her father's hiss of fury when she revealed her change of fortune and informed him that her brother would come the following week to help her move to London. His shouted response that by now both she and his heir should know better than to try and defy him. She stood her ground, having already planned a stealthy exit with her mother at dawn before Comeryn could imprison her again or devise some other means to foil her plans.

She felt anew the bitter satisfaction of knowing that never again would the tyrant be able to lock her away or control her.

'He wasn't happy,' she resumed after they'd sipped their tea. 'I informed him that I had sufficient funds in a London bank to support an independent establishment, and that I intended to take Mama with me to London and stay at an hotel until we found a suitable house. Unless he would allow us to reside, without interference, at Comeryn House.'

She let the Earl digest her words and smiled when, a moment later, he chuckled. 'What a devious female you are! He must have been doubly furious at that! Realising what a scandal it would cause if his wife and unmarried daughter established a separate residence. Only if you remained at Comeryn House, ostensibly under your father's authority, could you live in London without setting Society on its ear.'

'Exactly,' she confirmed. 'Although, frankly, were it not for my desire to have Mama resume her rightful place in Society, I would have insisted on living elsewhere. But she's endured enough all these years, married to him. I wanted her to finally be able to visit the friends with whom she's corresponded so faithfully and fully participate in the Society she's been denied, without a scandal of my making impeding her.'

'Living anywhere but Comeryn House would ruin your reputation, too,' Atherton pointed out. 'Or at least render you such an oddity as to compromise your eligibility and limit your acceptance by Society.'

Maggie shrugged. 'Now that I have funds and can live as I choose, I don't intend ever to marry, so I'm not concerned about what Society thinks of me. Even so, I will safeguard my social position long enough to accomplish my next goal. Which is why I ask that the true circumstances of my return to London remain concealed for the present.'

'Done. So, what is this "next goal"?'

'You may remember the two good friends I made during my debut Season—Lady Laura Pomeroy and Miss Eliza Hasterling?'

'The tall, graceful blonde and the quiet little brunette?'

'Yes. We became very close last Season—I now count them as the sisters I always wanted. So that they are safe and we can remain dear friends for ever, I intend to help them attain the same security and independence I now have. Unfortunately, neither has an obliging relation to give them money to invest, so they will have to follow the more traditional path—marriage. But I mean to find husbands for them who are wealthy enough and elderly enough to soon leave them rich widows. In our Society, the only female truly in control of her own life—aside from an oddity like me—is a rich widow.'

Atherton stared at her a moment. 'You're joking, of course.'

'Indeed not! I wouldn't joke about something as important as my dear friends' happiness.'

'But what you suggest is…preposterous!'

'Why so? Calculated, perhaps, but why is such a plan any more reprehensible than an ambitious Mama scheming to marry her daughter to a high title? Or a girl trying to snare a wealthy husband? Both aims are thought quite acceptable. I'm not suggesting they marry men for whom they care nothing. Respect and affection are essential.'

'It still sounds cold and calculating to me.'

Maggie waved an impatient hand. 'Given that, once married, her person, life, and fortune is entirely controlled by her husband, a female would have to be stupid not to carefully consider her choice—if she is indeed given a choice. Why should you think it despicable that I would match my dear friends to wealthy older gentlemen who will treat them kindly but leave them time to live their lives as they, and only they, wish? Doing so is a man's birthright!'

'Not so!' he countered. 'Gentlemen are often obligated to marry for family or financial reasons.'

'True. Another reason why my proposition shouldn't incite your disapproval. Marriage is often arranged for practical rather than romantic reasons—a much more reasonable basis for marriage, in my opinion. But once wed, a man still controls his own destiny. A woman does not. If she is neglected, her needs and desires ignored, the law offers no recourse, and often even her own family will not assist her. And that fact you cannot dispute.'

Her mother's married life was a vivid illustration of that truth. By now, Atherton knew enough about her family not to be able to argue the point.

After hesitating a moment, he replied, 'That may be true. But not every marriage becomes a sad union which the wife regrets. Only consider your brother's relationship with Marcella.'

'No, not every marriage is unhappy—at least at first,' she conceded. 'But over the long run, enough turn sour that I'd rather secure for my friends the most favourable circumstances. The plan I'm proposing is, after all, the same one I was following for myself before my last Season was abruptly curtailed.'

Atherton raised his eyebrows. 'You planned on finding an older husband? Is that why you encouraged me?'

Maggie grinned. 'Initially. But I soon concluded that, though rather older than me, you were too young and healthy to be a suitable candidate.'

And altogether too attractive for a girl determined never to fall in love, she added silently to herself.

Atherton stared at her, then shook his head. 'You are the most outrageous female! I'm not sure whether to feel gratified or insulted.'

'Besides, you're titled,' Maggie continued, 'and I wish them to wed wealthy commoners. Aristocrats like my father are too often arrogant and controlling, believing the world should accommodate itself to their views.'

'Which is why you tried to discourage Lord Tolleridge?'

Maggie shuddered, remembering the viscount's cold, snake-eyed stare. 'I would have discouraged him even if

he weren't Father's friend and titled. There's something…
so unpleasant about him.'

'You'd do well to avoid him now that you're back in London. I doubt he took your public rejection of his suit any
better than your father did.'

'A recommendation I am happy to follow, as I have no
wish to associate with him. Happily, *I* no longer need to
focus on marrying an elderly suitor to attain my independence. I shall employ all my efforts on behalf of Laura and
Eliza instead.'

Atherton raised a sceptical eyebrow. 'What do your friends
think of your Grand Plan?'

'I've not yet broached it with them,' Maggie admitted.
'But I will soon. Even now, Mama is calling on friends,
making discreet enquiries about the most promising candidates this Season. Of course, I would never promote to
my friends any gentlemen whose characters had not been
completely vetted, so you could help with—'

Atherton held up his hand. 'Stop right there! I appreciate your good intentions. I know you only want the best for
your friends. But rather than try to manoeuvre them into a
relationship of your making, wouldn't it be wiser for *them*
to choose who will make them happy?'

'And so they will!' Maggie countered. 'I simply intend
to bring promising candidates to their attention. Whether
or not to pursue any particular relationship will be entirely
up to them.'

'That relieves my mind—somewhat. I still feel your attempting to manipulate their suitors is a mistake. So don't
even think of asking me to help.'

'Not even to verify from your contacts—male contacts I
have no way to access—that the information I obtain about
them is correct?'

Atherton blew out a sigh. 'I suppose I can agree to confirming a prospective suitor's character. But nothing else. I would still ask you to consider abandoning this project entirely.'

Maggie grinned. 'You can ask. But, having secured my own freedom—oh, happy day!—I can't help wanting the same independence for Eliza and Lady Laura.'

'You realise they may not be as enthusiastic about this idea as you are.'

'Perhaps not. Though Lady Laura is wrapped up in her studies and caring for her father who, as you know, never fully recovered from that carriage accident, she must marry sometime. And Eliza just wants an establishment of her own. Why should considering kind, older gentlemen as potential husbands not be viewed as an acceptable option?'

Shaking his head at her, Atherton said, 'You're nothing if not tenacious once you've taken hold of an idea. But I suppose a female who can resist a man as strong-willed as the Earl of Comeryn has to be...determined. It must have taken tremendous strength of mind not to end up as controlled by him as your poor Mama.'

Maggie laughed. 'At the risk of tarnishing the shiny image you seem to have of my bravery, I must confess remaining independent didn't require much fortitude. As the youngest offspring, and a mere female at that, Comeryn simply ignored me. Elizabeth married while I was still a child, my brother James left for India shortly after and Crispin dealt with the Earl, so I was left very much to my own devices. Not until Crispin broke with Comeryn to forge his own path and I took up his role of supporting Mama did we begin to clash. Even then, the skirmishes were brief—I generally lost—and didn't become serious until I refused to bow to his matrimonial wishes. The affrontery of me, rejecting a man who'd agreed to forgo a dowry, thereby preventing the Earl from devoting the funds to his own use!'

'How could the Earl touch the money set aside for your dowry?'

'Mama's marriage settlements didn't specify that a certain amount be reserved for me. So, once they wed, all her funds were Comeryn's to use as he pleased. After he struck a deal with Tolleridge, he'd been priding himself on getting a useless daughter off his hands without having to part with any blunt. Hence his anger at me for spoiling his plans.'

'Any father worth the name should have gladly expended the funds to see you married to someone else.'

'Well, there you have it. Now, I intend to make sure my dear friends are much more comfortably situated than—save for Crispin's intervention—I would have been.'

'On that point, I can agree! Just don't push your friends too hard.'

'You'll be sure to restrain me if I try. I shall see you often during the rest of the Season, shall I not? You don't have plans to return to Atherton Hall?'

'I'll make periodic visits, but with the spring planting finished and everything proceeding as it should, I intend to remain here for the Season.'

And look for…suitable female company? It was well known that, since his bereavement, the widowed earl had made discreet arrangements with a succession of willing matrons, each liaison lasting no longer than a Season.

After viewing her mother's distress at her father's wanderings, she had no desire to experience such humiliation first-hand. Though Atherton was in all other ways far more admirable than her father, she wasn't sure he was capable of fidelity. Had he been faithful during his marriage?

It wasn't a question she could ask, of course—another reason she'd eliminated him as a matrimonial prospect.

Her determination to avoid the emotional entanglements that had doomed her mother didn't make her immune to Atherton's physical appeal, though. At the thought of the strong arm she'd leaned on while they walked to Gunter's wrapped around another woman, Maggie felt a pang of— surely it couldn't be *jealousy*?

She might find his touch thrilling, but the sad reality was, as a single lady rather than a dashing widow, she wouldn't be able to indulge in such pleasures.

Shaking away such thoughts, she said, 'Then I shall look forward to enjoying your escort—if you are not too occupied gratifying the desires of some voluptuous matron.'

A faint flush colouring his face, Atherton said, 'That's not a fit subject for discussion with you.'

Maggie waved away his protest. 'Come now, you wouldn't like me half as much if I were some die-away female who pretended to know nothing about what goes on between men and women. To say nothing of being hypocritical in the extreme, as I've been aware of my father's little "arrangements" since I was hardly out of leading strings. If I can persuade you to help me, if only to verify the character of my prospects, I shall be most grateful.'

'My help shall remain very limited indeed,' Atherton warned.

Satisfied to have coaxed from him even that concession, Maggie changed subjects. 'What of your boys? Are they all settled at school?'

She smiled to see Atherton's eyes light up. If he still mourned his late wife—the reason gossip said he'd never remarried, despite the many lures cast his way since he came out of mourning six years ago—he kept those feelings close. Not wishing to stir up unhappy memories, she'd always avoided asking him about the late Lady Atherton. But his delight in his three sons was charmingly apparent.

'They are back at school—I stayed in Kent until they had to leave for the next term. Stephen's become a crack shot and an excellent horseman, Mark is always up to mischief, and both have promised to look out for Edward. It's his first time at boarding school, you may remember.'

'I'm glad he'll have his big brothers to protect him. Boys can be brutal, I understand. You must miss them.'

Atherton sighed. 'I do. At ten, eight and six, they are now old enough to ride out with me to visit tenants, go hunting or fishing, play a rousing game of cards, and Stephen even challenges me at chess. But…they must be at school, so here I am.'

'I should get home,' Maggie said regretfully, setting down her tea cup. 'There's much to do to set up the house so Mama can entertain her friends. Fortunately, we expect Viscering imminently to help bring all to order.' She grinned. 'Now that our removal to London is a fait accompli, the *ton* would find it very strange if our butler had remained at Montwell Glen.'

Atherton laughed out loud. 'The cruellest blow of all! Stealing your father's butler out from under his nose!'

After chuckling herself, Maggie said, 'You must come for tea very soon so we can compare diaries and determine which entertainments we've both been invited to. I'm looking forward to dancing with you again. And you *must* partner me at cards.'

'Are you planning to fleece your friends even now that you are independently wealthy? Or are your funds tied up such that you need to augment your pin money?'

'No, I'll play for the enjoyment of it. Though a little extra income never hurt. It's always more entertaining to play with an intelligent partner, and we did make a good pair.'

'So we did. I'll be happy to dance and partner you—at cards or anything else you require.'

Maggie sobered. 'I left London so precipitously last year I never had a chance to thank you for all your help. Intervening to keep Tolleridge at a distance. Acting the suitor to protect me from my father while I evaluated other choices.'

'It was my pleasure.' Atherton stared down at her, his intent expression holding her motionless. Had she ever appreciated what a deep velvet green his eyes were? Like the depths of a verdant forest at midsummer. His eyes were as potently attractive as the rest of him...

Captured by the force of his gaze, she had to struggle to look away. 'Thankfully, with no need any longer to avoid suitors, we can simply enjoy our friendship. Promise me I'll see you again soon.'

Friendship will be enough, she told herself, squelching the lingering regret that there could never be more.

'Send me a note once you are ready to entertain. In the interim, perhaps we could go riding some morning?'

'I would love that! Once my schedule is settled, I'll let you know when I am free.'

'Excellent. Ah, I see Welsh nodding from the entrance— he'll have brought my phaeton around. Shall we go?'

Conscious of both the warmth of their renewed relationship and a tinge of regret at ending the interlude, Maggie reminded herself they would soon meet again. Hopefully, by then she would have thought of a way to persuade him to cooperate more fully with her Grand Plan.

She'd need to discuss it with Laura and Eliza first, of course. How wonderful it would be to see them again!

Even more wonderful to imagine them married to suitable husbands, on their own paths to eventually achieving financial and personal independence. What great times they could have together, once they were all free! She couldn't wait to begin the process.

During the drive back to Portman Square, Atherton gave her a summary of who among her former acquaintances had returned to London this Season and a rundown of which plays and entertainments were currently available. She sat contently beside him, enjoying the delicious thrill of his tall, virile body just a touch away.

And if she occasionally allowed herself to imagine what it might be like, were she one of the dashing matrons with whom he could establish a more intimate connection, what harm was there in that?

She would never try to entice him to it. Her sole purposes for re-entering Society were to return her mother to the city she loved and achieve the proper sort of marriages for her friends.

What she meant to do after, she wasn't yet sure. But while she worked towards getting them married, having Atherton's friendship, occasional escort and possible assistance in accomplishing her goals would be the sweet dessert to a satisfying meal.

The following day, Maggie sat in the parlour at Comeryn House, serving tea to Lady Laura Pomeroy and Miss Eliza Hasterling. After explaining how she'd come to return to town and accepting their congratulations on becoming an independent woman, she described her Grand Plan for them achieve a similar freedom.

Once Maggie finished, Eliza stared at her, open-mouthed, while Lady Laura said, 'You propose that we marry older commoners who will likely die soon and leave us rich widows?'

'Exactly,' she replied with an encouraging nod.

'You can't be serious,' Lady Laura said flatly.

'I'm entirely serious! It was the goal I was pursuing myself until, with Aunt Ulmstead and Crispin's help, I was able to become independent by other means.'

After Lady Laura and Eliza exchanged dubious glances, Eliza said, 'I suppose it wouldn't hurt to entertain the idea of an older husband. Quite frankly, my family can't afford to give me another Season. I'm not a beauty like Laura, possess next to no dowry, and generally remain mute in Society, so I'm hardly likely to arouse burning passion in some handsome young lord.'

'Which is a good thing! Falling in love is highly overrated, at least for a female,' Maggie asserted. 'Such rapturous fancy can blind a woman to the faults of a prospective husband—and once wed, she is trapped. Only look at my poor Mama! Despite the wealth she brought to her marriage, Comeryn wouldn't even allow her the funds to spend the Season in London. And once she'd produced his heir and spare, whatever charm he'd exerted on her early in their relationship was used to entice other women. Just recall the silly girls in love last Season—some sighing over men who ignored them, and even those with admirers who shared their ardour finding themselves in agony over every disagreement. I would have you both avoid such misery. Much better an amicable arrangement with an older gentleman— who might still give you the children you desire, Eliza, and be as intelligent and interesting a companion for you, Laura, as your father has been.'

'I'm in no hurry to wed,' Lady Laura said. 'I've been assisting Miss Rochdale, that young heiress I mentioned, to adjust to Society. And Father's condition seems to be gradually worsening, which…worries me.'

Maggie squeezed her hand. 'All the more reason for you to get settled! Your father would feel easier knowing you have a husband to protect you when he is no longer able to.'

'What of you?' Eliza asked. 'You have the independence you've always sought and no longer need to marry. But what of family? Children of your own?'

'Surely you don't believe all men are like Lord Comeryn,' Laura said.

As she'd never revealed to them the worst of her treatment at the Earl's hands, she couldn't expect them to understand the depth of her determination never to place herself again under any man's power.

'Not all are as bad as the Earl,' she conceded. 'But I shall not gamble my future on being lucky enough to end up with a man who remains as devoted after marriage as he appears when he's trying to woo a wealthy wife. I'll have Marcella and Crispin's children to spoil—she's increasing, you know. And never would I cede control over my wealth to a husband who could spend it however he liked while denying me a ha'penny! No, I intend to revel in my freedom. A freedom I am eager for you both to experience.'

'By becoming rich widows,' Lady Laura said dubiously.

'I do so want you both to be safe, secure and happy! I know what I'm proposing might seem somewhat…shocking. I just ask that you both consider it. Promise me?'

'I suppose we can promise that much,' Lady Laura said, while Eliza nodded agreement. 'But I should be getting home now. Papa is expecting me.'

'I've pledged to read to my sister's children,' Eliza said as both friends set down their cups and rose.

'We will get together soon and decide which entertainments we all wish to attend,' Maggie said as she walked her friends to the door. 'I'm so glad to be back in London and together again!'

Once they considered the matter, surely her friends would recognise the benefits of her plan, Maggie thought optimistically as she returned to the sofa. She must determine what sort of gathering would best show off the qualities of tall, blond, intellectual Laura. The musical talents of petite, quiet, retiring Eliza.

While she sat pondering her next step, Viscering walked in. 'This just came for you, Lady Margaret.'

Pleased to recognise Atherton's crest on the seal, she opened and read the short message proposing that they ride the following morning.

'Send Jackson to my sitting room in half an hour, won't you? I'll have a reply ready.'

Maggie walked back to her chamber, pleased by the day's progress. She would discuss potential candidates with Mama when she returned and, during their ride tomorrow, ask the Earl's insight into the characters of the proposed candidates.

The bright glow she felt at the prospect of seeing Atherton again, she told herself as she took up her pen, was just eager anticipation at the chance to forward her plans for her friends.

Chapter Two

As Julian directed his horse to the park the next morning for his ride with Lady Margaret, he thought again about their previous meeting.

As vivacious—and outrageous—as he remembered, she seemed...thinner, he recalled, concern setting his lips in a grim line. Though she'd mentioned nothing of the sort in her letters—which were invariably light-hearted, describing rides in the countryside and minor domestic disasters—he wouldn't put it past Comeryn to have locked her up for a time on bread and water.

He cordially despised Lord Tolleridge, who was rumoured to have an appetite for young females and few scruples about how he satisfied it. He had even less use for Maggie's father, the Earl of Comeryn.

Having observed the Earl's dismissive treatment of his gentle wife, Julian had been aware of Comeryn's selfish, controlling nature even before he banished his disobedient daughter. He'd both admired Maggie's courage and worried about her welfare when she defied her father by publicly rejecting Tolleridge.

After discovering she'd been whisked off to the country, he'd seriously considered going after her and offering marriage, just to allow her to escape the man's control. Even though, with three healthy sons to secure his earldom's succession, he had no desire whatsoever to marry again.

Julian couldn't help noting that, despite her loss of weight, Maggie's figure was still curvaceous enough to have stirred desire in an older gentleman who ought to think of her only as an amusing, innocent friend. But when he touched her hand…warmth zinged through his fingers at the memory and heat pooled in his belly.

Trying to banish the sensations, he recalled her comment about finding some voluptuous matron to gratify his desires. Magdalena Barkley had been that lady last Season. Though she'd entered the relationship with the clear and he'd thought mutual expectation it might be temporary, she had not been happy when he'd ended it.

Despite the urging of his deprived senses, weariness over the repeatedly disappointing course of such associations made him resist renewing the game of flirtation, innuendo and negotiation that could lead to another liaison. He'd begun each new relationship with the vague hope of finding a long-term companion and partner, perhaps even a wife who'd replace the mother his boys had lost—though Society women weren't known for being attentive to their own offspring, often consigning their care to wet nurses and nannies. But the affairs always seemed to end up, as the one with Magdalena had, with the lady wanting more of him than he had to give.

Through adolescence and university, he'd witnessed friends falling in love with various ladies, from ineligible bar maids to heiresses. Having never experienced such all-consuming emotion himself, by the time his father's ill-health prompted his sire to urge his son and heir to marry, he'd looked to make a sensible match based on mutual fondness and respect—and with Sarah Anne Mayfield, daughter of a long-time family friend, he'd thought he had.

Not until after they were wed did his wife begin showering him with a passionate, suffocating devotion, her needy gaze following his every move, begging for a reciprocal feeling he couldn't give her. Making him dread returning home to see the reproach and disappointment in her eyes.

Never a man who favoured hopping from bed to bed, he might long for permanent companionship. But never again did he want to put himself in the position of being responsible for—and always falling short of insuring—another lady's happiness.

Maybe Lady Margaret's goal of having her friends wed genial older gentlemen who valued companionship over passion wasn't so outrageous after all.

Though he'd still insist it should be the ladies themselves, not the managing Lady Margaret, who did the choosing.

Managing, and most unusual, he concluded with a grin. Without being a conceited coxcomb, as a wealthy earl, he knew he was considered a very desirable parti. Since becoming a widower, he'd been careful not to raise expectations in any marriage-minded maidens. It had been Maggie's sudden loss of interest in trying to attract him last Season that had prompted him to pursue a relationship he would otherwise have avoided. Her independent spirit and blunt, honest, often outrageous commentary on Society piqued his interest and fostered a desire to shield her from Tolleridge.

It was both intriguing and refreshing to spend time with a female who harboured no matrimonial designs—who indeed, unlike any other female he'd ever met, seemed to prefer *not* depending on a man. Over the course of that aborted Season, they'd developed a friendship—unusual as such a relationship between an unrelated and unmarried man and woman might be—that he looked forward to continuing.

A simple friendship, he reminded himself, was what they both sought.

No matter how potent the desire she aroused in him.

Besides, if she ever were to marry, the beguiling Lady Margaret deserved a man who *could* pledge a devotion as passionate as the one his late wife had offered him.

Riding through the park gates, Julian spotted Lady Margaret turning her gelding onto Rotten Row. He felt a warm glow of anticipation as she reined in and smiled at him.

'Good morning!' she called. 'Before we chat, shall we have a good gallop while the park is still deserted?'

'Midnight and I are ready. Shall we?' He gestured down the empty carriage way.

In answer, she clicked her heels and set off.

For few minutes, they simply enjoyed the rhythmic pounding of hooves, the rush of wind, the thrill of the ground-eating pace as their mounts raced side by side. Not until the horses began to tire did they pull up and slow them to a walk.

'That was splendid!' Maggie said, beaming at Atherton. 'I love being back in London, but I will miss riding for hours around the estate.'

'Nothing like a good gallop,' Atherton agreed. With a chuckle, he added, 'I enjoy it more without my boys. With them trying to outdo one another, I'm always worried one will take a tumble and break his neck. I counsel caution, but often as not, they don't listen.'

'Did you, at their age?'

'Probably not,' he admitted. 'Do you ride neck-or-nothing at Montwell Glen? It's rolling hill country, isn't it?'

'Yes, with pretty woods and some lovely vistas from

our park, but enough level paths to allow for a good gallop. Growing up with no siblings near in age, I'm lucky my temperament was suited to solitude and country rides. There's not much in the village beside a bake house, forge, livery stable and a single posting inn. I'd be starved for entertainment if I were not able to enjoy the wide outdoors and my own company.'

'Nothing to look forward to but a meat pastie from the bakery or perhaps a mug of cider at the posting inn? No window shopping for bonnets or consultations with the dressmaker?'

'A sweet from the bakery was the only treat on offer. But since until recently, I wasn't much interested in gowns and bonnets, I didn't feel the lack. Mama's maid is an expert seamstress, able to make up the fashions Mama chose from her ladies' magazines. Of course, for mine and my sister's presentations, gowns needed to be commissioned in London anyway.'

'Is there much visiting back and forth among the gentry?'

Maggie made a scoffing sound. 'As you can imagine, knowing my father, there are few individuals he considers worthy of being graced with his presence, and none in the vicinity. The Squire was occasionally invited to dine, and of course all the tenants and villagers came for outdoor gatherings during fetes and feast days, but with the closest family of rank more than a day's ride away, we didn't entertain very often.'

'Your mama truly was isolated all those years.'

'Yes, which is why I'm so delighted to bring her back to London. After the rest of my siblings left home, she had no companions of rank besides me to keep her company. One reason, I suppose, she carried on such a voluminous correspondence. I should go mad, were I not able to get out and walk or ride, but she has the inner serenity to make herself content whatever she was doing, spending hours on needlework, reading or the piano. A fortunate quality, as she was mostly ignored when Comeryn put in an appearance.'

'Did your father not at least dine with you?' Atherton asked curiously.

'Sometimes, though less and less after my brothers left Montwell Glen. As the Earl considered my mother an inferior conversationalist, he often took dinner alone in his library, or at the inn if he ended the day near the village. And he was frequently away, to London for Parliament or to visit the estates of other landowners. Believe me, we were both happiest when he was not at home.'

She frowned. 'Well, I was happiest. Comeryn's decades of neglect and indifference never completely extinguished Mama's memory of a time when he'd apparently played the gallant knight, loving her as she did him. Or seeming to. *Love*,' she scoffed. 'It…pained me to see the hurt in her eyes, always longing, always disappointed. I vowed then never to do anything so foolish as to fall in love.'

'With that sentiment I agree entirely,' Julian said feelingly.

'Too wrenching to lose your love, I suppose?' she asked softly, obviously referring to his wife.

For a moment, Julian was tempted to confess the truth. But the fear that admitting it might make her believe him as callous and unfeeling as the man who had scorned the gift of her mother's love kept him silent.

'How did you occupy your time if the weather was too inclement for walking or riding? I seem to remember you are *not* fond of needlework.'

Tacitly accepting his change of subject, she said, 'No,

I'm hopeless. No patience, and with me likely to end up with more holes in my fingers than stitches in the material, Mama soon excused me from sewing duties. I enjoy playing piano and my late grandfather ensured that the library at Montwell Glen was well-stocked. I've loved browsing there since I was old enough to know my letters. In the evenings, I would read aloud to Mama as she worked. Or we'd play cards.'

'Ah, practising your tricks to fleece your opponents once you had some?'

'Polishing skills, not tricks,' she protested. 'I admit, I am ready for more lively evenings. Which brings me back to discussing the immediate future.'

Atherton groaned. 'Is this where you start pressing me to support your campaign to marry off your friends?'

'You did agree to review the candidates Mama discovered and confirm there is nothing in their characters that might disqualify them. I wouldn't want to introduce to my friends any gentleman I later discover possess some vice, hidden in female company but known among men.'

'So I did,' Atherton confirmed reluctantly. 'But nothing more!'

'I shall hold you to it! Mama has come up with several possibilities. I'd like to name them to you and, if you cannot immediately vouch for them, have you keep a discreet ear out at your clubs for any rumours of indiscretion or vice. You could do that, couldn't you?'

He sighed. 'I can't talk you out of this?'

'Not a chance.'

'Would it not be better for your friends to find on their own the suitors they prefer?' Atherton said, trying once again to deflect her determination.

'I'll be delighted if they do. But there is nothing wrong with giving them a wider choice.'

Giving up the attempt, he said, 'Who am I to spy on?'

She gave him a reproving look. 'Discreet enquiries only are required, and only if you should hear something that demands further exploration. About the first candidate you need do nothing, as he is well known to my mother—Thornton Fullridge. The family is from Westmoreland; Fullridge's eldest son is now managing Greenlands, their manor there, as he lately purchased another estate, Fullridge Manor, in Essex.'

'Sounds eminently eligible,' he said without enthusiasm, already regretting he'd agreed to assist her.

'The other three candidates were suggested by her friends—Bixby Garthorpe, of Garthorpe Grange in Kent, Lyle Knottingsford, of Selby Green, Wiltshire and Arnold Wanlock, of Prior's Grove, Sussex. All older, wealthy commoners, therefore perfect candidates. Are you acquainted with any of them?'

Atherton frowned. 'Not personally. Garthorpe is a member at Brooks; I believe I've seen him in the card room. Knottingsford and Wanlock belong to White's. I don't recall hearing anything negative about the character of any of them. I suppose I could make discreet enquires, just to be sure. But I will consider you in my debt!'

'I'm happy to be in your debt, if it will insure the well-being of my friends.'

'You might consider the terms of repayment,' he said, looking over with a lazy smile.

'Why? Have you something in mind?' She angled up a teasing gaze, her lips slightly parted, immediately rekindling a desire he now realised had been smouldering under the surface since the moment he'd seen her riding towards him.

His gaze strayed from her eyes to focus on her mouth. Did those tempting, parted lips indicate she might be thinking about a kiss? He'd be delighted to oblige, he knew, his mouth tingling at the thought. Even better, to draw her close, feel her soft curves against him…

But he shouldn't be indulging in carnal thoughts—not about her. Jerking his gaze free, he said, 'I'll think of something.'

Forcing himself to refocus on the conversation, he continued, 'After you manage to get your friends settled, what do you intend to do? Since you've already stated rather emphatically you are not interested in trolling the Marriage Mart to find a partner for yourself.'

'No more than you have been!' she retorted. 'I'm…not sure. I might like to travel. I did a good deal of reading while I was incarcerated at Montwell Glen—'

'*Incarcerated*?' he interrupted, alarmed. 'What do you mean?'

Lady Margaret flushed, pausing before continuing, 'Well, you know. I should have said, while I was *exiled* in the country.'

'One doesn't usually lose several pounds, just rusticating,' he said quietly, his earlier worry about her welfare resurfacing. 'While he was confining you, did your father try to starve you into submission?'

Her flush deepening, she sat silent, as if not able or willing to reply. Uttering a curse under his breath, he said quickly, 'You needn't answer. I don't mean to pry. I'm just… concerned for you.'

To his distress, tears brimmed in her eyes. Dashing them away with one hand, she said, 'I suppose I can admit the truth, since you've guessed it already. Comeryn did lock me in my room for a time with…limited provisions. An…

unpleasant and embarrassing experience. I only hope it doesn't give you a disgust of me.'

'A disgust of *you*?' he echoed, his anger at Comeryn redoubling. 'It wasn't you who violated the trust and care every child deserves from a father! How could such a thing be allowed to happen?'

'You know my mother couldn't stand against Comeryn, nor would the servants dare disobey his orders. Crispin was travelling when the incident at the ball took place. When he returned to London and learned I'd been carried off to Montwell Glen, he came immediately—and insisted I be released.' Maggie laughed. 'I think by then Comeryn had realised no amount of deprivation would force me to yield. If anything, it only strengthened my resolve.'

Julian shook his head, still furious. 'Thank Heaven for your brother.'

'Yes, Crispin has played the guardian since childhood, bless him. At any rate, the episode did allow me plenty of time for reading,' she continued, obviously not wishing to discuss the experience any further. 'While I was in London last Season, my brother James, who works in India and is enchanted by the country, recommended several journals recently published by military gentlemen who were posted there. I was curious enough to snap some up—Captain Skinner's *Excursions in India*, Major Archer's *Tours in Upper India* and especially Godfrey Charles Mundy's *Pen and Pencil Sketches*, which revived my interest in drawing landscapes. Once my freedom to ride about the estate was restored, I began to exchange sketches with Eliza, who is a talented landscape artist. I'd love to travel to places new and old, where I could capture scenes like those travel writers did!'

Still concerned, but glad she seemed to have put the unpleasant memories behind her, Julian smiled. 'What, you'd become an intrepid explorer like Lady Hester Stanhope?'

'I'm not sure I'd want to live in such exotic places as she has, but I might visit as far as Venice or Paris. Much as one might deplore Napoleon, one must admire his transformation of the city from a medieval warren into a handsome expanse of wide boulevards and beautiful parks. Ah, to visit it! And while there, perhaps purchase some of those fashions I now enjoy so much.'

'Building on a more monumental scale is occurring here as well, you know. The expansion of the British Museum, the Bank of England. The new wharves recently constructed to facilitate movement of goods from all over the world.'

Maggie raised her eyebrows. 'What, are you a gentleman who, like Crispin, interests himself in what my father dismisses as "vulgar commerce"?'

Atherton laughed, a little embarrassed by her scrutiny. 'I do share with your brother the conviction that landowners in future who wish to maintain their property must invest in more than just agriculture. I first realised it as a lad, after the French wars ended, when the price for agricultural goods dropped precipitously while the cost of everything else rose. In many cases, rents alone could no longer fund necessary purchases of tools, seed and repairs, much less allow any new building. I argued then with my father that we should put some capital into other ventures, so we could continue to nurture and develop the land.'

'Sounds like the arguments Crispin used to have with Comeryn—who never relaxed his opposition to anything but acquiring wealth through property—or marriage. Were you more successful with your father?'

'He wasn't entirely persuaded,' Julian said, smiling as

he remembered his father shaking his head over his son's unconventional suggestions. 'But he couldn't argue with what the ledger figures revealed about expenses and profits. In the end, he allowed me a small sum with which to test my theory.'

Maggie angled a glance at him, looking impressed. 'I've always known you to be intelligent and broad-minded. I hadn't realised you, like Crispin, are also forward-thinking. How is it that I never knew about these interests?'

Julian shrugged. 'Commerce is not generally the stuff of discussion at balls, routs and musicales. Many, like your father, still consider it ill-bred for a gentleman to involve himself in business ventures.'

'Thick-headed autocrats willing to let their way of life disappear rather than admit any change is necessary,' Maggie said flatly. 'So, what did you do with your small stake? Put it into railways, like Crispin?'

'Canals, initially. After father's passing, once I had full authority over the estate, I bought some railway shares and kept an eye out for other promising ventures. Like the St Katharine's Wharf project. Trade with the East India Company.' He paused, impressed with her as well, her unexpected knowledge making him view her in a new light. 'How is it that I never knew *you* had an interest in such things?'

She chuckled. 'Because it's not the stuff of discussion at balls, routs and musicales? But how exciting to consider the world expanding around us! Railway will be the future of travel, Crispin believes. Unlike a horse, an engine never tires and can go as far and as fast as fuel and track permit, its rails unaffected by snow, rain or mud.'

Encouraged by her enthusiasm, he said, 'Have you ever travelled by rail yourself?'

'Not yet. Crispin is a principal investor in the Great

Western and promises to take me and Marcella on its initial journey.'

'There's a new line right here in the city, completed just last February—the London and Greenwich.'

'It's finished, then? I rode with Crispin and Marcella to view the construction work when I was in London with Mama a few years ago. I'd been meaning to revisit it, but going to view such a site doesn't make the list of *activities* favoured by the ton, either. I didn't take time to go by myself last year.'

'We should go together, then. Shall I get tickets? If you can find a maid intrepid enough to accompany us.'

'I'd like that! I'll bring my new maid, Anna. Though only a lower housemaid during my…restriction, she was indignant enough about my treatment to offer to carry messages for me. I didn't put her at risk by agreeing to that but did let her smuggle me books and art supplies. I rewarded her by bringing her to London as my new ladies' maid, a position to which she'd long aspired. I think she'd relish the adventure of riding the rails. Shall I carry along a sketchbook to commemorate the occasion?'

'An excellent idea,' he agreed, delighted to share the experience with so comely a companion and still marvelling that a ton maiden would have any interest in the commercial projects that fascinated him.

Though when that maiden was the unusual Lady Margaret, he shouldn't be so surprised. That shared intellectual interest would also help distract him from the physical attraction he was having increasing difficulty suppressing.

'While we're planning,' Lady Margaret said, pulling him back from his reflections, 'Mama told me we've been invited to the ball at Ashdown House. It will be our first Society excursion and Lady Laura and Miss Hasterling will both be attending. Will I see you as well?'

'Not if you're going to be manoeuvring your friends towards suitors,' he replied, thoughts of her project dissipating the delight produced by envisioning the railway outing.

'No, at this first event, we want to simply revel in being back together.'

'In that case, I suppose I can attend.'

She rewarded him with a beaming smile that made him glad he'd relented.

'I would like you to become reacquainted with my friends—so you may appreciate how dear they are to me and understand why I'm so eager to see them safe and happy! And I'd like to claim that dance you promised.'

'I suppose I can arrange that as well.' Might the dance be a waltz, where he could place a hand on her shoulder, another at her waist? Feel his torso brushing hers as they swept through the movements?

He tried, and failed, to stifle the wave of heat that washed through him.

'Excellent,' she was saying. 'The ball is in three days. Perhaps by then you will have discovered if there is anything untoward about any of the candidates.'

'Perhaps,' he said drily. 'There's only so much discreet enquiry I'll feel comfortable conducting.'

'I wouldn't wish you to do something that would make you uncomfortable.'

'I'd prefer to do something we both found…comfortable,' he agreed while, as if of its own volition, his gaze strayed again to her lips.

And again, she stared back up him, her eyes darkening and her lips slowly parting…as if she also envisioned a kiss?

But surely that was only his imagination—wasn't it?

She couldn't really feel the same physical connection he did. He was an *older* gentleman, after all, albeit not one decrepit enough to have made it onto her former list of marital prospects.

Before he could sort out his tangled thoughts, she said, 'Does your gelding have another gallop in him? It will be our last chance before the park grows too crowded.'

'He is as game as your mount.'

'Then, shall we?' She gestured down the carriage way.

Nodding his assent, he followed as Lady Margaret urged her mount to a trot, then a gallop. To the throbbing pound of the horses' hooves, he marvelled again to have learned they shared an unexpected interest, his enthusiasm over that discovery vying with concern over the growing strength of his attraction to her.

Perhaps he should look for some means to slake his unsatisfied desires. He'd always been too private a person to patronise one of the discreet establishments favoured by some of his contemporaries. And he still couldn't summon any enthusiasm for seeking another liaison in what had thus far been a fruitless search for a lady with whom he could share a more permanent bond, one who would be satisfied with only the fondness he was capable of pledging.

If he was able to restrain himself merely to companionship, he might have that friendship with Maggie, he thought, the possibility intriguing him. After what she'd revealed about her treatment at her father's hands today, he could understand better why she was so determined to see her friends settled, safe and eventually as independent as she was.

And why she was so opposed to marriage and the control over her it would give a husband.

He felt humbled and privileged that she'd trusted him

enough to share with him the distressing incident of her incarceration. And was more than ever ready to protect her and enjoy her unusual and fascinating company.

Even if he still disagreed about the wisdom of the marital project that seemed to consume her.

Chapter Three

Three nights later, Maggie strolled with her friends Lady Laura and Miss Hasterling back into Lady Ashdown's ballroom. They'd indulged in a long chat over refreshments, during which she'd offered a quick description of the candidates she intended to introduce them to at their next engagement. While neither looked enthusiastic about the meetings, both promised to give the gentlemen careful consideration.

That task accomplished, Maggie found herself impatient for Atherton's arrival. She was eager to claim the dance he'd promised her and perhaps partner him for a round of cards.

She'd been looking forward to seeing him again ever since their ride. She'd known he was kind but had been moved to tears by his compassion. Though she probably should feel mortified at having admitted to him the humiliating treatment her father had meted out, instead she felt somehow...better. The burden of the experience seemed somehow lighter now that someone else besides Crispin and her mother knew what had happened. And she was profoundly grateful that the knowledge hadn't seemed to lower her in Atherton's esteem, that they might move forward even closer friends.

She trusted without doubt that the Earl would never reveal the demeaning episode to anyone.

But she remembered most vividly how he'd gazed at her when he said he'd think of some way for her to repay him for his help in vetting her candidates. Those green eyes had seemed suddenly darker, his expression more intense, and his focus on her mouth so compelling she could almost *feel* the touch of his lips against hers...

Just recalling it made her mouth tingle and burn, while a strange, needy feeling swirled in her belly.

Had he been insinuating he might want a kiss as his reward? She'd known at once she'd be happy to grant him that. Maybe even more. The warmth within her intensified as she envisioned his arms wrapped around her, drawing her close, the heat and power of his body next to hers...

Then she heard his voice, jolting her out of her sensual spell. Looking in the direction of the sound, she noted that he stood with his back to her—facing a lady she recognised as Mrs Barkley, his paramour from last Season.

Something unpleasantly like jealousy extinguished her pleasant anticipation. She wasn't sure what emotion had appeared on her face, but Lady Laura put a hand on her arm, as if to keep her from advancing towards Atherton.

'It wouldn't be polite to interrupt,' Laura murmured.

'I didn't plan to,' Maggie replied, her tone sharper than she intended.

They found themselves near enough to the couple that Maggie didn't think she could sneak away without attracting their attention. Nor she could avoid overhearing their conversation.

'Where have you been keeping yourself these last few weeks, Atherton?' the tall, dark-haired widow was asking, leaning towards Atherton to better display her cleavage. One of the premier beauties of her debut Season, Maggie knew, the woman was still strikingly handsome nearly two decades later, her blue eyes brilliant, her porcelain face seemingly unlined.

'You're looking outstandingly lovely tonight, as always, Mrs Barkley,' Atherton replied—not answering the lady's question, Maggie noted.

'You used to think me so,' she said, eyeing him pointedly, though her tone remained light. So focused on Atherton was she, Maggie thought she probably could slip away unnoticed…but now stood guiltily mesmerised.

'My appreciation for beauty remains undimmed,' he replied.

'Does it? I hoped it might. Though I've had little indication that is case. Such a lonely spring it's been. You've been…disappointingly distant of late.'

'One can admire beauty from afar. Which I thought we'd agreed I'd do.'

'It's what you decided to do,' she corrected. 'I should remind you how much more…satisfying it can be to admire closer up.'

'But with beauty so striking, it would be unsporting not to let other admiring gentlemen bask in its light.'

'Beauty does have its preferences, though. Should those not be taken into account?'

At that moment, clapping a hand over her mouth, Miss Hasterling tried, unsuccessfully, to stifle a cough. Starting at the noise so close behind him, Atherton turned and spotted them.

An expression that looked like relief on his face, he exclaimed, 'Lady Margaret! How wonderful to see you again! And your friends, of course.'

Turning to bow to Mrs Barkley, he said, 'You must excuse me, ma'am. I've not chatted with Lady Margaret since last Season and must hear all her news.' Turning back to-

wards Maggie, he continued, 'I hadn't realised you'd returned to town.'

Well aware of Mrs Barkley's displeased gaze trained
on them, Maggie gave Atherton a puzzled look, but at his
minute shake of the head, didn't take him to task for that
blatant falsehood. Instead, she said, 'Lord Atherton, you
will remember my dear friends, Lady Laura Pomeroy and
Miss Eliza Hasterling?'

After an exchange of bows and curtsies, Atherton said,
'I'm delighted to encounter you ladies again. Might I escort you to take some refreshment?'

'Lady Margaret should accept your kind offer, but I fear
I must go find my protégé, Miss Rochdale,' Lady Laura re-
plied, while Miss Hasterling added, 'I, too, must decline.
My sister awaits my return.'

Anxious to give her time alone to hear Atherton's expla-
nations after she'd encountered him with his former lover?
Maggie wondered. Both girls had not so subtly encouraged
her friendship with the Earl last Season.

'Lady Margaret, then?' he said, offering his arm.

'Thank you, sir,' she said, giving him another specula-
tive look as she took his arm and let him lead her off.

Momentarily distracted as he put his hand over hers, its
warmth making her gloved fingers tingle, she recovered to
murmur, 'What was that folderol about not realising I was
in London? Both Laura and Eliza know we've met, and half
a dozen people saw us together at Gunter's.'

'Sorry. I needed an excuse to…extricate myself from
certain company.'

Not wishing him to realise she'd overheard much of their
conversation, she said, 'Was Mrs Barkley wanting to dispute her congé?'

Atherton's face flushed. 'What would you know about Mrs Barkley?'

Maggie shook her head at him. 'Didn't we already agree to dispense with silly pretence? Gossip about you and your *chère amie* abounded last Season. I may be still a maid, but I'm neither naïve nor sheltered. Looking around the room, I can spy two or three beauties who had similar arrangements at one time or another with my father—luring them with a charm he never bothered to display at home. Or perhaps he just rewarded them well,' she added drily. 'Mrs Barkley was at least discriminating about who she accorded her favours.'

He looked shocked for a moment before saying wryly, 'You do say the most outrageous things.'

'I only speak the truth. Is Mrs Barkley being…difficult?'

Atherton sighed. 'I shouldn't admit such a thing to you, of all people, but I fear she might be.'

More relieved than she should be by Atherton confirming that the affair, for him, was over, Maggie laughed. 'Well, one can't really blame the woman. She could hardly wish for a more handsome, virile or charming lover. I can sympathise with her mourning her loss.'

Atherton's eyes widened and he paused, seemingly at a loss for words. She probably shouldn't be so plain-spoken, Maggie thought ruefully. But the memory of having his intense gaze fixed on her lips still hummed in her blood. She felt driven to discover if the awakening desire she felt for him was mutual, or only a figment of her hopeful imagining.

'I'd be flattered if you truly found me handsome, virile and charming,' he said at last. 'Or are you only teasing this "older" admirer?'

'I wouldn't tease about so important a matter,' she murmured, hoping the heated appreciation in her expression would reinforce the answer she didn't dare word any more clearly. She felt her face warm at her boldness in having said as much as she already had.

He gazed intently at her for another moment before looking away. 'I—I see you are enjoying your reunion with your friends. They both seem charming. But no matchmaking schemes afoot tonight, I trust?'

Though excitement still simmered in her nerves at his nearness, she accepted the wisdom of redirecting the conversation to less dangerous ground. 'I did describe all the candidates to them, but will wait on introductions until a later event, as promised. Lady Laura presented her protégé, Miss Rochdale, a rich banker's daughter, whom she is tutoring in how to navigate the ton. Susanna is quite lovely and well-dowered, but very shy in company, which, given her merchant origins, I can understand. I've pledged mine and Mama's assistance in helping her feel more comfortable. I remember all the tales about the now amusing, but less so when they happened, incidents my sister-in-law Marcella, Crispin's wife, endured from haughty aristocrats during her presentation.'

'The "factory heiress" they called her, didn't they?' Atherton recalled.

'Yes. Weathering the Season was hard enough for Marcella, and she was self-confident and well-spoken. But enlisting Mama's support should go a good way towards smoothing Miss Rochdale's path.'

They'd entered the refreshment room, where Atherton plucked glasses of wine for them from a passing waiter. 'The approval of a well-respected countess must be helpful. However, if Lady Laura is going to be preoccupied tutoring her friend, she may have little time to devote to charming your candidates. A good thing, in my opinion!'

Maggie batted his arm. 'You're entitled to your opinion, however misguided. Laura will *have* to make time for them. Sadly, she confided this week her father, the Marquess, is not doing well. With his health so precarious, he must be anxious to see her settled. And as her family cannot give her another Season, Miss Hasterling needs to become more serious about securing her future as well. At our next ball, with Mama to assist me, we'll start the introductions. And I shall fervently hope they find one of the candidates agreeable!'

Atherton shook his head. 'Just make sure—'

'Yes, yes, I know,' Maggie interrupted. 'Don't push them too hard. Now, shall we have that dance?'

'With pleasure,' Atherton replied.

As he escorted her back to the ballroom, Maggie was guiltily aware that the music the musicians were tuning up indicated a waltz. She really shouldn't indulge in a dance that allowed Atherton to hold her close enough to breathe in his intoxicating scent of sandalwood while his chin brushed her hair and his strong torso brushed her body... But since he'd not refused this dance, she couldn't deny herself that treat.

They took their places on the floor, Maggie suppressing a sigh of pure pleasure as she settled in his arms, his hand on her shoulder, another clasping her waist. She thrilled to the music as he swept her into the graceful, rhythmic movements, intensely conscious of his nearness as they twirled together around the floor.

She looked up at him, smiling, to find his green eyes fixed on her with, she was certain, a sensual heat. He seemed to delight as much as she did in their proximity, content to *feel* rather converse. Without seeming conscious of doing so, he drew her closer still, until the pulse beating at her throat echoed the beat of the music, the captivating splendour of his gaze and the heady excitement of their near embrace.

When the dance ended, he simply stood with her for a moment. She relished the last moments of contact before he must release her, reluctant to let the interlude end. He continued to gaze down at her, smiling faintly, as if he too felt the bond that pulled them together and wished as much as she did to prolong it.

But end it must, of course. Lingering on the dance floor would provoke comment and speculation among the onlookers, so, resigned, she let him lead her off.

Would that he might ask her to waltz again, but that wouldn't be wise. Though both their friendship from last Season and his disinclination to remarry were well known, she knew on what slight evidence gossip about them could erupt. She neither wished to subject him to speculation nor be the centre of it herself.

'A game of whist before you re-join your friends?' Atherton suggested.

Maggie started, her misty gaze clearing, suddenly shocked back to the present. 'Y-yes. Yes, that would be sensible,' she said. Giving him another warm smile, she squeezed his arm. 'I would very much like to partner you.'

In so many ways, she thought—as her bold comments tonight must surely have informed him.

Before she let heady desire and fanciful imaging sweep her into uttering even more indiscretions, better to ground herself in a prosaic game of cards.

No matter how much the magic of the dance floor beckoned.

* * *

Julian walked Lady Margaret into the card room, the space nearly full of guests who preferred the lure of gaming to dancing or chat. As he must, before the heady delight of holding her in his arms encouraged him to indulge in even more outrageous conduct.

But how could he help being energised, when she'd seemed to confirm that she shared the attraction he'd been trying so hard to deny or suppress?

Her shocking affirmation that she found him 'handsome, virile and charming' had gone straight to his head—and to his loins. Desire, and a deep sense of masculine gratification, filled him at the possibility that she might consider him a desirable lover.

But if the strong attraction he felt was mutual, how would that complicate the friendship they were trying to maintain—friendship being the only relationship she wanted? The only relationship possible, save the marriage she firmly rejected, between a gentleman and a well-born maiden.

Alas, he'd never be able to hurry through his day, counting the hours until the evening, knowing Lady Margaret would be awaiting him, her slender body wrapped in a thin veil of silk, as eager for his caresses as he was to give them...

He jerked that line of thought to a halt before it rampaged any farther.

As their dance ended, he'd felt a strong urge to spirit her out to the moonlit terrace, where they might waltz again undisturbed. Where in the concealing dimness of that torchlit space, he could pull her even closer...

As he struggled to resist that temptation, his gaze had lit upon the door to the card room, presenting an alternative that would allow him to keep her company while avoiding doing something rash enough to give rise to gossip. They had often been partnered at cards last Season, and her skill and zeal for games of chance was well known.

And so, resisting the pleading of his aroused senses, he'd led her here. Cards might be a poor substitute for the embrace he longed for, but he could still gaze at her loveliness and admire her wit.

'There's Lord Innesford,' Lady Margaret was saying, pointing to a tall gentleman who waved at her. 'Shall we join him and his partner?'

'If you like,' Julian said. As they walked over, Lady Margaret murmured, 'He seems to have quite an affection for Lady Laura. If he weren't going to inherit a title, he might make her an eligible parti—but then, she tells me he's not interested in marriage.'

'If you're planning on joining him to continue your marital intrigues, I'd rather sit elsewhere,' Julian replied, her reversion to concentrating on her matchmaking schemes a more effective damper on his ardour than the scrutiny of a disapproving dowager.

Wrinkling her nose at him, Lady Margaret said, 'No intriguing tonight. I shall just enjoy the play—with a skilled partner. As long as you can keep your attention on the game.'

'I'm not the one involved in matrimonial schemes,' he retorted as he walked her over.

'No, you were trying to avoid schemes of a quite different sort,' she said, giving him a mischievous smile.

Trying without success to come up with a retort that would chastise Lady Margaret for tweaking him about Mrs Barkley while being innocuous enough not to reveal the subject of the conversation to anyone who might overhear, Julian didn't notice until after he'd helped her to a seat that one of the matrons at an adjacent table was Lady Bellingame—younger sister of Lord Tolleridge, the suitor Lady Margaret had so publicly rejected the previous Season.

As Innesford's partner dealt their hand, Julian winked at Lady Margaret, then angled his head towards the neighbouring table. Following his glance, she looked over and grimaced. 'Least it's not the man himself,' she murmured.

Julian's hope that they might play their game undisturbed lasted halfway through the rubber—until Lady Bellingame, glancing idly in their direction, suddenly stiffened. Her eyes narrowed and her expression turned hostile.

'Did you know Lady Margaret d'Aubignon had returned to town?' she said to her partner, her voice deliberately raised.

'Indeed?' gasped the matron, who since her back was to their table wasn't aware that the lady they were discussing was seated behind her. 'Shocking! I wonder she dares show her face.'

'Such an embarrassment for Lord Comeryn! Imagine, after coaxing my poor brother into making her an offer, having her repudiate the engagement to her father's face in front of a ballroom full of guests. The sheer, ill-bred nerve of it.'

Lady Bellingame had to be well aware her conversation was audible not just to Lady Margaret, who sat expressionless, but also to the guests at every nearby table. Even now, the murmur of conversation hushed, the onlookers doubtless agog to discover what would happen next. Would the girl who'd shocked Society by creating an appalling scene the previous Season jump up to confront her detractor? Flee in embarrassment?

His anger building, Julian once again caught Lady Margaret's eye and angled his head towards the door, silently offering to escort her out.

Her eyes sparkling, she gave him a minute shake of head, then looked back at her hand and calmly played the high trump. 'My trick, I believe.'

Julian released a breath. He should have known Lady Margaret wouldn't back down. If she could stand up to her formidable father and forced starvation, she wasn't likely to be cowed by a maliciously gossiping matron.

'Why in the world would she return to London?' the other woman asked. 'I can't imagine any man being desperate enough to consider wedding such a scandalous jilt—no matter how vast her dowry.'

Lady Bellingame tittered. 'Nor can I. The jade must have harangued her poor father into it. Though much good it will do her! You will recall what my brother dubbed her after his lucky escape—when she'd declared she would *never* marry him? "Never-Marry-Margaret, she is indeed," he said. "For now no one would have her!"'

The matrons chortled. At the glare Julian swept over the nearby onlookers, however, other sniggers ceased and the players looked back to their cards.

Though Julian knew Lady Margaret's lack of response was the best way to handle the matter, he couldn't help being furious on her behalf. But to his surprise, she chuckled. 'Lord Atherton, you're not paying proper attention,' she scolded. 'You've just wasted a trump.'

He grimaced. She was right; in his distraction, he'd overplayed the trump with which she had already won the current trick. 'Sorry,' he muttered.

If she could rise above the insult, so should he. Fixing his attention back on his cards, he assisted her to win the hand. Meanwhile, having been unable to provoke a response from Lady Margaret, Lady Bellingame refrained from further incitement and returned to her own game.

His partner coolly continued her card play until, after two more hands, they had soundly beaten Lord Innesford's team. 'That's rubber, gentlemen,' she said, placing down her last cards. 'I believe I could use some refreshment. If you would be so kind, my lord?' she said, looking over at Julian.

'Of course,' Julian replied, rising to pull out her chair. 'You'll excuse us, gentlemen?'

'Save me a dance later,' Innesford said loudly. Julian gave him a nod, pleased at his gesture of support for Lady Margaret.

Who looked over at Innesford, her smile mischievous. 'If you are sure you dare.'

Innesford grinned. 'I believe my courage is up to the task.'

'Then I should be delighted.' Nodding to Innesford and his partner, she took Julian's arm and walked out with him, her steps unhurried—as if she were unaware of being the focus of the surreptitious gazes of half the guests in the card room.

Bravo, he thought. What an exhibition of sangfroid and restraint!

To his surprise, once they'd exited the chamber and walked into the hallway towards the refreshment room, rather than give vent to anger, as he expected, or embarrassment, which he doubted but would have been understandable, she burst out laughing.

It took several minutes, while he looked on in bewilderment, before she was able to control her mirth.

'Never-Marry-Margaret!' she gasped at last. 'I never credited Tolleridge with an ounce of wit, but I must concede him a hit for that. I love it! And it's quite apt.'

'It's meant to be an *insult*,' Julian protested, still angry on her behalf.

'Oh, pish-tosh. Perhaps if I really did wish to marry, I might be annoyed, but as I have no intention of altering my blessed single state, I'm only amused. Indeed, the so-briquet might even be useful. Since, based on the charming Lady Bellingame's comments, Society might believe I came back to London still hoping to marry, presumably with my fat dowry intact, it might help discourage any would-be fortune-hunters from annoying me. I didn't expect I'd have to worry about potential suitors this Season, but can I count on your help to repel any persistent aspirants, if the need arises?'

'Of course. I'll be happy to protect you, as I did from Tolleridge last year.'

'Then I am content. Or I will be, if you will grant me another dance. Then I must catch back up with Eliza and Lady Laura and make plans on how to proceed. Tonight was for enjoyment, but after this I must get to work. The Season will end all too soon, and I'm determined to see them settled. For now—is that our dance?'

Fortunately, Julian could tell from the introductory music that the next number would not be a waltz, with its temptation to hold her too close and dream of forbidden delights. 'I believe it is. If it is your pleasure, my lady?' He offered his arm.

'The only pleasure in which I can indulge…at the moment,' she murmured, pressing his arm as she took it.

Putting out of mind any contemplation of what double meaning she might have intended, Julian walked her back to take their place in the set forming up. He was still angry on her behalf at Lady Bellingame's mean-spirited attack. But he was also immensely proud of her restraint.

Looking up at him as he clasped her hand for the first figure, she murmured, 'One can't be made a laughingstock if one doesn't allow it.'

'Indeed. Trump and rubber to you in that contest as well.'

'One should have a little sympathy for her, poor lady. She does have Tolleridge as a brother.'

He was still laughing at that as they began the next figure.

Chapter Four

$\infty\!\!\sim\!\!\infty$

As Atherton handed her into the next movement of the dance, Maggie was glad that a slight indisposition had kept her mother at home tonight. The incident with Lady Bellingame would have distressed the Countess, though had she been present a mere baron's wife might not have dared insult her daughter. In any event, she would make light of the exchange to Mama after she got home, before her mother heard about the contretemps from someone else.

It would take much more than Tolleridge's sour sister to dispel the glow created by claiming Atherton's escort, she thought as she watched him link hands with the other lady in their pattern. She'd even quite shamelessly given him undeniable hints of how attractive she found him. Why had she allowed herself that unprecedented freedom?

Perhaps because, secure now in her independence, she no longer need worry that her remarks might make him think she was trying to attract him. Though giving those hints was ultimately futile—it was too dangerous to take the game to the conclusion it had produced with Mrs Barkley. But if she were a widow beyond childbearing years who might dally with a lover without fear of consequence? Ah, then she might well be angling to take Mrs Barkley's place.

But she wasn't an older widow. And even if she tempted

Atherton, which she was almost certain she did, that honourable gentleman would doubtless recoil from the idea of debauching an unmarried lady of quality. No matter how much she tempted him.

But acknowledging the sensual bond that had always simmered between them could signal a new phase in their friendship. That bond could add a delicious zing to their already enjoyable encounters.

As long as she didn't let it distract her from her quest to see her friends settled.

For tonight, though, she could relax and just enjoy his company, she concluded, giving him a brilliant smile as the movements of the dance reunited them.

She was walking with him off the floor when a familiar voice hailed her from behind. She turned, delighted to confirm it was indeed her brother Crispin approaching.

'Dellamont, good to see you,' Julian was saying, holding out his hand for her brother to shake. 'Did you have a successful investment tour?'

'Very,' her brother said, giving Maggie a quick hug.

'You did get my note saying there was no need to collect me from Montwell Glen? I do hope you didn't make a wasted trip! And is Marcella not accompanying you tonight?'

'No Marcella tonight. She's feeling somewhat better after the illness of her early months, but ton balls were never something she enjoyed. And I did get your note, but stopped at the Glen anyway, as it was on our route back.'

'Shall I leave you two to catch up?' Atherton asked. At Maggie's nod, he continued, 'I enjoyed meeting your friends again tonight and hope to see all of you soon.' After bowing, Atherton walked off.

Maggie's high spirits sagged a bit as he disappeared into

the card room. But, she reminded herself, her Season had just begun, and despite her need to focus on her friends, she would have many more opportunities to spend time with Atherton. Soirees, balls, routs, dinners—she intended him to be present when her friends and their perspective suitors were invited to Portman Square—as well as morning rides, musicales, cards games—and maybe even an outing on the new railway.

Plenty of time to enjoy his agreeable company and indulge in the delicious thrill of his nearness.

Turning to Crispin, she said, 'You stopped at the Glen, then. Is Comeryn still furious?'

Crispin gave a noncommittal shrug. 'Probably. You can't imagine how relieved I was to discover a means for you to escape him. When I think of you locked in that bedchamber... Comeryn is fortunate I didn't do him an injury—despite the respect a son owes his father.'

Touched by his concern, Maggie squeezed his hand. 'Thanks to your brilliant investments, we'll never have to worry about such a thing again. For that blessed change, I can never sufficiently express my gratitude.'

Crispin squeezed her hand in turn. 'You are entirely welcome.'

'Did you try to soothe his ruffled feathers?'

Crispin laughed shortly. 'I just repeated what you doubtless told him—that he could protest about his ungrateful child to anyone who would listen, thereby making himself a subject of derision or pity, or he could tacitly support your removal to London and keep his reputation as master of the family intact. Which would mean resigning himself to behaving cordially if he should come to the city.'

'I doubt he would cause a ruckus here. He was always careful to commit the worst of his dictatorial acts at Montwell Glen, where no one in Society was likely to learn of them. Now that Mama is in London, her many friends will be watching.'

'You seem to have had a good friend yourself tonight. Especially in the card room.'

'Oh, dear,' Maggie said with a grimace. 'You've already heard about that?'

'Innesford cornered me when I arrived, not wanting me to be blindsided if someone else mentioned it. From what he described, you acquitted yourself well.' He shook his head at her. '"Never-Marry-Margaret". You're probably proud of the title.'

She grinned. 'I am, actually.'

'You've matured remarkably. I can't imagine the hot-blooded scamp you used to be letting Lady Bellingame's insult stand. Whereas tonight, you treated it—and her—with just the right indifference to defuse its ability to injure.'

Maggie shrugged. 'Now that I'm independent and don't need Society's approval to escape Comeryn through marriage, gossip can no longer injure me. Besides, I had to mature. After you went away, there was only me to shield Mama.'

Crispin looked away. 'I'm sorry I left you alone to deal with him.'

'No, don't be sorry. You *had* to leave—you couldn't have stood his interference much longer. Besides, had you not followed your interest in railways and your talent for investment, neither you nor I would now be free of Comeryn's control. Besides, it did me good to concern myself with the welfare of someone other than myself.' She sighed. 'Even if I didn't accomplish much.'

'You stood up for Mama, despite his berating you and the punishments he inflicted. That was enough. And I can see you've landed on your feet in London! Well, I can now return home to my wife, secure in the knowledge that you are in no further need of my help.'

'I shall always need your support, dear brother.'

'You shall always have it,' he said, kissing her forehead.

'Give my best to Marcella, won't you, and tell her Mama and I will visit soon.'

'She'll be delighted to see you both.' Pushing her to arm's length, he looked down and shook his head again. 'My bold little sister.'

'Your very *independent* little sister,' she corrected with a grin.

'My very independent little sister,' he agreed. 'If you can defy Comeryn and rout beldames like Lady Bellingame, I believe you can accomplish whatever you desire.'

She blew Crispin a kiss as he walked away, then scanned the room for Lady Laura and Eliza. If she could accomplish getting her friends advantageously settled, she'd be satisfied indeed.

Ah, that she might accomplish *whatever* she desired! But though some pleasures might be beyond her reach, while her campaign to marry off her friends required spending a good deal of time in Society, she could look forward to the delight of Lord Atherton's company.

Four nights later, Maggie stood at the top of the grand stairway at Covent Garden, scanning the crowded vestibule below. She'd not seen Atherton since their last dance together at the Ashdown ball. But he'd sent a note today saying that, knowing how fond her mother was of Shakespeare's comedies, he would look for them in the Comeryn box tonight for the performance of *Much Ado About Nothing*.

However, the first interval was about to end and he'd yet to appear.

With a frown, she acknowledged that she'd been waiting impatiently ever since receiving his note, anxious to see him and eager to consult him about the progress of her campaign. More disappointed than she liked to admit, she was about to return to the box when, just after the bell sounded to announce the end of the interval, she spotted him striding into the vestibule.

A leap of gladness and excitement lifted her spirits as he looked up and saw her. Feeling the smile he gave her mirrored on her own countenance, she waved, then waited, trying to avoid being jostled by the crowd returning to their seats, until he joined her at the top of the stairs.

'Here you are at last,' she said, making a quick curtsey to his bow. 'I'd about given you up.'

'Sorry to be so late. Some business correspondence arrived from the estate today and I lost track of the time.'

'Nothing alarming, I hope,' she said, putting her hand on his arm—and feeling that little tingle of contact down to her slippers.

She heard him suck in a quick breath—as if he, too, felt the connection between them. A moment later, he continued, 'No, just a rather lengthy accounting of the status of crops and livestock. How have you been faring? Have you your protégés in tow tonight?'

'Lady Laura is here—with *her* protégé, Miss Rochdale— and Miss Rochdale's brother, who has been squiring Laura while Lord Innesford entertains his sister.'

'What of Mr Garthorpe and Mr Fullridge?'

She sighed. 'Neither was able to attend. Which I suppose is just as well, for Miss Hasterling wasn't able to come, either. All the parties will meet at the ball tomorrow night, with Mama present to make the introductions. Miss Rochdale will not be present, which will allow Laura to concentrate on her own prospects.'

Her tone must have turned a bit tart, for Atherton laughed. 'You think her too preoccupied by Miss Rochdale?'

'I do. She told me when Mama and I called on her two days ago that she'd begun her "lessons" with Susanna. I must concede, the girl is so shy, she really does need coaching. Her brother, who accompanied her tonight, is much more self-assured. Though he was nothing but polite when we chatted, I got the distinct impression that he did not favour his sister having a Season.'

Atherton cocked an eyebrow. 'Why ever not? The Rochdale bank is doing well, from what I've heard. Surely he doesn't begrudge the expense.'

'I don't think it's that. Susanna told us he attended Oxford, where he seems to have developed as much disdain for titled gentlemen as I have and would rather not have his sister wed one. I can't help but sympathise with that opinion!'

'A youth from a merchant background would likely have suffered a good many snubs from the well-born sprigs who didn't feel the offspring of a "tradesman" belonged among them,' Atherton acknowledged.

'I asked Crispin about the Rochdale enterprises and he confirmed that the bank is one of the most well-run and progressive firms in the City. Mr Rochdale is quite well-spoken and appears sensible and intelligent, as well as strongly protective of his sister—a quality I can only admire. Indeed, aside from his youth, with his wealth and other qualities, were he gentry born, I'd consider him a suitable candidate for Lady Laura.'

'Now who is being top-lofty?' Atherton teased.

'I'm the first to admit it's quite unfair,' she acknowledged. 'His sister, with her sizeable dowry, could marry an aristocrat and be elevated to his rank, though the highest sticklers might not accept her. But were Lady Laura to wed a man who wasn't a gentleman, she would be dropped by all but her closest friends.'

'You would still befriend her, were she to make such a misalliance?'

'Of course!' Maggie exclaimed, giving Atherton an indignant look. 'I only wish her to marry a man of character who appreciates her worth! That said, I'd not want her to forfeit the position into which she was born. Her true friends would stand by her, but Society certainly wouldn't. Much as I might disdain the ton and its artificialities, even I acknowledge that it would be rather lonely to be permanently exiled from almost everyone you've ever known.'

By now they'd reached the door to the Comeryn box. Peeking inside, Maggie noted her mother, Lady Laura, Miss Rochdale and her brother already seated within. Tugging at Atherton's sleeve to halt him, she said, 'Before we join the others, please tell me quickly anything you've discovered about my candidates.'

Atherton heaved an exaggerated sigh, making Maggie frown at him reprovingly before he began, 'Very well, I've mentioned the names to members at my club who pride themselves on knowing all the latest gossip. I've heard nothing untoward about any of the gentlemen.'

Maggie blew out a relieved breath. 'Thank heavens! I knew Fullridge was beyond reproach, but couldn't be sure about the others. Now I can proceed with no qualms! I do thank you for your efforts.' She gave him a grateful smile. 'I know that making those enquiries, however discreetly, went much against the grain.'

He put his hand over hers, pressing it as he gave her a

rueful smile—and once again sending a tingle of warmth through her. 'I appreciate your acknowledging that fact. Now, am I excused from any further participation in your schemes?'

'No more active participation,' she promised, savouring the feel of his hand still covering hers. With a flash of dismaying doubt, she added, 'You will still dance and chat with me, won't you?'

'Of course. I may disapprove of your scheming, but other than that, I quite enjoy your company. Perhaps as the Season goes on, I can persuade *you* to give up interfering and let your friends find their own resolutions.'

'I do want them to find their own resolutions,' she countered. 'I just want to offer some sensible, advantageous possibilities.'

'We shall continue to differ then,' Atherton said. 'Shall we join the others?'

'Yes, and speedily, so you may greet everyone and I can introduce you to the Rochdales before the next act begins. I expect *you* are not too top-lofty to make the acquaintance of a merchant banker and his sister.'

Atherton chuckled. 'Certainly not! With agricultural prices so unstable, I might have need of a loan myself one day. Being personally acquainted with a prominent banker could be quite advantageous.'

Maggie let him escort her into the box, buoyed by the knowledge that no defect had been found in the gentlemen she had chosen—and considerably relieved that her persistence in pursuing a matter about which he disagreed was not going to drive Atherton to abandon her.

Even ending up with her friends well situated would seem a hollow victory if pressing forward caused her to forfeit Atherton's regard and company. Indeed, the very possibility was so dismaying she quickly dismissed it.

Somehow, after beginning as an amusing diversion, having his friendship had become as essential to her well-being as her brother's support. How much she looked forward to continuing, even deepening that relationship!

After the necessary greetings and introductions, Maggie took the chair next to Atherton and crowded pleasantly close to him within the narrow confines of the box. Secure in his continued regard, her marriage campaign on hold for the night, Maggie could simply enjoy the rest of the evening in his company.

'Lady Laura's Miss Rochdale is quite a beauty,' Julian murmured to Lady Margaret during the next interval. 'If she's as well-dowered as she is lovely, her brother is wise to fear some aristocratic suitor will try to snap her up.'

'Rumour says she is,' Lady Margaret replied. 'But Laura will be at least as diligent as Rochdale in making sure she's not courted by anyone unworthy of her,' she assured him, patting his hand.

Julian felt his fingers tingle at the contact and suppressed a sigh. Her chair was positioned close enough that he need only lean ever so slightly to be able to whisper in her ear and he could inhale her soft rose perfume without even moving. The knowledge of her proximity having its inevitable effect on his body, he shifted somewhat uncomfortably. In the semi-darkness, with the lamps dimmed for the performance, he could easily bend down unobserved and brush a kiss along that soft expanse of neck below her ear, bared beneath the curls pinned atop her coiffure…

'Quite a fitting play for you and Lady Margaret to be

viewing,' Lady Laura said, her comment jolting his wayward thoughts to a halt.

'Indeed?' Lady Margaret said. 'How so?'

'Beatrice and Benedick, of course,' Lady Laura replied with a grin. 'You, like Beatrice, vowing to remain always a spinster, and Lord Atherton disinclined to remarry.'

'We may banter, but never as cruelly as those two,' Lady Margaret objected. 'I would never insult Atherton's appearance by telling him that scratching could not make worse a face such as his, as Beatrice does.'

'You can't deny you both seem as opposed to matrimony as the characters of the play,' Lady Laura insisted, then laughed. 'What a fine joke it would be if someone plotted to trick *you two* into wedlock!'

'Pernicious thought, when I've only just won my independence!' Lady Margaret retorted. 'Thankfully, such plots unfold only on the stage.'

'Besides, although I may be disinclined to wed again, unlike Sir Benedick, rather than thinking ladies unworthy of trust and incapable of constancy, I hold them in the highest esteem,' Julian said.

'As they do you,' Lady Margaret said. 'Indeed, by arriving late, you missed the best line thus far, Atherton: when Benedick declares he is "loved of all ladies, save only Beatrice". *I* am quite safe from matrimonial traps, but you must be ever vigilant to avoid female scheming.'

'Like Miss Gwendolyn's last Season?' Lady Laura said. 'As I recall, she was always trying to manoeuvre Lord Atherton onto a deserted balcony.'

While Julian groaned, recalling it, Lady Margaret chuckled. 'I do remember. Much as I owe Atherton gratitude for shielding me from Tolleridge, I did return the favour a few times, saving him from Miss Gwendolyn's blandishments.

And shall be happy to offer assistance again this Season, should the need arise.'

'Much obliged,' Julian said drily. Fortunately, the marriage-minded Miss Gwendolyn had managed to bring another gentleman up to snuff, so he'd not have to be on his guard against her stratagems. He only hoped he'd not have to continue avoiding Mrs Barkley's.

As the actors resumed their places, conversation lapsed and they turned their attention to the stage. Settling back in his chair, his whole side humming with the consciousness of Maggie sitting close beside him, Julian recalled her remark about wedding him being a 'pernicious thought'. Would she find marriage to him so unpleasant? he wondered, a bit stung.

'You may not have insulted my looks, but you did tell me I wasn't old and feeble enough to make a good marriage partner,' Atherton murmured in her ear.

She choked off a giggle. 'That wasn't insulting,' she whispered back, 'merely the truth. Besides, I've lately told you other truths I should think you would find…much more appealing.'

Julian's thoughts flashed back to the remarks she'd made earlier. 'When you said Mrs Barkley could hardly find a more handsome, virile or charming lover?'

A becoming flush coloured her face. 'Hush now, the players are beginning.'

He'd hoped she would reaffirm the observation—but it had been shockingly indiscreet, and perhaps she now regretted making it. He wished he might also enquire if she'd meant more than cards when she'd said she would like to partner him.

Had he merely imagined an underlying innuendo in both cases?

Although, other than adding a teasing fillip of excitement to their exchanges, it really couldn't mean anything more. There'd be no 'partnering' of a well-born maiden outside of marriage, and Maggie had made it quite clear she was firmly opposed to wedlock. A 'pernicious thought' indeed.

Sighing, Julian sat further back in his chair—which didn't place him farther away the temptation that was Maggie, but did allow him to view her lovely profile as he followed the action on stage. He had to smile when the play reached that part where Claudius and Don Pedro conspired to have Benedick overhear them proclaiming Beatrice's supposed love for him, inspiring that gentleman to realise he must be in love with the lady, too. And that character's resulting observation that, despite having up until that moment railed against marriage, one's 'appetite could alter.'

Would his ever? The years since Sarah Anne's passing had muted the revulsion he'd initially felt for the idea of wedding again, even as the uncomfortable ending of his affair with Mrs Barkley made him reluctant to attempt to form what would probably be a just another short-term relationship. Marriage would solve the problem of the loneliness that often gripped him, perhaps provide his boys with the mother they lacked and end the frustration of his long-denied sensual appetites.

Marriage to the right woman, of course. His friendship with Lady Margaret must not blind him to the fact that most women were more like his first wife, wanting a husband who would take care of them, protect them and become the centre of their life—a position he still had no desire to occupy. He'd only met one fiercely independent female who craved freedom and was adamantly opposed to having a man run her life—Maggie.

And since that fiercely independent woman couldn't

become a mistress and didn't want to become a wife, he should remember that, as she'd pointed out, plots like the one that paired up Beatrice and Benedick happened only on the stage. He should enjoy the fiction, but keep his expectations fixed on what was possible.

Enjoy the play he did, but as the action moved along to the part where Beatrice, outraged at the insult to the honour of her cousin Hero, said she would give her love to the man who could right the wrong done her kinswoman, Julian found himself wondering what feat might win Maggie's love.

Not that he'd want to win it himself—knowing he wouldn't be able to return such devotion. And then Maggie had already condemned even more adamantly than Beatrice the whole idea of falling in love.

Intelligent and practical, she was fully capable of managing the everyday business of life without a man's guidance. If she should decide she needed assistance, she had a concerned brother to call on.

If Lady Margaret d'Aubignon were ever to marry, he speculated, it would have to be because she'd decided she wanted to share her life with a kindred spirit and fully indulge the passion he sensed in her. Even at that, she'd first have to overcome the distaste for wedlock that her parents' disastrous union had engendered. A tall order, on every count.

Whereas…he already knew himself strongly attracted to her. He admired her wit, her courage, her undaunted spirit and sheer audacity as much as he did her beauty. What a splendid companion she would make, if he could keep her so over the long term! He'd have to be on his guard, not against the matrimonial schemes he usually had to watch out for with unmarried females, but against letting his admiration for her lead him into pushing for the physical possession he craved but could never claim.

And so, unlike the characters in the play who would end happily wed, he'd need to make sure he didn't let his thoughts stray beyond the bounds of friendship. He'd have to find another answer to the problem of his unsatisfied physical longings.

The next interval arrived, allowing him to escape the sensual tension of her nearness—and his wayward thoughts—by first offering to fetch refreshments, then chatting with the Countess while Maggie spoke with Lady Laura and the Rochdales.

As the interval ended, he returned to his chair beside Maggie, feeling that magnetic pull between them as he took his seat and determinedly refocused his attention on the stage. With the rest of the audience, he laughed when both Beatrice and Benedick denied their love for each other— only to be brought up short when Claudius and Hero each produced scraps of the love poems the two had written to each other.

When Benedick stopped Beatrice's final protests with a kiss, Julian's fist clenched on his chair, his breath suspending as Maggie, drawing in a sharp breath of her own, reached over to seize his other hand.

All his good intentions to concentrate on remaining friends melted in the heat of that contact. His imagination immediately flamed into wondering whether she wanted as badly as he did to share a kiss like their alter egos on stage. Before he could order his thoughts and beat back his imaginings, as if suddenly realising what she'd done, she snatched her hand back.

Julian watched the remainder of the play in somewhat of a daze. It was fortunate the box contained so many witnesses, else he might have committed the folly of leaning over to give her that kiss.

Would it have earned him a slap—or a passionate response?

He reminded himself that it did not matter. He must not kiss a woman with whom passion couldn't proceed any further and around whom he was already struggling to control his responses.

Perhaps agreeing to remain friends wasn't wise after all.

But the idea of breaking off their relationship was completely unacceptable. Perhaps he should just limit their contact?

He would do better, he promised himself. He wasn't a callow youth, after all, unable to control his appetites, but a seasoned, responsible gentleman. Besides, after having promised to support her during—if not in—accomplishing her goal of settling her friends, it would be ungentlemanly as well as cowardly to completely abandon her now.

Thankfully unaware of the turmoil the play had evoked in him, as the performance ended, Maggie rose and turned to him. 'Fortunately, we can leave the subject of marriage upon the stage. Will you see us out?'

'Of course.' Julian offered her his arm, telling himself he would simply enjoy their interplay, as Beatrice and Benedick had before the avowals of love complicated everything. Her companionship would assuage his loneliness, and that would be enough.

As he escorted Lady Margaret and her mother down the grand stairway, she said, 'Will you be attending the Harkness ball two nights hence?'

'Is that when you'll be embroiled in all your matchmaking?'

'Only to introduce all the parties to one another. Once

they are acquainted and have got past any initial awkwardness, I will leave them to their own devices. By then, I shall be wanting to dance and perhaps to win a little blunt in the card room. I'd be most grateful for your company.'

A little voice in his ear repeated that it would be wiser to create more distance between them. He stifled it.

'Then you shall have it. But I warn you, I'll not arrive until later, to be sure your matchmaking efforts have been completed.'

She shook her head at him. 'Very well. As long as you appear eventually.'

As he bid goodbye to Lady Laura and the Rochdales, then went to summon the Comeryn carriage, Julian wondered if by ignoring the voice of prudence, he was being more foolish than the jester in Shakespeare's play.

Chapter Five

Shortly before midnight two nights later, Julian proceeded up the stairs to the Harkness ballroom. It was late enough that the receiving line had long ago dispersed. A throng of dancers crowded the ballroom floor, others had drifted into the card room, refreshment room, or one of the adjoining salons where couples could enjoy a quiet tête-à-tête. Keen to avoid being drawn into Lady Margaret's matchmaking schemes, he trusted by now she and the Countess would have made the requisite introductions, started the new acquaintances off conversing and dancing, and Maggie would be free to dance or join him for a game of cards.

It would be wise to do more of the latter and less of the former, in spite of—or rather because of—his simmering eagerness to have her in his arms again. Pattern dances only, if he did indulge, he promised himself. Absolutely no waltzes.

He scanned the room, where the current dance was in its final movements, and spotted her at the far side. After staring a moment to identify her partner, he muttered an oath and set off through the throng, ignoring the occasional exclamations of annoyance from the dancers.

Sir Reginald Wardener, a widower on the shady side of forty, would never have made it onto Maggie's eligible bachelor list. A well-known gambler possessed of a heavily mortgaged estate, he'd been trying to snag a wealthy bride to support his gaming habits and secure the succession to his title ever since his downtrodden wife died after providing him three daughters but no heir. Julian was certain she wouldn't willingly have partnered the baronet, but as he was possessed of a pomposity and self-importance not even Maggie's sharp tongue could deflate, short of fleeing the room, she could not have escaped him.

Julian was not above using some strong-arm tactics to sweep her off to the card room as soon as the dance ended.

He saw the relief in her eyes when she spotted him approaching and grimaced. He'd prefer to escort Sir Reginald onto the shadowy terrace beyond and inform him, if he valued his teeth and his straight nose, not to approach Maggie again. But it was more important at this moment to escort her away from the baronet's clutches.

He'd deliver the warning later.

The last strains of the music hadn't yet faded when he reached them, pulled Sir Reginald's arm off Maggie's sleeve and planted himself between them. 'Lady Margaret is pledged to partner me at cards,' he said, gave the baronet the barest hint of a bow, and pulled Maggie away.

'My hero to the rescue,' she murmured as they crossed the floor, leaving the baronet gaping after them. 'Apparently Lady Bellingame's gossip has done its work. Sir Reginald must believe I'm still angling for a husband—and am somewhat desperate—to have approached me so confidently.'

'He'd believe you looking for a husband, but the man is thick as a stump, supremely confident of the worth of his name and title, and oblivious to the desires of females he pursues. The only factor that matters to him is how large a dowry the girl possesses.'

'He must be thick, for he's been refused by half a dozen

ladies already. I should think by now he'd have started hunting for a wealthy merchant whose daughter wants a title and isn't particular how she gets it.'

'He's too vain for that, he'd never sully his name by wedding a woman of inferior birth.'

'Well, my slighting remarks certainly didn't seem to dent his sense of worth.'

'You did attempt to dent it?' Julian asked, amused.

'In truth, we exchanged very few words. He bowed and asked me to dance, I said I wasn't dancing this set, he said, "Not yet" and grabbed my hand. I was tempted to jerk it free and slap him, but he's not worth causing a scene over. I then told him I never dance with men who ignore my wishes.'

'And what did he say to that?'

'He ignored me and half dragged me onto the floor. Honestly, does he truly think he can drag some female to the *altar* against her will? We're not living in medieval times, thank the Lord!'

'He probably thinks females don't have wit enough to know what is good for them, and that a woman as scandalous as you should be grateful for the opportunity to marry a man of his rank and impeccable lineage.'

Maggie laughed again. 'That's exactly what he told me. Somewhat regretting I'd chosen not to jerk my hand away and slap his face, I remained mute for the remainder of the dance. Since, as you observed, though I be as disparaging as Beatrice was to Benedick, not the most barbed of comments would have discouraged him. He has the self-protective carapace of a tortoise! Though I thank you for intervening, I would have managed to escape him after the dance. Even Sir Reginald isn't bold enough to pursue me into the ladies' withdrawing room.'

'Where you would have hidden out all night? I'm glad I intervened, then!'

'I would certainly not have "hidden out" for long. I'll not let any man force me into anything ever again! If he were still persistent when I emerged, I *would* make a scene, if it were necessary to avoid dancing or talking with him.' She sighed. 'Hopefully, my "scandalous" reputation is scandalous enough to dissuade less desperate fortune-hunters from annoying me. I'd not like to have to give the cut direct to a more deserving man.'

By now, they'd reached the corridor outside the ballroom. Maggie halted him with a touch that sent another shiver through him.

'Before we try our hand at cards, can we take some refreshment? After having to refrain from uttering the blistering remarks that occurred to me during the dance with Sir Reginald, I could use a glass of wine. Besides, I wanted to let you know how this evening has gone.'

Julian groaned. 'No more matrimonial plotting, I beg you.'

'No, just a report. You would like to know things are progressing, wouldn't you? So you will have a sense of when my quest might end?'

'A consummation devoutly to be wished,' he said with feeling. Though what project would the ever-busy Maggie come up with once she achieved her aims in this? Last Season, she'd been driven to escape her father; now she was campaigning on her friends' behalf. Julian didn't think she'd be content with merely buying gowns, attending teas, balls and routs and exchanging Society gossip for the rest of the Season, much less the rest of her days.

Maybe she'd embark on the travels she'd mentioned? He felt a wave of protest deep within at the thought of her journeying far away from him, to Paris or Venice or with her brother in India. Especially if she chose the latter; with the dangers of travel, he might never see her again.

Shaking off those disturbing thoughts, he procured two glasses for them and walked with her to a quiet window alcove where they might converse without interruption. 'Since I can't avoid it, you might as well make your report.'

'I'm glad to find you so enthusiastic,' she said drily. 'Garthorpe and Fullridge both attended tonight, so Mama was able to introduce them to Lady Laura and Miss Hasterling. The six of us chatted for a bit, then the gentlemen asked the ladies to dance, Garthorpe claiming Eliza and Fullridge pairing off with Laura. The couples adjourned for refreshment afterwards, then re-joined Mama in the ball-room, where they shared a second dance, then parted with good wishes all around and promises to call.'

'Sounds…pleasant,' Julian said noncommittally, not wishing to prolong the topic any longer than necessary.

'A promising beginning, I think. I didn't note any signs of a particular, immediate attraction in either case, but neither did any of them seem to take a dislike to one another. One always hopes initial cordiality, then friendship, might develop into much more.'

She looked up, her hazel eyes fixed on him. Might there again be another meaning beneath her words—that she hoped for more to develop between *them*? But what else could they share besides friendship, unless her attitude towards marriage changed? And his, he added hastily to himself.

'One can always treasure a deeper friendship,' he said after a moment.

She uttered a sigh, her bright eyes dimming. 'Yes, a deeper friendship is to be treasured,' she murmured and looked away.

Julian studied her averted face. Had his reply…disappointed her? That ever-present sensual connection urged him to take her hand, tilt her face up so he could examine it…but that wouldn't be wise. Frustration stirred along with curiosity, for if she remained set against marriage, what else could she possibly hope for between them?

After sipping the last of her wine, she set down the glass. 'If you are ready, let's seek out that card game.'

'Whist again?'

'It's the most interesting play available. The stakes are high enough to make it exciting, but not so high as to attract rabid gamesters.'

'You wouldn't want to burden your conscience by winning too much blunt from your acquaintances.'

'Exactly,' she confirmed with a smile.

They approached the door to the card room just as two matrons were exiting. Lady Margaret halted him with a touch to the wrist, nodding towards the couple, one of whom he recognised as Lady Bellingame.

'I've resolved to try to make peace her, though my attempt may well be rebuffed,' she murmured, then walked to the ladies and curtsied.

After a moment's hesitation, the two returned her courtesy, the expression on Lady Bellingame's face turning hostile. 'Lady Margaret, Lord Atherton,' she murmured tonelessly, and made as if to pass by them.

Lady Margaret stayed her with a hand to her arm. 'A moment of your time, please, Lady Bellingame. I wanted to assure you my refusal of your brother's suit had nothing to do with any ill opinion of his character. Your sobriquet is more apt than you could know. Unusual as the resolve might be, I truly don't wish to marry—anyone. My father made the public announcement to try to force me into wedlock. The battle was between me and Comeryn, with Lord Tolleridge unfortunately caught in the middle, something I truly regret. I had no desire to bring scandal to his name.'

Lady Bellingame looked her up and down disdainfully. 'You regret having made a mockery of a gentleman who'd done you no harm, impugning his spotless character?' She sniffed. 'A tawdry game for a supposedly well-bred maiden.'

She transferred her disapproving glare to Julian. 'If you *truly* "don't wish to marry" you choose your company well. Lord Atherton has avoided all inducements to remarry these six years.'

'I, too, am perfectly content in my single state,' Julian confirmed.

Lady Bellingame harrumphed. 'Then I expect you will experience some bother the rest of the Season, Lady Margaret, fending off those who would overlook your...deficiencies in hopes of securing your fortune. Something, as you know, my brother never sought. Good evening.' With the barest of curtsies, she swept past them.

'After all your efforts to avoid the man last Season, did you really expect her to believe you didn't hold a negative opinion of Tolleridge?' Julian asked as the two ladies walked off.

Maggie sighed. 'I can't believe she could assert with a straight face that Tolleridge possesses "spotless character"! Surely she's heard the rumours about his...questionable tastes. I hoped to find a way to establish cordial relations, but apparently that's not possible. But give me credit, I did try.'

'And a handsome effort it was, given that the lady had no qualms about making disparaging remarks about you. I suppose she is still outraged at the insult of your refusing her brother's suit, no matter how much you tried to wrap it up as a quarrel with your father.'

'Well, that's an end to it. Unless…if she continues to harbour animosity towards me, knowing I truly don't wish to wed, she might encourage sluggards like Sir Reginald to pay me court, just to annoy me.'

Looking at the rigidly disapproving back of the lady now disappearing into the ballroom, Julian said, 'Unless she has a massive change of heart, she's not going to be wishing you well.'

'As long as she doesn't try to sabotage my efforts to see Lady Laura and Miss Hasterling settled, I shall be content. I can handle any negative comments she sets circulating about me.'

'I would hope she's not vindictive enough to harm innocent ladies just because they happen to be friends of yours,' Julian said.

'Well, a countess trumps a mere baron's wife, so with Mama's backing, I think Laura and Eliza are safe, whatever mischief Lady Bellingame might come up with. On that note, shall we go trounce some opponents?'

Julian laughed. 'Take out your frustration on some poor innocent card players?'

'Winning a few pounds will certainly do much to relieve my irritation.'

And so it did. Julian found he was able to relax, observing Maggie as she skilfully played her cards. He sat close enough to watch every reaction on her expressive face, appreciate her witty banter—and be amused by her evident satisfaction in besting their opponents and pocketing a few pounds. The width of the table between them left him far enough away that only a wisp of her rose perfume teased his nose, not close enough to her tempting body that he was unable to rein in the simmering desire her proximity always aroused.

In short, he was able to enjoy her company while behaving as a mature, principled gentleman, just as he'd assured himself he could.

The card game ended, Maggie looked over. 'A few more dances, and I will pronounce the evening perfect. My thanks for the game, my friends! Will you excuse me?'

'And me,' Julian added.

Rising among their opponents' good-natured complaints about having been fleeced again by the skilful Lady Margaret, Julian escorted her towards the ballroom.

'You must erase my ugly memory of being hauled around the floor by Sir Reginald,' Lady Margaret said as they walked away. 'I sincerely hope I won't have to spend the rest of Season fending him off.'

Recalling his earlier resolve, Julian said, 'I can assure you it won't come to that.'

She angled her head up at him enquiringly. 'Can you? And how do you intend to manage that?' Her eyes widened. 'Are you going to…threaten him with bodily harm?'

'Absolutely. I have a well-deserved reputation as a pugilist. Sir Reginald might be too self-important for a verbal warning to have any lasting effect, but he wouldn't want a broken nose to spoil the aristocratic profile he prizes so much. He's obtuse about many things, but he understands the unspoken rules governing gentlemen well enough to know that if he doesn't heed my warning, he couldn't evade my challenge to stand up with him without being branded a coward in all his clubs. Which would be anathema to a man like that, for whom his standing among gentleman is all.'

'He thinks a reputation as a hopeless gamester is more acceptable than one as a coward?'

'Of course. All gentlemen gamble. Far too many of them lose for them to be overly disdainful of Sir Reginald.'

'There but for grace of God…'

'Exactly.'

The next set was forming as they entered the ballroom—fortunately, not a waltz. 'Shall we?' Julian asked.

'I'd be delighted.'

As he walked her onto the floor, he said teasingly, 'See, I *do* listen to my partner.'

'You don't always obey her, though. I seem to recall a strong reluctance to assist in my efforts to settle my friends.'

'Isn't it the lady who pledges to obey?'

She laughed. 'Never this lady. Exchanges must be…mutual.'

He shouldn't bandy provocative words, but he couldn't resist. 'What…mutual exchange would you propose?'

'Ah, that I might suggest what I know would give us both…pleasure.'

'Would you dare?'

She stared at him, looking as if she were truly considering an answer. Julian felt his pulse quicken, that always-simmering desire flaming hotter as long-denied need surged in his blood, fogging his brain from acknowledging the danger and futility of such questioning.

He offered his hand for first figure, hardly aware of the dancers joining the set around them. She squeezed his fingers, sending a sharp pulse of sensation through him. 'I don't dare…yet,' she murmured, and swayed into the first move of the dance.

Julian spent the rest of it trying to clear his head of sensual imaginings and wrestle her back from the object of his desires to untouchable, innocent, plain-spoken friend.

Which is all she can be; he tried to beat the refrain into his brain. No matter how much he wished it could be otherwise.

When the dance finished, the two remained standing motionless, gazing at each other. Then suddenly she started.

'Mrs Barkley is bearing down on you, a determined smile on her face,' she warned.

'Heaven help me,' he muttered.

'Heaven may not, but I will. We can escape—this way.' She grabbed his hand, the shock of her touch delaying him from realising for a moment that she was headed for the terrace.

Swiftly she led him out into the cool night air. Lit dimly by torches at each corner, the space was nearly deserted, the several couples who'd escaped the heat of the ballroom passing them as they returned inside for the next dance.

She walked him to a far corner, where in the low, flickering light they would be all but invisible to anyone gazing out from the ballroom. Looking over her shoulder, she frowned.

'Drat and blast. She's still following.'

Then her eyes brightened with mischief. 'Let's see if I can discourage her.'

Before Julian had any inkling what she intended, Lady Margaret threw her arms around his neck, pulled his head down and kissed him.

A blast of sensation suspended all thought. In a blaze of pent-up longing, Julian pulled her closer and deepened the kiss.

Chapter Six

Kissing Atherton truly did begin only as an impulsive ploy to save him from the persistent Mrs Barkley. But as soon as his lips brushed hers, shock hammered her senses, igniting heat and need and a craving for more. And when, after a second of immobility, Julian pulled her closer, cradling her body against his and intensifying the kiss, any thought of ending what she'd meant to be a brief caress evaporated.

Instead, she wrapped her arms more tightly around his neck. With a murmur of approval, he drew her closer still, his lips nuzzling, brushing, teasing hers. With another shock that set off an even hotter wave of sensation, the soft, wet blade of his tongue traced her lips and probed at the edges of her mouth.

Instinctively she opened to him. His tongue entered slowly, caressing her lips, then seeking her tongue, igniting another wave of swirling heat that made her feel as if she were melting from within, until she clung to him for support, weak and boneless. Tentatively she pursued his tongue with her own, stroking and suckling, and was rewarded with a groan and tightening of his arms around her shoulders.

A buzzing filled her ears, drowning out sounds from the night around them and the ballroom beyond. She felt as if her body were lifting, soaring, racing like a galloping stallion urgently seeking some unknown destination, desperate to find it.

Meeting his tongue stroke for stroke, she would have continued the pursuit, but suddenly Atherton broke the kiss and jerked away from her. Uttering an inarticulate protest, she held on to him, not sure her legs would support her. She stared up at him breathless, her body still pulsing with that urgent need.

His breath was coming in pants, too, as if he were running the same race. Before she could gather wit enough to whisper, 'Kiss me again,' he stepped away.

'Don't...go!' she gasped.

Though he kept both hands on her arms to steady her, he did not move closer. Instead, he simply stared down at her, his expression somewhere between awed and horrified.

As sanity slowly returned along with a sense of time and place, she realised they were still on the dim-lit terrace—and thankfully alone. Touching her lips wonderingly, she murmured, 'That was...amazing.'

He uttered what sounded like a half-laugh, half-groan. 'And incredibly foolish,' he said roughly, seeming to have difficulty steadying his voice.

'If you dare say you are sorry, I will slap you!'

His expression turning wry, he shook his head. 'It was ill-advised. Dangerous. Unconscionable of me to respond and prolong, but no. I'd be uttering the biggest lie ever voiced in Christendom if I claimed I was sorry.'

Gladness filled her, along with a tangle of emotions and a residue of sensations too overwhelming to sort out at the moment. Shoving them all aside to examine later, she said, 'Also effective. It certainly discouraged Mrs Barkley, who is now nowhere to be seen.'

Atherton gave a pained laugh. 'Effective on that score,

certainly. I only hope your noble attempt at rescue doesn't backfire, leading to gossip about us so compromising that it might bring up calls for marriage.'

'I hardly think we need to worry about that—not from *this* observer. I expect that Mrs Barkley believes if you were to marry, she would never regain her position. That is, you wouldn't take a mistress if you had a wife—would you?' she asked, seizing the unexpected opportunity to pose the question she'd never before dared to ask.

'Of course not! How ever…trapped I sometimes felt during my marriage, I would never have shamed my wife by finding solace with another woman. Nor would I, were I ever to marry again.'

Her shock over what he'd just revealed overshadowed her relief that she'd read his character aright. 'You felt… *trapped* in your marriage?' she echoed, her eyes widening. 'I thought…everyone thought…'

Sighing, he wiped a hand over his eyes. 'Having blundered into that admission, I suppose I must explain. Even at the cost of your good opinion.'

'Only if you wish to,' she replied, not wishing to pry—though his last remark made her even more curious.

'Everyone believes my disinclination to remarry stems from grief. But they're wrong,' he said wearily. 'Never having been in love—if such a thing exists, I don't believe I'm capable of it—I hadn't any inclination to marry, though I knew my duty as the heir would require it eventually. When my father's health began to fail, he persuaded me to offer for the daughter of a friend. I liked Sarah Anne, believed she liked me, and thought we could forge an amicable union based on respect and mutual esteem. Only after we were wed, she developed this…fanatical devotion, an almost obsessive desire for my presence and a deep need for me to express for her the same passionate love she felt for me—an emotion I just didn't have to give her. Her continual efforts to evoke that love, her silent disappointment that she could not, rebuked me every time I came home. Until the point that I dreaded coming home. So, yes, I felt trapped. And though I never wanted to cause her pain, when she was suddenly taken, I felt…more relief than grief. Monster though that makes me sound.'

'Not a monster,' she said quietly, compassion filling her at the difficult situation he'd stumbled into, all unaware. 'Just a man pressed to produce an emotion he never promised and could not manufacture. Love can be a terrible burden. It was for my mother. Which is why I've vowed never to succumb to it.'

'So you won't…repudiate our friendship?'

'Of course not! It was one thing for my father to promise my mother love and then withdraw it, leaving her bereft. But apparently you never offered more than fondness. You shouldn't feel responsible for not meeting greater needs when, through no fault of your own, the nature of your relationship changed.'

'But I did feel responsible. Guilty, and resentful for feeling guilty. Unable to make my wife happy, or even lessen her disappointment, the situation became…impossible.'

'No wonder you never wished to remarry.'

'Indeed.' He blew out a breath. 'Thank you for…understanding. I've never confessed the truth about my marriage to anyone. I'd appreciate you keeping my secret.'

'Of course. I'm honoured that you entrusted it to me.'

He blinked rapidly, looking as if he might say more, then simply took her hand and kissed it. 'You are an incredible lady.'

The tingling of her fingers where his lips brushed them

recalled their interlude on the terrace. She stilled, filled with a nearly irresistible desire to step closer and kiss him again, to underscore with that gesture the true depth of her understanding and sympathy—and her undiminished desire.

Before she could commit such an indiscretion—when, at any minute, a wave of dancers escaping the ballroom might join them on the terrace—she made herself step away. Atherton stepped back too, ending the fraught moment.

Forcing her attention away from the sensations still coursing through her to focus on their previous conversation, Maggie said, 'Well, since Mrs Barkley still entertains hopes of luring you back, spreading rumours that might force you into marriage would be the last thing she would do.'

'You may be right. Would you also agree that, though neither of us is sorry about what happened here, it mustn't be repeated? Mrs Barkley might not want to compromise us, but she's perhaps the only person in Society who'd refrain.'

Maggie shuddered. 'Yes. Practically everyone else would be thrilled to spread such delicious gossip about the scandalous Lady Margaret.'

'Unless you've changed your mind about marriage, we shall have to be much more careful.'

The idea of marrying Atherton burst like a tiny flare of excitement in her brain before flaming out in a shudder. 'I've not changed my opinion one wit. Having just, finally, gained a hard-won independence, I'm not willing to sacrifice it for anyone. Not even you, Atherton, dear as you are to me.'

Dear, and much too attractive. Could she resist falling in love if they were joined in daily intimacy, sharing passion as well as companionship?

Thrusting out of mind the terrifying possibility of losing control over both her emotions and her life, she continued, 'Besides, you can't tell me you are any more eager than I am to forfeit your single status.'

He looked as if he might say something, then closed his mouth and shook his head. 'True enough. We should step back from the abyss. Return to the safe, familiar path of friendship.'

'Difficult as that might be,' she remarked with a sigh. Marriage might be too risky, but kissing him? That, she was certain she could handle.

'If I'm truly honest, I very much enjoyed kissing you and would willingly do so again.'

Atherton sighed himself. 'You make it difficult for one to remain a gentleman. But encouraging you in that direction would be the actions of blackguard. I may have just committed a regrettable lapse, but I'll not allow myself to stumble down the path of becoming a man I could no longer respect. No matter how much you entice me.'

A deep satisfaction filled her. 'Do I entice you?'

'Don't gloat, minx. Leave me some tatters of dignity! And for Heaven's sake, let's get off this balcony before someone like Lady Bellingame *does* see us. Having just assured her how much we both wish to avoid marriage she'd probably think it a fitting revenge for the insult you did her brother to force us into it.'

Maggie groaned, recognising the truth of that. 'Very well, it's back to the ballroom. But—' she gave him a mischievous smile '—you still owe me thanks for what was a quick-witted and effective rescue. However risky.'

Atherton bowed. 'My thanks. But take care not to repeat the stratagem.'

Maggie made him an elaborate curtsey. 'I promise to devise some other means if I must rescue you again from the threat of Mrs Barkley—or some marriage-minded maiden.'

Though she was not sure she could find another means as thrilling or delightful—or one she wanted, despite her avowal, so very much to repeat as kissing him.

As they entered ballroom, Atherton said, 'To remove temptation and give us both time to embrace being just friends, I'll return you to the Countess. Besides, I'm sure you're eager to check with her on the results of your matchmaking efforts.'

Maggie found herself strangely loath to leave his company. She was relieved to dismiss the threat of marriage and reluctantly agreed there could be no more kissing—now, anyway. But the tingling thrill of her hand on his arm, the feel of his strong arms around her when they danced, even his smile at her across the table as they played cards, made every activity more vivid and thrilling, as if she'd passed from a room dimly lit by candlelight into a garden gilded with brilliant noonday sun. She loved her mother and her friends, but being near them didn't create nearly the same joyous sense of being…*alive*.

She craved continuing that experience, as long and as often as possible.

Still, he was right to counsel defusing the sensual tension. 'It would be sensible to part for a time. Are you off to card the room?'

'No, I'll return home. I don't want to give Mrs Barkley an opportunity to ambush me again if she's still here. Are you sure you will be safe from Sir Reginald?'

'I can handle him if he reappears. Besides, he might ignore my protests, but under Mama's watchful eye, he wouldn't dare force me to dance.'

Atherton nodded. 'Then, thank you for the game that left me a few pounds richer, and the dance.'

'And the rescue?' she dared ask.

For a moment he stood silent. Then he unexpectedly lifted her hand and kissed it. 'I will *never* forget that rescue. Or your compassionate understanding. Now, let me return you to Lady Comeryn.'

He walked her across the ballroom to where her mother stood with some friends, her brain barely functioning as she suppressed the maelstrom of sensation and wildly conflicting emotions still churning within. She'd have to wait until she was alone in her chamber at Portman Square to sort them all out.

And decide what to do next. How to re-establish the calm equilibrium of the friendship she must maintain while she accomplished her mission. Perhaps, all her senses awakened by that kiss, daring to speculate what might happen between them…after.

Several hours later, Maggie sat in a wing chair before the hearth in her bedchamber. Her maid had helped her into her night rail and brought the glass of wine she'd requested, but after finishing it, she was still unable to sleep.

Not while she was still reliving that kiss.

If she were honest, she'd been wanting to kiss Atherton for a very long time. Only her desperate preoccupation with escaping her father last Season had subdued the simmering desire he had evoked from their very first meeting. Although she'd even at the time acknowledged that sensual pull, soon recognising that the Earl didn't fit the picture of the rich, elderly husband she needed she'd ruthlessly suppressed it.

Wanting to also counter the threat his compelling personality might make to her heart, she'd focused on turning him into the friend who'd proved invaluable in protecting her from Tolleridge and a few other fortune seekers her dowry had attracted. Though their strong connection had not progressed farther than bantering exchanges before her Season was abruptly terminated.

But now, though she still needed to keep a safe emotional distance, she no longer had any pressing need to prevent her from acknowledging her physical attraction. So, what was she to do about it?

She knew what she *wanted*. But the risks of a physical liaison had not disappeared just because the fervency with which she desired him had exponentially increased after sharing that kiss.

Despite how much the prospect of passion tempted her, she was not willing to wed. Not when she'd only begun to explore the tantalising, delirious possibilities of having complete control over her life and fortune, able to do virtually anything she wanted. Save, perhaps, becoming Atherton's mistress.

And not when she was determined to safeguard her heart from a man she already found far too appealing.

Compassion stirred as she recalled his confession about the true state of his former marriage. He was no villain like her father; indeed, despite the cost, it seemed he valued fidelity as much as she did. While his devastating experience doubtless made him even more resistant to marriage than she was.

Even if wedlock didn't mean a proximity that threatened her ability to remain heart-whole, she doubted she could long tolerate performing the duties of wife, mother and housekeeper. Duties that would restrict her movements and limit the travel she'd begun to think would be her first priority, once her friends were settled.

After all, one couldn't just haul a household of babies

to Paris, the Levant, or India. She didn't think she would be content exchanging the novelty of adventure for the familiar domesticity of England.

And sadly it was a risk beyond insanity to embark on an extramarital affair—even if she could seduce as honourable a man as Atherton into it.

Which meant, like a mariner studying a map with a final line inscribed 'beyond here be dragons,' she must chart a course back from passion's abyss into the safe waters of friendship if she wanted to keep him in her life.

She might not want to lose her heart, but neither was she ready to give up spending time with him. So, if passion must be restricted to safeguard their friendship, how to avoid being tempted into another amorous interlude?

Prudence said she must limit their interaction to card games or pattern dances in crowded ballrooms; avoid waltzes and walks on deserted terraces—or daytime strolls in intimate gardens.

At that depressing conclusion, her spirits dipped.

But there could still be rides, perhaps sketching expeditions, she rallied herself. That outing he'd proposed on the London and Greenwich railway. While they rode or strolled in these safe, public places, she could enquire more deeply into the mechanics of investments in things like railways and canals, which he apparently understood as well as her brother Crispin. There were dock projects, he'd mentioned—the East India Docks where the treasure from India would be brought in, like the goods her brother James dealt in. Tea, spices, luxurious silks, fine muslin and brightly patterned cottons.

She would love to visit those places and sketch the scenes. Especially the East India ones, where she might catch a glimpse of treasures from the land she'd read about in the accounts of Captain Skinner and Major Archer, viewed in the illustrations of Mr Mundy, a country James described so enticingly in his letters.

Yes, she thought, encouraged, there would many ways to keep company with Atherton and avoid temptation while learning more about things that interested and intrigued them both.

She'd write him a note this very night, proposing another ride.

Chapter Seven

Three days later, Julian was astride Midnight, riding to meet Lady Margaret at her home for the excursion she'd proposed.

He was glad to be seeing her in a neutral environment. Despite his attempts to put it out of mind, over the intervening days, his thoughts kept returning to the kiss, unsettling him all over again every time with strong feelings of regret, shame, deep sensual delight and bittersweet yearning.

That *kiss.* Audacious as Maggie had been on several occasions, he'd never anticipated she would make so unexpected a move. Still, shocked as he'd been, he should have immediately ended it. *Should* have. But lowering as it was to admit it, he wasn't sure he *could* have immediately ended it.

Visions of tasting her lips and exploring her mouth had glimmered like chimeras in his dreams for so long, and the desire of his deprived senses was so powerful, he couldn't help himself responding. Especially when, instead of recoiling in alarm when he intensified the kiss, she'd enthusiastically responded.

That she was an innocent, he had no doubt. But it took her only a few moments to adjust to his movements, to respond to the touch of tongue and begin, not just to permit his exploration, but to initiate her own.

A wave of heat washed through him and sweat broke

out on his brow, just remembering it. A man would have to have been a saint carved of stone to have resisted, and he was far from that. He was only grateful there'd been enough honour remaining within him that he hadn't succumbed to base instinct, pulled her into the garden and onto the nearest bench and completed her ravishment, attaining the fulfilment every molecule of his body had been demanding.

But that tiny core of honour and sanity held, forcing him to step away before he could commit that unforgivable betrayal. He'd betrayed her and his own sense of honour enough as it was.

In the immediate aftermath, when he returned her to her mother, he'd been unable to meet the Countess's eyes. Though honest in assuring Maggie he didn't regret the kiss—who could regret having a forbidden taste of Heaven?—he'd been disturbed that his control turned out to be so flawed. Her mother would have expected a gentleman to protect her, from herself if necessary. Not to almost ravish her.

He made a wry grimace. If he'd ever had wondered about the depth of passion Lady Margaret possessed, that few minutes on the terrace put all speculations to rest.

It wasn't entirely his fault, his self-esteem tried to argue. She had initiated the kiss. With no warning. He was only a man, made of fallible flesh and blood, and he'd been caught off guard.

He now knew just how unexpected her actions could be and must be careful never to be caught off guard again. Much as he might welcome a repeat of her bold initiative, he must forestall it. Otherwise, honour would compel him to deny himself her company, and he wasn't prepared to go to that extreme...yet.

Though if he committed any further lapses, he might have to.

* * *

A few minutes later, Julian pulled up his mount at the mews, handed his horse over to a groom, and walked through the garden to the front of the house, where the butler showed him in. He discovered Lady Margaret just coming down the stairs and braced himself for whatever reaction he might receive.

He hadn't seen her since he left her with her mother at the Hardwick ball. Would having time for reflection have changed her reaction to what had occurred between them to regret, alarm—even distaste?

She gave him a little wave, not meeting his eyes. Unease still roiled in his gut, but she hadn't cried off from the ride, so if she were angry or disappointed with him, at least she hadn't decided to break with him completely—much as he might deserve it.

'I already had Viscering ask the grooms to bring our mounts around,' she told him as she accepted her crop and gloves from the butler. 'So we can depart immediately.'

Sadly, he acknowledged there was a subtle tension between them that hadn't been there before. Maybe this would be their last ride, he thought, his spirits sinking.

The next few minutes were taken up with the business of mounting, settling in side-saddle, adjusting reins. 'To the park, then?' she asked, still not looking at him.

'As you wish.'

The usual bustle of morning traffic prevented much conversation during their transit down Portman Street onto Oxford Street and then into Hyde Park through Speaker's Corner. Not until they drew side by side and set the horses to a trot, the groom dropping a respectful distance behind, did Julian try to speak.

'I'm glad you still wanted—' he began.

While simultaneously she said, 'I'm relieved my audacity—'

They both fell silent, gazing at each other. His spirits rose as he realised she looked as uncertain as he felt. Was she as concerned about his reaction to the incident, now that some time had passed, as he was about hers?

'Ladies first,' he invited.

'I was saying, I'm relieved that my…lack of decorum didn't give you a disgust of me. I half expected to receive a note saying you'd been called away on business, or some such excuse to cancel the ride.'

She'd truly feared her boldness would disgust *him*? His spirits rebounding even further, he said, 'Not at all! Indeed, rather the opposite. I've been wondering if I might receive a note saying *you* no longer had time to meet.'

'So…my forwardness didn't alienate you?'

Happiness that they were not to be estranged bubbled up. 'It was a near-run thing, but in the end, I decided I must make allowance for the fact that you were attempting to help me.'

Her eyes widened in alarm before her ear recognised his teasing tone. 'Wretch! If you were closer, I'd whack you with my riding crop.'

'No longer the penitent? Now, that's more like the impetuous Lady Margaret I know.'

She sighed. 'Impetuous for certain. Immodest and unmaidenly it might make me, but honesty compels me to admit that though, after reflection, I cannot help but be somewhat appalled by my shocking behaviour, I still cannot bring myself to regret it. Have you…regretted it?'

'I can hardly accuse *you* of shocking behaviour when a true gentleman would have accepted a chaste brush of your lips and immediately set you free. Instead of…responding as if you were a high-flyer trying to entice me. For that, I am ashamed and beg your pardon.'

Her smile faded. 'Would you have kissed me senseless, had I not made the first move?'

A little shocked, he said, 'Of course not! What sort of rogue do you take me for?'

'And you only responded because you were surprised out of your normal restraint and good judgement?'

'Well—yes.'

'Then how can you possibly take responsibility for a lapse that I initiated? I'm not a brainless rag doll, to be mindlessly led by some controlling man. I'm responsible for my own behaviour—and my own lapses, thank you very much!'

He stared at her. 'You're…angry because I regret not meeting the standard of behaviour to which I hold myself?'

She slapped the crop against her palm, her annoyed expression telling him she'd rather be slapping him with it. 'I'm angry that you regret kissing me, when you promised me you wouldn't be!'

'It's not that simple,' he protested. 'Regret kissing you? Never! Regret the lapse in the proper behaviour due to an innocent maiden? Yes, I do regret that. I should be *protecting* you, not…debauching you.'

Looking somewhat mollified, she said, 'I hardly think I could be "debauched" by some kissing—no matter how delicious it was. It's just that, as *I* initiated the reprehensible behaviour, the fault belongs to me, not you. Freely admitting that, I must ask if…if you feel you can no longer associate with a female whose behaviour caused you to react in a manner so far beneath what you expect of yourself.'

He blew out a breath. 'I'm rather considering whether I should deny myself the pleasure of your company because you…affect me so much I can't be sure of maintaining that standard.'

Her eyes widened in what looked like alarm. 'And what have you decided? Is this to be our last excursion?'

'I don't want it to be. But if we are to spend time together, it's essential that we set some guidelines on how… and when. Much as I deplore my lack of control, I'm honest enough to admit that, were the circumstances similar, it might happen again.'

'You mean—if I surprised you?'

He gave her a severe look. 'I shall try not to be surprised again. I want to continue being your good friend. But there's no question that having once acted upon this…attraction between us makes that more difficult.'

She nodded. 'I've come to the same conclusion. I admit, I've wanted to kiss you for a very long time, though you mustn't think I *planned* to do it that night. I suppose in the back of my mind, I thought perhaps kissing you once would satisfy my curiosity and extinguish the desire.'

She looked so serious; he suppressed his chuckle at her naivete. 'And did it?'

She sighed. 'Not at all. Rather the opposite. But I agree that kissing you is far too dangerous an activity to repeat. I enjoy your company, too, and I don't want to deny myself either. So I've compiled a list of activities we might do together without subjecting ourselves to excessive temptation. If that is agreeable to you?'

As touched as he was relieved—and amused—he said, 'Quite agreeable. I'd like to recapture the ease I've always felt around you.'

'Have you truly always felt easy? I've always sensed this…something under surface.'

Julian shook his head, amazed anew that she spoke so

openly and honestly about desire, a topic most females approached only obliquely, flirtatiously or not at all. But he shouldn't be surprised. Hadn't she always been painfully honest—as when she told him he was too young and not decrepit enough to be suitor? Small wonder he found her company so enjoyable, a breath of fresh air that dispensed with the stale artifice almost always present in the dealings between men and women.

'You're right. I did as well, from the very first.' He laughed ruefully. 'I did try to ignore it or tell myself I was imagining it. After all,' he continued, meeting her honesty by voicing the lowering thought, 'I told myself that being so much your senior, I *shouldn't* have such feelings towards you.'

She made a scornful noise. 'Nonsense. You are a man in your prime! Granted, you are a few years older than me, but I hardly look at you as a father figure.'

He chuckled. 'I'm relieved to hear it—especially given your feelings towards your father. I admit, it is a relief to have all the desires and pressures we've both been struggling with expressed openly.'

'How else to deal with them sensibly? Anyway, here are my conclusions. We may ride and drive—although we have yet to drive together, I intend to purchase a phaeton. I've never had so daring a vehicle, and I'd rather have you instruct me in handling it than a coachman.'

'That would certainly force us to keep our minds on our task, lest we both end up in a ditch, unstable as that vehicle is.'

'So I thought. I'd like to explore some of London and do some sketching. Continue to attend balls and routs—no more waltzes alas—and have you attend Mama's dinners at Portman Square. You play pianoforte, do you not? We could participate in some musical evenings. I shall certainly be going, as Eliza is an exceptionally fine musician and it's a good opportunity for her to display her skills.'

'Are these to be matchmaking evenings? I'm not sure I want to agree to that.'

'Perhaps initially. But remember, though I intend to set things in motion and help them along—' she held up a palm as if giving court testimony '—I pledge to leave them alone afterward to make their own choices.'

'I suppose I can agree to that.'

'Eliza has been telling me about the beautiful façade on the new King's Library at the British Museum. After having a good gallop here, I propose we ride there and let me do some sketching.'

'The new entry is impressive, but the surrounding area is basically a construction zone. The King's Library occupies the east gallery, the north and some of west gallery has been finished, but the south gallery is still a work in progress, as is the rest of the west gallery, which cannot be completed until Montagu House is demolished. May I suggest another location that is already complete, and in my opinion, just as interesting to an artist looking to draw Roman-inspired architecture?'

'Of course. What would that be?'

'The Bank of England on Threadneedle Street. Though the portion I'm recommending is actually on the corner of Prince and Lothbury Streets. Called "Tivoli Corner," it's a decorative feature modelled after a Roman temple Sir John Sloane, the architect, saw in Italy during his Grand Tour.'

'It sounds perfect. Shall we go today?'

'It's a bit farther of a ride than Great Russell Street. Perhaps we could go another day, when you are prepared with your sketching supplies?'

She patted a small saddle bag on the cantle. 'I have them

here. Since I began sketching again after my release from "captivity" at Montwell Glen, I always have my materials with me when I ride. We can go now, if you have time.'

Riding a spirited mount, supporting Maggie in an activity she enjoyed, basking in her company without the worry of temptation overcoming him—a bubble of delight rose at the prospect. Compared with the deep unease with which he'd arrived at Portman Square, the relief that all would be well with them despite his shocking lapse—no, *her* shocking lapse, she'd insisted—made his chest expand with a happiness that was almost giddy.

Spend time with a female who not only didn't look to a man to assure her welfare, but fiercely insisted she alone was responsible for her actions and woe betide any man who tried to tell her what to do? He suppressed a laugh. How could he resist?

'As I've no immediate tasks demanding my attention, I'd be happy to escort you.'

'Shall we make an excursion of it, then? I promise tea when we return, before you head back to St James's Square.'

'Then let's be off, before the roads get any more congested.'

With Lady Margaret's groom trailing, they picked their way through streets that grew narrower and increasingly busy as they entered the City proper. Merchants, businessmen, tradesmen, hawkers and maids with baskets on their arms walked, rode, pulled handcarts or drove heavy vehicles past them as they navigated towards their destination. Fortunately, their mounts were well-schooled and they arrived at the imposing Threadneedle Street entrance without incident.

'This is the Roman architecture you spoke about? Quite impressive!'

'So it is, and you may sketch this prospect if you wish. But it isn't what I brought you to see. Shall I take you to it?'

Her expression curious, she nodded. Julian led her onto Prince Street and down to the corner. As a small, semi-circular pediment supported by four fluted Corinthian columns appeared, she gave cry of delight.

'How lovely! The proportions are so harmonious, they are more pleasing, though less grand than the façade. Yes, I'd love to sketch this.'

The groom dismounted, holding the reins while she slipped from the side-saddle and extracted her supplies from the small cantle bag. Dismounting as well, Julian stood beside her to prevent her from being jostled by the stream of clients and clerks passing by the pediment towards the entrance beyond.

It was delicious torment, having embraced her and learned the passion of her response, to stand close beside her, breathing in her rose perfume and the scent of her skin, that tempting bit of neck below her ear bared to him beneath her bonnet as she bent her head down to the sketchbook. How wise they'd been to choose a public space in which to meet, where the constant traffic of pedestrians, carts and merchants helped restrain his desire to kiss her again.

To distract himself from the temptation, he said, 'The corner is a handsome structure as well as Sir John Sloane's clever solution to the problem of what to design for the awkward angle at which these two streets meet. The architrave above with its graceful garlands, the urns embellishing the two sets of columns flanking each side, create a graceful, pleasing whole, do you not think?' he asked.

'Absolutely! The inspiration comes from a Roman original, you said?' she asked, not looking up from her sketching.

'So I've read. The Temple of Vesta in Tivoli.'

For a half hour, conversation lapsed while she worked, from time to time studying the building, then returning her attention to the sketch pad. Julian was content to watch her, enjoying her total absorption in her task, their comfortable silence and her apparent lack of need to try to impress him or chatter to keep his attention focused on her while she worked.

He didn't know any other unmarried female who could remain so oblivious to the presence of an unattached male, not instinctively driven to try to please or engage with him. Despite the edgy undercurrent of attraction pulsing between them, spending time with her like this was...exhilarating.

Providing just the sort of intellectually stimulating, intriguing companionship he'd been craving.

At last, she looked back up. 'I believe I'm finished. What a joy and inspiration to have something so beautiful here in the City! The statues in the niches are handsome, as is the Doric gallery farther down the street, but I love this the best. Perfect classicism in miniature. I hope the merchants who do business here appreciate the art in their midst! To think, I never imagined to find something like that here, in the heart of the City.'

'It's not surprising you don't know of it. The ton isn't much interested in commercial London. Although your Lady Laura's Mr Rochdale is probably familiar with it.'

'I expect he is. I wish I knew more about the mysteries of investing, especially since I owe my current freedom to its happy outcome! Perhaps I can ask Mr Rochdale to explain it to me sometime.'

Julian felt a sharp stab of something uncomfortably like

jealousy at the thought of her closeted with the handsome young man. 'I can't claim to possess Rochdale's expertise on banking, but I've done a bit of investing myself. I think I could explain the basic concepts.'

She closed her sketchbook and walked over to put her supplies back in the cantle bag. 'I imagine you could. Perhaps I'll ask you, or Crispin, for a lesson later.'

Julian didn't examine too closely why he was much happier with the idea of her consulting her brother. 'I'm sure he'd be as agreeable as I would be to tutoring you.'

'Thank you again for bringing me here. Shall we head back now? You must be gasping for some tea. I know I am.'

Though Julian was ready to return, he'd found the time here, standing and doing nothing but watching her, surprisingly fulfilling. Not only had he introduced her to an unusual place, a part of the world that fascinated him that he'd never expected a ton maiden would enjoy, she'd appreciated it as much as he'd hoped she would. And he'd had her all to himself, he thought, before another idea set him chuckling.

'Would you like to share what amuses you?' she asked, an eyebrow raised at his mirth.

'I'm just imaging the reaction, if someone told Lady Arbutnot or one of Society's other high sticklers that Lady Margaret had spent a good chunk of her morning outside the Bank of England.'

She gave a peal of laughter. 'I don't know whether she would be more incredulous or disapproving! Best not to let that secret out until my friends are settled. Even Mama's credit might not be sufficient to offset my dawdling in a place Her Ladyship would surely condemn as "unseemly and vulgar".'

He nodded agreement. 'Our only saving grace is it's

highly unlikely she, or anyone she would know, would be in the vicinity to spot us.'

'That's a blessing! Shall we flee while we can?'

This time, instead of turning to the groom to give her a leg up, she gestured to Julian, her chin lifted, a hint of challenge in her eyes. It was borderline reckless, inviting the temptation of having him touch her, but offset by the fact that they were in a place where they dare do nothing more, regardless of the desire even a brief touch could ignite in them.

Her way of indulging her sensual longing, while insuring they would not go beyond the bounds of propriety?

He'd be happy to meet the challenge. And if he let his fingers slide slowly, caressingly along her boot and his hands linger at her waist just a few seconds longer than strictly necessary to steady her in the side-saddle, that would only be just retribution for teasing him.

He knew from the tremor he felt ripple through her body how immediately she reacted to his touch, even as the feel of her under his fingers sent a surge of sensation through him.

Teasing with temptation, courting danger? he thought as he turned to remount his gelding. Perhaps. But that little interlude proved he was no more ready than she to abandon the game completely.

Which meant he must be doubly on his guard. Fortunately, Lady Comeryn would be joining them for tea.

With Higgins riding watch behind them, Julian escorted her back to Portman Square.

Chapter Eight

Knowing she would be occupied overseeing her campaign for her friends, Atherton had declined to appear at the next several balls that Maggie and her two charges attended. So it wasn't until a week after their ride that she finally saw him enter the ballroom at Lady Tallaford's entertainment. By then, almost beside herself with fury, anguish and worry, she practically ran across the ballroom to his side.

'Thank heavens you are here at last!'

His eyes widening at her fervency, he gave her a puzzled smile. 'Delighted to see you, too. But what calamity inspires so frantic a greeting?'

'Come to the anteroom with me. We must talk!' She seized his hand, a testament to the depth of her agitation that she barely noticed the inevitable frisson of connection sparking between them.

By the time they reached the salon next door where she thankfully found an unoccupied settee near the fire, Atherton's smile had faded, a look of concern taking its place. 'What's happened to distress you so? Not your family—your brother, his wife, the babe, your mother?' He gave her wry look. 'I don't expect you would be quite so distraught if something had happened to Comeryn.'

'No, thankfully my family is all well. It's Lady Laura. Have you not heard?'

'You know I try to avoid talk about matrimonial intrigues,' he said drily.

'It's not about matrimonial plans. Or at least, not directly.'

'I've heard nothing at all about Lady Laura. She isn't ill, is she?' His look of concern deepened. 'Or is it her father? You told me Lord Carmelton's health was failing.'

Maggie gave a despairing laugh. 'Her father is well, and so is she—at least physically. It seems her father, on his banker's advice, invested almost all his available capital in a new railway venture recently approved by Parliament. The generous returns on earlier projects—to which I can attest—have apparently generated a frenzy of new development plans, with no coordination between the different projects. Not only did this particular venture duplicate a route already under construction, the terrain proved so challenging that the cost of building soon far exceeded the capital the engineers had available. To sum up, the venture has gone bankrupt.'

'Which, I assume, means Lord Carmelton has lost all of his investment, with no hope of recovery?'

'Exactly. But it's worse than that. He put into it not just the ready cash he had available—he also invested the whole of Laura's dowry. Which has also been lost. Indeed, she told us that the shortfall of coin is so extreme, they will have to rent out the London house and return to the family estate in Warwickshire.'

Atherton frowned. 'Cutting short her Season—and throwing all your plans in disarray. You will need to work faster, it seems.'

Maggie gave a bitter laugh. 'If only it were that easy. Only think, Atherton! Lady Laura may be a marquess's daughter, but with no dowry, her value in the Marriage Mart has been suddenly and drastically reduced. Over this last week, as news of her father's reverses made its way around the ton—and as you can expect with a titbit so shocking it didn't take long—I've had to stand by helplessly and witness the humiliating drop in the number of gentlemen conversing and dancing with her. Even two of my own candidates have distanced themselves, which is ridiculous, since both are wealthy enough not to need a bride's dowry.'

'Few gentlemen do not wish marriage to add to their coffers, even if their money chests are already overflowing.'

'Nothing about the excellence of her person, talents or character has changed one whit! Yet she is being punished for circumstances over which she had no control—because her father, hoping to increase their wealth, put his trust in an adviser who turned out to be reckless. This whole debacle orchestrated by *men*, of course, who can cut their losses and move on to other things. Whereas she, with no other way to secure her future but by marriage, has hers ruined! Galthorpe hasn't abandoned her, and Fullridge has been faithful, but so few others. It makes me so angry I could—could do someone an injury! Starting with the City banker who advised her father.'

Though relieved to have confessed the distress weighing so heavily on her to Atherton, the recital did little to ease her agitation. She sat back, pressing her lips together to hold back the tears that threatened.

Atherton regarded her soberly. 'I wish I could offer some optimistic words of advice, but you've summed up the situation accurately. I'm so very sorry. The best I can do is make sure not to take you near the City again armed with a whip or pistol. I'd not have the situation made worse by having you attack the offending banker.'

Though she appreciated his attempt at levity, her spirits

were too depressed to respond to his humour. 'Mama and I both assured her we'd be delighted to have her stay with us at Portman Square for the remainder of the Season, if it does become necessary for them to vacate Carmelton House, but I'm not sure we could persuade her. Most of her ton suitors have already abandoned her. Galthorpe and Fullridge have proved faithful, both of whom she should seriously consider.'

She sighed. 'Eliza warned me not to push either of them on her, saying I should let her have time to recover from the shock of the financial reversals.'

'Wise advice I would second. The last thing she needs in so distressing a situation is someone forcing solutions on her. And you can be quite…forceful,' he added mildly.

Maggie waved a hand. 'I know, I know! But it's infuriating to stand by, watching girls of lesser charm and character claim the attention of men who formerly ignored them to court Laura, while the snide make disparaging comments or express falsely sweet sympathy for her "situation". I could do them all an injury, too!'

'My fierce and loyal Maggie,' Atherton said, taking her hand and squeezing it.

She put her hand over his, her anguish somewhat eased by the comfort of his presence. 'I *hate* feeling so helpless! Rest assured, anyone now snubbing her will receive the cut direct from me for ever after.'

'I'll take care that you don't have a whip or pistol while you're near any of them, either,' Atherton said wryly. 'Come now, you must put on a brave face. I can't think at the moment of anything that might help rectify the situation, but having Lady Laura see you so distressed can only deepen her own anguish.'

Maggie blew out a breath. 'You're right, which is why

thus far I've masked my agitation when I'm around her. It's been difficult to conceal, though, when I've been so worried and angry. Thank you for listening. Since I don't want to distress Mama either, I've avoided discussing Laura's situation with her, but I was beginning to feel that if couldn't vent some of my agitation and outrage to someone, I would explode.'

Atherton tipped her chin up. 'I'm always ready to listen. I'd do anything I could to alleviate your distress.'

She did feel better. Once again, Atherton was proving himself both understanding and compassionate, qualities never shown her by any man but Crispin. Thank heavens they had devised a way to retain their friendship, for she wasn't sure what she would have done without his comforting presence tonight!

Indeed, now he'd soothed the edge off her agitation, as she looked up into his eyes, she suddenly became intensely aware of his thumb stroking her chin, his head bent down towards hers, the warmth of his nearness, the strength of his solid, muscled body close to her.

She saw his eyes darken with the same desire flaring up in her. She felt her eyes flutter closed as she leaned her face up to him.

Until she remembered herself, and the fact that the kiss she longed for couldn't happen, especially not here in an anteroom where at any moment someone might walk in. Hastily she sat back, even as Atherton, obviously also recalling the danger, dropped his hand and moved away. Both sat motionless for a moment, simply staring at each other, their unspoken longing simmering in the air between them.

Pulling herself from its spell, Maggie said, 'We should get back to the ballroom. You could help in one way—you could dance with her.'

'Of course I will.' He smiled ruefully. 'Not that I'm sure it will help much, since I'm known to be as firmly opposed to wedlock as her friend Innesford.'

'It will help to show that a handsome, desirable parti still approves of her. It wouldn't hurt either if you could blast with a disapproving look or blighting word anyone who cuts or disparages her.' She huffed out a frustrated breath. 'It's less effective when I do. As usual, a gentleman's actions are more likely to sway others.'

Atherton stood and offered his arm. 'Back then to the fray.'

Maggie rose, then hesitated. Taking a quick look around to insure they still alone in the room, she rose on tiptoe to brush a quick kiss on Atherton's cheek—not the full lips-to-lips engagement she would have preferred, but enough to express her appreciation as well as her longing. 'Thank you again, my best of friends.'

'Always the best of friends.'

She walked out on his arm, unable to suppress a little voice that said, after that terrace kiss, she might not be satisfied for much longer with simply 'best of friends'.

As they walked back into ballroom, Maggie inclined her head to the opposite side of the room, where Lady Laura waited with her chaperone. Though she stood proudly erect, her expression serene, Maggie could tell the strain in the rigidity of her figure. 'This set is already forming, so we won't rush across the floor to her, but invite her to dance the next one, won't you?'

'I'll be happy to. As long as you promise to dance with me for the one after that.'

'An easy promise to give,' she replied, anticipation at being in his arms—even briefly, in the movements of a pattern dance—further lifting her spirits. Then she halted, frowning. 'There's Eliza—dancing with *Lord Markham*? I didn't know they were acquainted.'

After a glance in that direction, Atherton nodded. 'He's a widower, and certainly old enough to make your list.'

'True, except as a viscount, he's too highly ranked. Indeed, I'm surprised he would deign to dance with a girl who's only a vicar's daughter with a very modest dowry.'

'Perhaps he's not a high stickler. And appreciates beauty, modesty and charm.'

Maggie made a scornful noise. 'Perhaps. I'll have to enquire more closely of her later. Now, let's make our way around the floor and keep Laura company.'

She'd barely spoken the words when she spotted a young man approaching her friend. After a brief exchange, Laura put her hand on his arm and the man led her into the dance.

Looking closer, Atherton said, 'Isn't her partner Mr Rochdale?'

'Indeed it is,' Maggie said, mystified. 'I don't remember seeing him earlier! Perhaps he came to check on his sister.'

'I understand Miss Rochdale is being sponsored by a baronet's wife, but I'm surprised that her banker brother received an invitation to a ton gathering. Not that I object, of course.'

'Miss Rochdale told us her brother became great friends at Oxford with Thomas Ecclesley—a baron's younger son, you may recall. With no money settled on him, he had few prospects until Rochdale helped him obtain a position in banking, which eventually earned him the independent income he lacked. In thanks, the son insisted his extended family and friends invite Mr Rochdale to any entertainments they hosted—they have a family connection with Lady Tallaford. Although his sister said he almost never attends such functions. Given the disdain I noted in him regarding members of the aristocracy, I'm not surprised.'

'He's definitely here tonight. And dancing with Lady Laura.'

Maggie sighed. 'Much as I appreciate his support of her, interest displayed by a banker will not help her prospects very much.' At Atherton's raised eyebrow, she said, 'I'm not being top-lofty! It's simply the truth. You know how snobbish the ton is.'

'Sadly, yes. Though Lady Laura seems not at all worried about any negative opinions her escort might elicit. She seems quite…taken.'

'Miss Rochdale's brother is charming and handsome. I'm sure it's a relief to dance with someone who probably understands better than anyone the gravity of her situation. Someone with whom she doesn't have to pretend that everything is fine.'

Satisfied that her friend was supported for the moment, Maggie was about to turn away when Laura suddenly dropped her partner's arm and fled. After a moment of immobility, Mr Rochdale hurried after her.

'Something's wrong!' Maggie exclaimed. 'I must help her!'

Dodging the waltzing couples, she wove her way across the floor, Atherton at her heels. Looking around frantically after reaching the far side, she suddenly spotted them. 'They're on the terrace,' she murmured to Atherton under cover of the music.

Not wanting to call attention to the couple, she slipped silently out the door, Atherton shadowing her, then halted. Lady Laura stood in the shadows, Mr Rochdale beside her. She heard his urgent murmur offering to escort her back inside to the ladies' withdrawing room and find her chaperone to take her home. Only then did Maggie realise that Laura was weeping.

'I must go to her!' she whispered urgently to Atherton.

He stayed her with a hand before she could move. 'Do you have any reason to distrust Mr Rochdale?'

'Not at all! He's very protective of his sister. I'm sure he's just trying to help Laura.'

'Let him. It would only embarrass and further distress her to know you've observed her loss of composure. If you trust Rochdale to ensure she gets safely home, don't interfere. Wait and call on her tomorrow, after she's had a chance to recover herself.'

As Maggie hesitated, irresolute, Atherton murmured, 'Would you want her to discover *you* so overcome?'

'No,' she admitted with a sigh. 'Very well, I'll trust Mr Rochdale to see her safely home. But,' she added as they crept silently back into the ballroom, 'I'm even more eager now to do someone an injury.'

'Then why don't we forgo dancing and proceed straight to the cardroom? Perhaps some of her faithless swains are there. You could relieve your frustration by fleecing them of as much blunt as you can manage. '

Maggie gave short laugh. 'That *would* make me feel better. Very well. Cards it is.'

As they entered the card room, Maggie surveyed tables, her eyes narrowing. 'See—over there? You know Mr Pyrtonby, the baron's son?' At Atherton's nod, she continued, 'He was one of Lady Laura's most faithful courtiers…until he heard she no longer possessed a fat dowry. I'd be delighted to relieve him of some of the ready. Mr Linkworth is with him. Pyrtonby's sycophant, he follows everything the man does, so he snubbed Laura too. Perfect targets.'

Though Atherton sighed and shook his head, he followed without protest.

Arriving at the gentlemen's table, Maggie stopped and smiled sweetly. 'Good evening! May we join you for a rubber?'

Pyrtonby stood and bowed, returning her smile. 'Lady Margaret, you are always welcome! It would be my delight to partner you.'

Probably because she had the reputation of always wining, Maggie thought acidly—and shook her head. 'Sorry, but I've already agreed to partner Lord Atherton. Shall we settle for being opponents?' she asked, unable to hide an edge from her voice.

'I'd never wish to oppose you,' Pyrtonby replied—doubtless for the same reason. 'But I could never refuse the request of so lovely a lady.'

Maggie gritted her teeth at his saccharine gallantry before replying, 'How very chivalrous of you…on this occasion.'

Anger simmering under the surface, she ignored a reproving look from Atherton that seemed to warn her to watch her behaviour. 'Focus on the cards,' he murmured as pulled out a chair for her.

Rather than distract, her impotent fury seemed to sharpen her wits. In record time, she and Atherton annihilated their opponents and won the rubber, as well as a significant amount of blunt, for she'd staked far more than the trifling amounts she usually waged when gaming only for amusement. Linkworth, blanching at some of the amounts, was white-faced by the time the rubber ended.

'You certainly demolished us, Lady Margaret,' Pyrtonby said gamely as he pushed towards her the final stack of coins.

'That was refreshing,' she said, feeling a tiny bit better at having discommoded the man who'd slighted her dear friend.

Pyrtonby blew out a breath. 'After that trouncing, I could certainly use a liquid restorative! May I escort you for glass of wine, Lady Margaret?' He gave her an ingratiating smile. 'Basking in the company of a beautiful lady would do much to relieve the pain of having my pockets emptied.'

Maggie frowned. Pyrtonby had played a significant part of Lady Laura's court not just because her friend was well-born, lovely and charming; she had also—formerly—been reputed to possess a significant dowry.

Were rumours that Maggie was desperate to marry prompting Pyrton's unusual gallantry? He'd never paid much attention to her before. She hadn't heard that he was in dire need of cash, but his family wasn't one of the ton's wealthiest. The fact that she was keeping company with Atherton, who was known to have no interest in wedlock, might be giving Pyrtonby the idea that snagging *her* dowry could be possible.

'It's kind of you to ask, but I need to consult Lord Atherton about strategy for future games.'

'Perhaps I should listen in. It appears I am in need of new strategy myself,' he said, and had the audacity to give her a wink to underline the double meaning behind his words.

'Better make plans elsewhere,' Atherton intervened, giving Pyrtonby a look that wiped the ingratiating smile from his face. 'Good evening, gentleman. Our thanks for the game.'

At that, Atherton took Maggie's elbow and led her off.

'My, how masterful of you!' she said, a little annoyed by Atherton's seizing of control. 'Not that I don't appreciate your concern, but I think I was doing a fair job of discouraging him all on my own—the little weasel!'

'In my defence, you did ask me to shield you from fortune-hunters,' Atherton protested. 'Believe me, I have no doubt you can handle almost any situation without help from some overbearing male.' He gave a quick laugh. 'You are nothing if not forceful.'

Mollified and a little contrite for immediately assuming he was being high-handed, Maggie said, 'My apologies. I did indeed ask your help and shouldn't have snapped at you for offering it. Though Heavens, if I'm going to have to discourage every potential fortune hunter in the ton, I may flee to the Hebrides as soon as I get Laura and Eliza settled!'

'You won't have to worry about Sir Reginald.'

She looked up at him, her eyes widening. 'Deliver him a warning, did you?'

Atherton nodded. 'In terms plain enough that even that blockhead understood.'

'And how did he respond?' she asked, amused and curious.

Atherton's lips thinned before he replied, 'He said he'd known all along that you were not worthy of his pursuit. Which made me ready to plant him a facer anyway, just for that disparaging remark. He must have realised it, for he speedily took himself out of the room.'

By now they'd reached the refreshment room. Maggie took a glass of lemonade offered by a passing waiter and downed it.

'Better now?' he asked, his tone turning to compassionate enquiry.

Maggie felt tears threaten at the concern on his face. 'Winning Pyrtonby's blunt was satisfying, but it wasn't enough. I wish I could have planted *him* a facer!'

'In the middle of the card room? Think of the scandal!'

he said, obviously trying to lighten her mood. 'Your poor mother would be distraught!'

'The only good reason to refrain,' she said mulishly. 'As if I'd accept him switching his court from Laura to me, even if he hadn't insulted my dear friend! If he thinks to win back his blunt by getting his grubby hands on my dowry, his wit is as lacking as his manners.'

As they approached the table where the wine was set up, Maggie realised Lady Bellingame had just approached as well, trailed by one of her friends. Halting abruptly, she gave Maggie her usual disdainful glance.

Wishing she could give this woman the cut direct, Maggie steeled herself to offer the curtsey politeness demanded. 'Lady Bellingame.'

'Didn't I just see you playing cards with Pyrtonby? Apparently, you've lost the interest of Sir Reginald but gained another *highly* desirable parti there. A coup, if you could bring him up to snuff, and quite a suitable match for one of your character and temperament.'

Meaning a self-absorbed individual who thought only of her own gain, uncaring of the sensibilities or reputation of anyone not of use to her?

While Maggie pressed her lips together to prevent uttering a scathing reply, Lady Bellingame turned to the matron accompanying her. 'Shall we take our wine elsewhere? The air here seems rather…foul.'

'Foul indeed,' Maggie muttered as the two walked away.

'I half expected you to throw your wine in her face,' Atherton said with a sympathetic glance.

'I very nearly did,' she muttered. 'I think it's time to follow Laura's example and leave. If I have to stomach any more insults from Lady Bellingame or more cloying courtship from man-milliners with eyes on my dowry like Pyrtonby, I *will* do someone an injury.'

'Then let me help you find Lady Comeryn.'

Setting down his unfinished glass, Atherton offered her his arm. Maggie took it, her anger fading, a sense of helplessness and hopelessness that was as infuriating as it was enervating taking its place.

Listlessly she bid goodbye to her friends, noting with relief that Lady Laura had managed her escape. Telling Eliza she'd call on her shortly to discuss strategy after the 'latest development,' she let Atherton walk her downstairs, where he reclaimed her wrap and waited with her for her mother, who was bidding goodbye to her own friends.

'Again, thank you for listening.'

'I wish I could do more. I will put my mind to Lady Laura's situation and see if I can come up with anything useful.'

'I doubt anything save a miraculous infusion of cash from some now unknown source would be of any help. But you have helped, just being here.'

'I'll always be there for you.'

Warmth, gratitude and something deeper and more powerful stirred within her. 'Will you?' she asked, marvelling at how much she'd come to value his support.

'If it's at all within my power.'

'Can you come for tea day after tomorrow? Laura told me the Harris-Smythe ball will be the final Society event she attends. She said she refuses to subject herself to any more snubs, snide remarks or infuriating pity and I can't say I blame her. I assured her she mustn't give up hope, even if she abandons *ton* entertainments. Mama and I had already planned to give a dinner for her, with Eliza, Fullridge and Garthorpe in attendance and will now include other friends who've not deserted her. Like you, I hope. Could you come for tea, so I can discuss it further?'

Looking resigned, Atherton said, 'If you want me there, I'll be there. For tea and for the blasted dinner.'

The tenderness in his face was echoed in his voice, in the protectiveness that sheltered her from being buffeted by passing guests. Much as Maggie was determined not to let herself need any man, his quiet concern once again touched some deep cord within her. Angry, tired, distraught, she wished she could throw herself in his arms, lay her weary head on his chest and pretend for a few moments that everything would be all right.

But of course, with the butler standing nearby, milling footmen and a continuous stream of departing guests, seizing such comfort was impossible.

She limited herself to squeezing his hand. 'Your support means more than you could know.'

Squeezing her hand back, he simply nodded. The strong sensual attraction was still there, humming between them undimmed. But paralleling that a deeper bond was developing, something that soothed and comforted. When she was with him, she knew she could voice her opinions, express what was troubling her, be *herself,* and still be accepted, valued and cared for. She'd never experienced that sense of belonging with anyone.

She would have to be very careful not to let the unruly desire he evoked spiral out of control, causing him to withdraw from her the friendship and support that was becoming so vital. And, at the same time, guard against a deepening connection that could leave her too dependent on him.

Chapter Nine

Two days later, Julian walked up the steps of the Comeryn townhouse. Despite his disinclination to assist in what he still felt were Lady Margaret's ill-advised matrimonial schemes, he was too concerned about her distress over her friend— and too concerned for Lady Laura herself—to fail to support either of them. Even if that meant sitting through what might be an uncomfortable dinner.

He stifled a sigh. He'd spent a few hours the last two days sitting in his own library over port, examining every angle of Lady Laura's situation, looking for any possible solution, without success. As Maggie confided at the Talla-ford ball, her friend's few alternatives were to retire unwed to her family's country home, probably to remain a spinster for ever, to marry one of Maggie's candidates, or to hire herself out as governess or companion.

Much as Julian disliked Maggie's scheming, he had to agree that marriage to a kind gentleman who'd care for Lady Laura would be the best alternative. Unlike Maggie, who was often far too strong-willed about imposing her well-meant solutions on her friends, he wouldn't go so far as to press that option on the lady himself. But for once, unless Lady Laura had in mind an alternative marriage candidate of her own, he was willing to support Maggie's attempts to see her settled. Including remaining congenial during the upcoming dinner.

Perhaps he'd get a few enjoyable hands of whist by the end of it. In the interim, he'd try his best to put the smile back on Maggie's lovely face. He found it unexpectedly disturbing to see her so distraught, a discomfort that inspired in him a deep desire to do something, anything, to alleviate her distress.

Good thing the vestibule at Tallaford House had been so crowded, or he might not have been able to resist a strong urge to pull her in his arms, hug her close and offer comfort.

That desire to shelter and protect was perhaps more shocking than his undimmed desire for her. After the suffocating neediness of Sarah Anne, he'd thought he would never again want to be a source of solace to anyone but his sons.

Apparently, he'd thought wrong.

Maybe it was just the shock of seeing Maggie—fiercely independent Maggie, I-can-take-care-of-myself-thank-you-very-much Maggie—so in need of comfort. Comfort she'd not requested, asking only that he listen to her express her distress. Touched that she'd allowed him to see her so vulnerable, he'd found himself wanting to offer it unbidden. And meaning that offer sincerely, even to the point of ignoring his still strong objections to her matrimonial designs.

She felt things so deeply, passionate not just in her physical desires but in everything she cared about—horses, sketching, architecture and especially her love and loyalty to friends and family. It would be difficult to soothe her anxiety over someone she loved so well, but he would try.

Determined to rally her, he walked into the parlour as Viscering announced him.

To his surprise, the Maggie who jumped up and hurried

over to greet him wore an expression of excited delight. Both taken aback and relieved, he gave only a distracted bow to Lady Comeryn, who smiled at him from the wing chair by the hearth.

'Oh, Atherton, I've just had a note from Laura,' she cried. 'It's the most wonderful news!'

'Her father has recovered from his reverses?' he guessed.

'Yes. Come, sit, I'll tell you all about it.'

'What brought about this miraculous rescue?' Julian asked as he took a seat. 'Did Lord Carmelton find an investor to buy up his debts?'

'Apparently. I don't understand quite how it works, but her father told her the debts had been assumed by another creditor. One who fixed such favourable terms for repayment, they would be able to remain at Carmelton House. There would even be enough to restore her dowry! Is that not amazing?'

'That's excellent news,' he said, surprised and wondering who would have both sufficient cash reserves and the desire to take on such an obligation. Agricultural earnings, as he knew only too well, were unreliable in the best of times; it could take years for the Marquess to repay the amount he'd borrowed from his estate's returns alone. Most serious investors sought ventures that offered a much quicker payback.

Perhaps one of Carmelton's friends had stepped in—but whoever it was would have to have a very ample supply of liquid assets to manage such a thing, something few aristocrats possessed, their wealth being mostly tied up in land.

'Probably the investor bought the debts at a discount, but even so, it's a very fortunate development,' he said after a moment.

'At a discount?' Lady Margaret wrinkled her brow. 'I'm

not sure how such a thing works. I should just be happy her situation is resolved, but I am curious. Could you explain it to me, Atherton?'

'Let the poor man drink his tea first,' Lady Comeryn chided as Viscering brought in the tray. 'The very idea of managing such accounts makes my head spin!'

Chat about Lady Laura's situation halted while the Countess poured them each a cup. She then turned the conversation to asking about Julian's sons and how the youngest was adjusting at school.

'From the brief notes I've got, as well as can be expected away from Nurse's indulgent care. Fortunately, Ned has his older brothers to smooth his way. But it did sound as if he were a bit melancholy. So I'm planning to surprise the boys with a visit and a trip back to town. I must admit, I miss them as much as they miss home. I'm rather glad Stephen's note gives me an excuse to fetch them.'

'What a kind Papa you are,' the Countess observed. 'Not many ton gentlemen would interrupt their Season to entertain three active youngsters.'

'How can I not? They miss having a mother, though little Ned never knew her and even Stephen, the eldest, barely remembers her. He does remember her sweetness and the love she lavished on him. I can't fill the gap left by her loss, but I do make an effort to show my concern for them.'

'I'm sure your sons will do fine as long as they have the loving care of one parent—as I have!' Lady Margaret said, patting her mother's hand. 'What treats do you plan for their visit? Astley's, I'm sure. The theatre?'

'Definitely Astley's. Probably also Tattersalls and Burford's Panorama.'

'You should take them to the British Museum,' Lady Margaret advised. 'They might not be too impressed with the Elgin Marbles—though the carving of the horses is magnificent—but what boy could resist the Bird Room with all those stuffed specimens? Or the displays of minerals, fossils, reptiles and bugs?'

Julian lifted an eyebrow. 'You visited all these curiosities?'

'During our trip to London several years ago, before I was out, Crispin took me to see the Marbles,' Lady Margaret said. 'While at the Museum, I insisted on seeing the other exhibits.'

'No little boy could be more interested in viewing reptiles and insects than my daughter,' the Countess said, shaking her head. 'Such a scamp she was, growing up! Always riding about the estate, climbing trees, catching frogs, jumping through streams.'

'And as often as I could manage to escape undetected, doing so wearing a pair of Crispin's cast-off breeches,' Maggie said with a grin. 'You must allow, Mama, it's much easier riding and climbing when one is not encumbered by skirts.'

'I wouldn't know,' the Countess said drily. 'I sometimes despaired of her! But she's grown into a delightful young lady,' the Countess said fondly.

'I completely agree,' Julian said, winking at Maggie. She might have grown up with a boy's curiosity, but there was nothing a bit masculine about her curvaceous figure...or those tempting lips.

It suddenly occurred to him that having her accompany his boys to the Museum would make the trip even sweeter—along with providing a safe venue for him to spend time with her. Nothing remotely romantic was going to occur with them surrounded by his boisterous offspring.

Besides, he realised, he'd like them to meet her. As there

was not a particle of anything reserved or missish about her, they were sure to enjoy her company.

'Perhaps you should accompany us, since you seem to possess the same turn of mind as the boys.'

'If that is a challenge, I accept,' she said.

'Excellent. I'll let you know before I fetch them to London. Lady Comeryn, would you like to come along?'

Not surprisingly, the Countess shuddered. 'Heavens, no! No insult meant to the company, but I have no desire to view skulls, bugs or stuffed birds! I would be happy to entertain them if you want to bring them for tea.'

'I'm not sure I could trust them in a lady's drawing room,' Julian said. 'But thank you for the invitation.'

As Julian set down his cup, Lady Margaret turned back to him. 'Now that you've had your tea, may I ask my questions? The success of my investments has made me curious about all things financial. I would like to learn how a debt like Lord Carmelton's could be discharged.'

Before Julian could answer, Viscering bowed himself in to announce that several of the Countess's close friends had called.

'Please send them in and bring another pot of tea.' Turning to Julian, Lady Comeryn said, 'It's a lovely day. Since any talk of finance is beyond me, would you mind taking your discussion into the garden? While I chat with Lady Augusta and Mrs Schilling about things I do understand. Viscering can send for Anna to bring your wrap, Maggie, and accompany you.'

'A walk sounds delightful,' he answered, giving the Countess a bow as he stood.

Her eyes merry, Lady Margaret took Julian's arm and walked him out, pausing in the hallway to greet the Countess's new guests. While they waited in the entryway for Lady

Margaret's maid, she threw off his arm, lifted her skirts and danced around the space, laughing at her own foolishness. Laughing with her, Julian felt his chest swell with relief and fondness, her happiness making his own heart beat faster.

A few minutes later, he walked her through a side gate onto the manicured gravel path leading to the small allées of shrubbery behind Comeryn House, the maid trailing at a discreet distance.

'Now for my finance questions,' Maggie said. 'Lord Carmelton still owes the same debt, doesn't he? How can having another investor have improved the situation so dramatically?'

'To have run so deeply in debt that assets like his townhouse were threatened, he must have put not only his available cash into the railway venture, but also borrowed additional funds to invest,' Julian explained. 'When the project failed, he would have had to take out further loans to pay the interest on the first borrowing and to support his current expenses. Paying off those loans would have required virtually all the income he earned from the estate's harvests over the next few years, as well as anything additional he could generate by renting out the townhouse or selling unentailed property. Apparently, some other investor bought up the debts, paying off the original loans immediately and assuming the obligations while offering the Marquess an extended repayment period, so he wasn't forced to liquidate all his assets. Even, apparently, extending the loan so he might use part of the money to fund his London expenses and Lady Laura's dowry.'

Maggie nodded. 'I think I understand. Laura certainly would. She's a genius at numbers, you know. Attends lectures given by Mr Babbage about his "Difference Engine" with her friend Lady King, another mathematical prodigy.'

'All's well that ends well,' Atherton said, smiling.

'It's not ended yet! Her dowry is restored, which gives her back her options, but that doesn't settle her future. She still needs a husband, which means I still intend to arrange that dinner. Her note didn't indicate whether she intends to return to Society—after the way she's been treated, I would understand if she wanted to spurn most of it! But she'll have a better chance anyway to become acquainted with her suitors in a smaller gathering attended just by friends and carefully chosen guests.'

'A better chance to become uncomfortable with your manoeuvring,' Julian retorted. With the immediate crisis resolved, he couldn't suppress his strong disapproval of her whole strategy.

'It won't become uncomfortable,' Maggie countered. 'I've dined with Fullridge on several occasions. He's quiet but well-spoken, and too considerate to press or embarrass Laura. If it seems they are not getting on, he will withdraw. Laura is well able to hold her own, too. You'll see.'

'Will I?'

'You promised to support me during dinner,' she reminded. 'You don't intend to go back on your promise, do you?'

Trapped, Julian grimaced. 'With a happy end to the financial matter, I was hoping the dinner wouldn't be necessary. But if you feel you must continue with your plans… No, I won't renege on my promise.'

They'd been walking some distance ahead of the maid. As they reached the spot where the allée turned the corner, Lady Margaret gave a quick glance over her shoulder, as if to ascertain just how far ahead of the girl they were.

Then, seizing his arm, she pulled him quickly around the corner out of sight, leaned up and kissed him.

Startled, but not shocked this time, he should have moved away immediately…but once again, he couldn't make himself. Keeping his hands rigidly at his sides to prevent himself from drawing her closer, he simply stood motionless. And let her kiss him.

Fisting her hands in his lapels, Maggie brushed her lips against his, then opened her mouth to him and began a leisurely exploration that aroused him instantly. The kiss was sweeter, less frantic than the one she'd given him on the terrace but no less urgent, more tender but no less thrilling.

Apparently, she retained enough awareness to realise the maid would soon catch up, for after a few seconds of pure sensual bliss, she broke away, brushing a fingertip across his lips as she stepped back. Though every impulse shouted at him to pull her back into his arms, he let her retreat.

'That was to thank you again for your support,' she said as she placed her hand back on his arm and set off a bit unsteadily down the allée. 'With Lord Carmelton's financial debacle the most unusual situation I trust, please Heaven, to ever encounter, I don't expect anything that dire to happen again. So there shouldn't be another occasion more deserving of my thanks. In any event, I promise I won't steal any more kisses.'

'Can you promise that?' Arousal still coursing in his blood, he wasn't sure he could. But none of the reasons to refrain from the risk of kissing her had changed, so he would have to remain vigilant. And simply savour this unexpected opportunity to share one final kiss.

She sighed. 'We might both be better pleased if I couldn't, but we've already agreed indulging in more would be too dangerous. Fortunately, the shrubbery here is thick and Anna is very discreet. But as you pointed out at the ball, one can't count on every place—or every person—being as obliging.'

'True,' he admitted. They simply must be more discreet, lest they risk disaster.

Their discussion of financial matters having reminded him of her keen interest in such things, it suddenly occurred to him there could be another public venue where he might safely spend time with her.

'Before you drag me to that matchmaking dinner you won't agree to cancel, let me invite you to share something I'd find more enjoyable—and equally safe.'

She turned her face, which she'd cast down at ending their tête-à-tête, back up to him, her eyes brightening. 'What might that be?'

'You've expressed an interest in commerce, have you not?' At her nod, he continued, 'You may remember I invested in the St Katharine Docks, which are located just east of the Tower. Not that far a ride from Mayfair, and only a bit further from there to the East India Docks. I could drive you in my phaeton, you could bring your sketchbook and we could make a picnic of the journey. You'd see goods being unloaded by the unique and very impressive equipment at St Katharine's—an apparatus well deserving of being sketched—and perhaps observe some exotic stores brought ashore at the East India Docks.'

As he expected—unlike the response he presumed would come from any other ton maiden—she cried, 'That sounds wonderful! When do you propose to make the trip?'

'One needs tickets to visit the East India Docks, which I must obtain in advance.' Julian gazed up at the sky. 'One can never predict English weather, but it's fair enough today and the clouds indicate that clear skies should hold for a few more days. Shall we say in the morning two days hence, unless it's pouring down rain?'

'Unless there's a heavy downpour, I'm willing to go. You may recall I'm thinking of purchasing a phaeton for my own use. I'd like to try driving yours.'

'I won't promise you that! Not along the streets in London at any rate, which are much too busy for a novice driver.'

'In the park then, another day?' she coaxed.

'Perhaps,' he returned, unwilling to promise more. 'Now, we should return you to the house before your mother's guests begin to speculate about our absence.'

Trying to ignore the aroused senses still smouldering in the aftermath of her kiss, Julian walked her back in. He was more relieved than he could express that Lady Laura's crisis had been so happily resolved, lifting that burden from Maggie's concerned shoulders, and thereby from his own.

However, her normal sunny disposition restored, she'd now focus on single-mindedly pushing forward with her marriage project. Though he might, regrettably, still be obligated to assist at her dinner, at least he had the docks outing to look forward to.

And her curious and enthusiastic company on the visit. Most females, like Lady Comeryn, had neither the inclination nor the desire to comprehend the intricacies of commerce or finance. Lady Margaret was the only lady he'd ever known, with the possible exception of numerically talented Lady Laura, to display any interest at all about investigating them. Indeed, honesty provoked him to observe even most members of his clubs would consider such topics vulgar and taking an interest in them beneath the dignity of a true gentleman.

It was energising to share the commercial concerns that excited him with someone other than his man of business.

Someone open-minded enough to be curious about them. Someone who seemed to appreciate as he did what their development could mean for the future of commerce and England's place in the world.

That that someone was also lovely to look upon with a touch that thrilled him made the prospect of the upcoming excursion just that much more attractive. Even if he must firmly dismiss any possibility of stealing another kiss.

Chapter Ten

As it turned out, despite Atherton's hopeful assessment of the sky during their walk at Portman Square, inclement weather delayed their outing to the docks for several days longer than anticipated. Which turned out to be fortunate, for the afternoon before their ride, Laura had asked Maggie and Eliza to Mount Street for tea and made an announcement so shocking, if she'd not been already scheduled to see Atherton the next morning, Maggie would have sent a note asking him to meet her as soon as possible.

As it was, she'd slept little the night before, frustrated that propriety prevented her from leaving Laura's house and going directly to call on him in St James Square. Forced to wait almost eighteen hours to convey the news, she'd been up since dawn, trying to distract herself with a book after packing her sketching supplies and collecting a basket of provisions for their picnic.

She'd spent the last hour before he was due to arrive pacing the parlour, her book abandoned on the side table, when at last she heard him greeting Viscering in the hallway.

Unwilling to wait a second longer, she rushed to the entryway, basket of victuals and pelisse over her arm, portfolio in hand. 'I'm ready, Lord Atherton,' she said, handing him her burdens while Viscering helped her into her pelisse. 'I wouldn't want you to keep your horses waiting.'

'My tiger is walking them. I'll have to keep a close eye on Henry while we're at the docks. Fascinated with foreign places, he might try to stow away on a merchantman.'

Nodding thanks to the butler, she took Atherton's arm and headed down the entry stairs. 'I sympathise with his fascination. Intrigued by the letters from my brother James, I'm eager to see the ships and their goods myself. But first, I must tell you another bit of shocking news.'

Atherton paused in their descent of the stairs to gaze at her, frowning. 'Not another alarming development, I hope!'

'Not alarming, exactly. More…concerning.'

'Then tell me at once, before we set off. Once driving the vehicle, I'll have to focus all my attention on the team to safely navigate the streets. So—what is it?'

'I won't need to organise a dinner at Portman Square after all. At least, not for Lady Laura. She told us at tea yesterday that she is engaged to marry.'

'Not to one of your candidates, I take it. Then to whom? Did Innesford come up to snuff after all?'

'No. She's to wed Mr Rochdale. The banker.'

As she expected, the astonishing news stunned Atherton to silence. After a moment he said, 'That will certainly set the cat among the pigeons. Does she believe they will be received? Though Lord Ecclesley's family supports Mr Rochdale, it will be heavy going getting the rest of Society to accept him.'

'She doesn't intend to try. Though after how she was treated, I really can't blame her. She plans to abandon Society entirely. Except for the company of family and close friends like us.'

'He seems a worthy young gentleman. Whether he's deserving of that sacrifice I suppose is Lady Laura's decision.'

'His not being a gentleman is truly the only fault I find

with him. Especially after Laura revealed that *he* is the investor who bought up her father's debts. Using not just his bank's assets, but also his personal savings—so she might have her place in Society and all her choices restored, she said he told her.'

'Did he not offer for her at once, then?'

'Not at all! He knew what marrying him would mean for her position in Society. Once she determined, by baldly questioning his sister, that he truly loved her, she had to almost blackmail him into admitting his feelings.' Maggie laughed. 'She told him she intended to withdraw from Society and begin dealing in investments, which, with her flair for mathematics, she ought to be able to do quite successfully. So, she told him, since she would be ruined anyway, if he cared at all for her, he might as well marry her.'

Atherton laughed. 'Now that's a determined young lady.'

'As many times as I've abandoned proper maidenly behaviour, I can hardly criticise her boldness.' Maggie sighed. 'She told me I should be pleased, for her choice fulfilled two of my requirements: Mr Rochdale is wealthy and he's not titled. And I suppose being able to enjoy youthful passion is a blessing not to disparage. But…youth can also be a drawback, for they will be wed a very long time. I only hope his devotion will endure, and he will always treat her with the courtesy and care he seems to offer her now,' she said, recalling her mother being deceived and distressed.

'Lady Laura is intelligent and sensible, isn't she? And Mr Rochdale seems very honest and trustworthy. I doubt your friend would wed unless she believed Mr Rochdale's vows of devotion and is certain he feels for her the same love and respect she does for him.'

'No, I suppose not,' Maggie replied, though *she* was still not entirely convinced. 'He'd *better* always treat her well, or he will have me to deal with! Well, there's no more to be done about it. I'll just have to redouble my efforts with Eliza.'

'I would rather hope this resolution to Lady Laura's dilemma would dissuade you from any further scheming. Isn't it better to let your friends find their own solutions?'

'Eliza still can, if she chooses. But since her need to be settled is even more urgent than Laura's was, I don't see why I shouldn't continue to offer alternatives. And no, you can't dissuade me from going forward, so don't try.'

Apparently realising the truth of that, he shook his head at her, but made no further comment. 'When are the first banns to be called?' he asked instead.

'No banns—they are to wed in two weeks by special licence. Laura didn't want to wait any longer than necessary. She's only delaying that long because she wants to choose a place for them to live. Eliza and I are going to help her find a suitable house and furnishings.'

Atherton studied her. 'You look…melancholy. Aren't you happy for her happiness?'

'Oh, she's glowing, and I am happy for her. It's not that.' Maggie felt again that odd, unexpected sense of abandonment. 'I didn't fully comprehend when doing all this planning that having a friend wed means…losing her. And since Laura is wedding a young man instead of an older gentleman who would before long leave her a widow, losing her for a long time.'

'You're not losing her. Lady Laura will just transition to another phase of life. Change is inevitable, you know.'

'But our closeness can't help but diminish—marriage will mean she must focus upon her husband. Her very *young* husband! Another reason for me to dislike the institution. But enough, let's talk of happier things. I refuse to be downcast on a day when I can drive a phaeton—'

'Ride in one,' Atherton corrected as her helped into the vehicle.

'Sketch,' she continued, determined to recover her spirits, 'and view new wonders like the commercial docks. Let us be away, then!'

Conversation did halt as Atherton guided the high-perch vehicle along the crowded streets. Maggie had visited the Tower of London before with Crispin, but except for their previous journey to Threadneedle Street, had never spent any time outside Mayfair and the theatre district.

She'd been riding on their excursion to the Bank of England, which had required her to focus on guiding her mount around carts, wagons, carriages, pedestrians and other obstacles. Now, as a passenger in an open vehicle, she was free to gaze about her and observe the city as closely as she liked.

Atherton obligingly followed a route that took them down Oxford Street to High Holborn, past Cutler's Hall and the Stock Exchange to New Change and St Paul's Cathedral, where he drew up the team to allow her to admire Wren's magnificent building. From there they proceeded past the north side of the Tower before heading down where the road opened up into a vista of warehouses and water.

Pulling up at the street's edge, Atherton gestured towards the buildings beyond. 'There, for your sketching delight, I give you the St Katharine Docks.'

Maggie gazed in awe at the large expanse of basins in which about thirty tall-masted ships were moored. The basins were bordered by five-storey brick warehouses, their ground floors embellished by graceful arched arcades. A bustle of workmen covered the decks of several of the ships, while men she assumed must be warehousemen, supervisors, clerks and factors bustled in and out of the buildings.

'There isn't much quayside area to allow for unloading,' she observed.

'No. The esteemed engineer Thomas Telford designed the project with a unique unloading system that moors the ships very close to the warehouses, allowing cargoes to be transported directly from the ship's hold into storage. I'm told the unloading process take a fifth of the usual time.'

Atherton paused a moment, scanning the area. 'If you are truly curious about industrial mechanisms, the unique system I mentioned is being used to unload that ship on the far side of the basin.' He pointed with his whip. 'Would you like to see it operate at closer range?'

'Absolutely,' Maggie said, fascinated. She'd seen sailing craft on lakes and in the river, but never anything as massive as the merchantmen. 'As we go, can you tell me how it works?'

As he set the horses in motion, he said, 'The apparatus looks like a giant treadwheel, sixteen feet in diameter! The workers, instead of walking on the exterior of the wheel, pace along on the interior of a large wooden cylinder, six or eight of them abreast. Treading in rhythm to raise the attached winch, the men can lift sixteen to eighteen hundredweight of cargo off the deck and into the warehouse, forty times an hour.'

'Gracious! That's little more than a minute per load. Astounding!'

'Wait until you see for yourself.'

A short time later, Atherton pulled up the phaeton a safe distance away from where the merchantman was being unloaded. While his tiger came to take the reins, he helped Maggie down and waited while she took her sketching sup-

plies from her bag. He then once again stood guard to prevent anyone from jostling her while, her rapt attention fixed
on the men and their apparatus, she rapidly sketched their
likeness into her book.

The stamping feet of the workmen had a pleasing rhythm
about it, accentuated when one burst into a sailor's ditty, the
others soon taking up the tune. Other men were working
winches on the ship, hauling up what appeared to be wine
casks and rolling them to where the treadwheel mechanism
could pick them up. The bustle and efficiency were impressive, as was the amount of goods conveyed into the warehouse even in the short time she stood sketching.

Atherton's high-bred carriage horses, however, were
made demonstrably nervous by the noisy activity, forcing
Atherton's tiger to struggle to restrain them. Noting his dif-
ficulties, Maggie hurried to complete her sketch.

'Thank you for bringing me so close! But now we should
move to a quieter area, lest your horses mutiny and leave
us to walk home.'

'Not an environment in which they are comfortable,'
Atherton agreed. 'The East India Docks have few warehouses, those merchants already having storage facilities
within the city itself at the time the docks were constructed.
So there'll be no hundredweight wine casks lifted over my
horses' heads. Even so, I'll have Henry walk them outside
the enclosure while we stroll around the docks. I'd take you
by the West India Docks, which we will pass on the way,
but because of the prevailing winds, ships arrive there only
from July to October.'

After speaking some soothing words to his team, Atherton helped her back into the phaeton, handed her portfolio
to his tiger and, hopping up himself, put the team in motion.

The St Katharine Docks, still close within the city, were

surrounded with buildings housing workers as well as taverns and a multitude of various shops. But as they proceeded eastward, the buildings grew less numerous and farther apart, until most of the area bordering the road appeared country-like, a patchwork of fields interspersed with a few houses. Then in the distance, Maggie saw the masts of the merchantmen riding at anchor over the high walls surrounding the dock area.

Still some distance away, Atherton pulled up the team near a copse of trees. 'Shall we have our refreshment before we visit the enclosure? We've been travelling for few hours now.'

'I would appreciate that, thank you.'

While the tiger tended the horses, Atherton helped Maggie from the vehicle, then brought over a blanket and the provisions. Spreading the woollen covering over the grass, she seated herself with her back against a convenient tree and set out the meat pies, cheese and jugs of water and cider cook had provided.

After dispensing some provisions to the tiger, Atherton returned and lowered himself beside Maggie. Her avid interest in the sights she had observed during their transit through the city, then her absorption with sketching the workers in their treadwheel mechanism had been distracting enough to mute the effect Atherton's nearness normally produced. But now, with him stretching his tall form out beside her, she was only too aware of him.

The soft breeze wafted to her the faint sandalwood scent of his shaving soap. She could feel the warmth emanating from his shoulder and side as he reclined against the tree just a few inches away. Even relaxed and taking his ease, he still emanated a strength and confidence she found, not imposing or challenging as she had her father's, but...appealing.

She gazed up at his profile, the desire to kiss him welling up again. Fortunately, she thought ruefully, his tiger lounging nearby, sharing his apple with the horses, made an even better chaperone than her maid.

To distract herself, she poured Atherton a glass of cider and handed him a meat pie.

Engage your mind, ignore your senses, she told herself.

She was curious about Atherton's dabbling in commerce; now was a perfect opportunity to enquire further.

'Do I recall correctly you saying you invest in docks as well as canals?'

'You do. I was already handling affairs for the estate when the St Katharine Docks project was approved by Parliament. Although most investors in dock ventures are merchants, factors, businessmen or property owners involved in trade, anyone can purchase shares. To be sure, I was a rarity among my Oxford classmates in having any interest at all in them. Commercial investment by men of our class has become more common with the advent of railways, with quite a number of aristocrats putting money in them or helping sponsor bills. But the India trade in particular has been very lucrative; the returns have been very helpful in financing improvements on the estate.'

'What am I likely to see at East India Docks? You said there are not as many warehouses.'

'There are fewer, yes. The quays are broader and there are no unloading mechanisms like the one you just sketched at St Katharine's. All goods must be handled by individuals or a smaller team of men, which results in a great bustle of activity.'

'Sounds exciting! I look forward to sketching it.'

He gazed at the sky, gauging the position of the sun. 'We should have sufficient time. The dock gates open at ten and the whistle blows at three o'clock, signalling everyone must leave—supervisors, labourers, clerks, horses, wagons, carts and all—before the gates are locked for the night. It's been a huge improvement in security. Before the docks were constructed, merchantmen, which are too large to sail further upriver, had to anchor out, unloading into lighters and smaller vessels. Not only did the unloading take much longer, with no way to control the water traffic around the vessels, theft was rampant. The loss of so much valuable cargo was the major impetus for construction of the docks.'

'Seems a wise investment.' Finishing her cheese, she took a last sip of cider. 'If you are ready, shall we go? I'm eager to see everything!'

'As my lady commands.'

She gave him a sharp look. Would he obey her commands? He was only reluctantly assisting in her plans for her friends.

The vision of their kiss, hovering always at the edge of memory, recurred to send a flare of heat through her. He'd followed her lead there—so far. Could she lead him further—if ever she dared?

Thrusting that question out of mind, Maggie packed the jugs, glasses and leftover bits back into basket, then accepted Atherton's hand to help her up.

He didn't immediately release it after he'd steadied her on her feet; instead, his thumb caressed the top of her gloved hand, producing prickling eddies of sensation as he looked down at her, holding her gaze. The smoulder in his eyes increased the warmth spiralling in her body.

Though the gesture was far less intimate than a kiss, it stirred her senses just as readily. The intensity of his expression hinted that though he might refrain from leaning down to take her lips, the thought of kissing remained as near to his mind as it did to hers.

Then, with a sigh, he released her hand and went to stow the basket and blanket back in the carriage. With a quick squeeze of her fingers, he helped her back into the vehicle, jumped beside her and they set off.

A few minutes later, they reached the imposing main entry to the East India Docks. A triumphal arch with a large central gate and two smaller ones on either side supported a central attic story surmounted by a clock and bell turret. The gates flanked by narrow wings gave way to a tall brick wall that surrounded the entire dock area.

'Very grand,' Maggie noted, gesturing towards the entry.

'I have our tickets ready. Let's disembark, get your sketching supplies, and set Henry to walking the horses. Would you like to draw the gate before we enter?'

'I would.'

Once again, Atherton stood guard while Maggie made a quick sketch of the entry gates with their handsome pilasters, the tall tower and its clock, and the bristle of masts and the upper storeys of warehouses visible over the enclosure walls. When she finished, Atherton walked her to the entryway, where he handed their tickets to the guard, who reminded them to listen for the whistle signalling the closing of the docks for the day.

Inside the gates, the dock area was as busy as Atherton had described. There happened to be a merchantman moored at the first warehouse beyond the entrance—and hardly an unoccupied space to be found where she could retreat from the fray to do her sketching.

Large rectangular boxes stacked in piles ten or twelve wide at the base and towering to two or three times her height took up much of the dockside space. Around them a multitude of men were rapidly pushing what looked like small ladders on wheels, each supporting two wooden trunks, round casks or several bales of what looked like cotton. Other workmen operated winches on the decks of the vessel, hefting boxes or bales and lowering them to the quay or directly into wagons brought alongside. Supervisors walked among the crowd, overseeing the activity and calling out orders.

And over it all drifted the enticing scents of tea, coconut, jute fibre and tamarind.

Maggie looked over at Atherton, enchanted. 'It's wondrous! One can almost taste the tea and spices. Is that what is packed into the chests?'

Atherton nodded. 'With coconut oil in the casks. The scent is even more exotic at the mill across from the north dock, where they grind various spices. One can inhale the odours of cinnamon, cardamon, ginger and the tang of pepper.'

Maggie busied herself, first recording an overview of the bustling scene, then using another page to sketch a vignette of a workman pushing his cart, another of the men working the winch to unload cargo into a wagon, becoming so absorbed in her work that she almost forgot Atherton's presence.

Sometime later, she looked up to see him inspecting her sketchbook with a nod of satisfaction.

'Pleased with your drawings?' Atherton asked. 'I think them very fine.'

She felt a little glow of pleasure at his praise. 'I've captured the scene fairly well, I think. I only wish I could imbue the drawing with the aromas of tea and spices.' Looking around them, she frowned. 'It seems less busy now.'

'It's almost the end of the workday. Most of the wagons

that will carry goods back into the city have already departed and the workers will be getting the last of the bales and boxes into the warehouses for the night.'

As if waiting for Atherton's cue, they heard the piercing blast of a whistle.

'That will be our warning to depart. Have you completed all the sketching you wish to do?'

'Yes, I have enough. The whole scene is so vibrant, I may do some additional pictures at home later, in pastels to better capture the colour of it.'

'If I am particularly obliging, might I have one your sketches?' When she angled her head questioningly, he added, 'To remind me of my investments.'

As a reminder of his investments—or because he'd value having something she created? The latter thought filling her with a warm satisfaction, she said, 'I suppose. If you are truly obliging.'

'Then I expect I must resign myself to attending the dinners and musicales for Miss Hasterling, since I suspect I know what your definition of "obliging" will entail.'

She chuckled. 'It just might. Now I suppose we must make our exit before the gates are locked. A shame—I wish we could linger here and have tea, surrounded by the ships that bring it to us and the aromas of the land from which it comes. Perhaps I will travel there myself one day.'

'A long voyage...and still dangerous,' Atherton observed.

'What is life without adventure—and a delicious bit of danger?' From the sharp glance he gave her, she knew he understood she was referring to more than just travel.

'Delicious indeed,' he murmured, gazing at her lips. She felt them tingle and burn before he looked away.

After packing away her supplies, Maggie took Atherton's arm, navigating her through the groups of departing workers and the last few exiting carts and wagons. They found the phaeton across from entry, Henry slowly walking the horses.

'I wondered if you might run off and leave us, Henry,' Atherton teased. 'I'm sure one or two of those ships will soon be headed back to India.'

'Cor, Yer Lordship, them boats be enormous. I never seed one up close afore. Talked with some of the stevies that was moving cargo, 'n they said first job a new crewman gets is hauling sail up there on the topmast. Made me right queasy, just looking at it from here. Reckon I'll just stay in England.'

'Given that the top will be heeling over violently in wind and storm, staying in England is undoubtedly safer. Have the horses done well?'

'They liked it better here, grazing on the grass verge, than at them docks with the barrels swinging over their heads. But I reckon they're longing for their stable.'

'We'll get them there soon enough.' He helped Maggie up, savouring the delight of his fingers lingering on her waist a bit longer than necessary, before he climbed up himself. 'Back to Portman Square, then.'

During the transit back, while she again watched the passing streets with interest, Maggie's mind drifted over all the unique sights she'd viewed on the tour today. She was particularly eager to look over her drawings and choose several to copy in pastel, so she might capture the light and colour of the docks.

Henry might have been intimidated, but she'd been excited by the grandeur of the ships and their exotic cargoes, giving her a suggestion of what travel might offer—the vista of strange new places, people in many and varied dress speaking languages and performing tasks she'd never before witnessed, the scents of unique products and foods different from anything she'd known. She was grateful for Atherton's indulgence in bringing her somewhere most gentlemen would never think to visit themselves, much less carry a lady.

Atherton's knowledge of the equipment and business of the trading in which he'd invested further impressed her. Most aristocrats, if they cared about anything beyond the earnings brought in by their lands, put their money in banks to increase their wealth, leaving its management to others. Atherton, with his curiosity and keen, probing mind, wanted not just to pocket returns, but to know the details of how his investment was turned into the trade that earned the wealth. Which again reminded her of her brother Crispin and his zeal for learning all he could about railways.

How enjoyable it had been, going on this adventure with someone whose views and interests marched with her own! Learning more about this unexpected side of the Earl further increased his appeal.

That she could savour the small touches of hands as he helped her in and out of the vehicle and ride with her body brushing his in the carriage provided an additional secret delight. Though it didn't begin to satisfy her growing desire for them to be closer still.

Even so, investigating this new world she'd hardly imagined existed in company with a man she admired as much as she desired him had given her the most perfect day she'd ever spent in London.

Chapter Eleven

Several hours later, Julian guided the horses into Portman Square where, to his surprise, Maggie asked him to drive around to the mews. With his tiger available to hold the team while he escorted her in, he was mystified why she would want to enter her home via the stables, but didn't question the request.

After handing her down, he said, 'I'll walk you in. A gentleman always sees a lady safely inside her door.'

'I won't object,' she said with a smile. 'In fact, I'd appreciate if you could stay a bit longer. I've been very impressed with the speed and handling of your phaeton. I'd like to talk with Russell about purchasing one and would appreciate having you give him your advice.'

'I'd be happy to,' Julian replied. 'But the horses are tired, let me send Henry home with the team. I'll get a hackney after we've consulted with the head coachman.'

'If you're sure it won't inconvenience you.'

'No trouble at all.' After giving the tiger his orders and instructions to give the horses an extra ration for their good behaviour, Julian walked Maggie inside the stable gates.

'Like most aristocrats in Society, the horses will consider they've spent the day in surroundings beneath their dignity,' he explained to Maggie.

'Only Hyde Park and Mayfair for them?' she asked, chuckling at the analogy.

'I'm pleased that you approve of my investment interests. It's not just high-bred carriage horses who'd be indignant at the surroundings we visited today. I'd never mention such an outing at my club. The kindest reaction I could expect would be puzzlement as to why I would wish to visit such an area. At worst, they would say taking such a personal interest in commerce betrays my breeding as a gentleman.'

Maggie nodded. 'Crispin says that Comeryn often told him he was a disgrace to the family name for "dirtying his hands with vulgar commerce". Whereas for me, the expansion of travel and trade doesn't just represent a vision of the future. "Vulgar commerce" has gifted me with independence, for which I can never be thankful enough.'

Julian was not sure he was quite so thankful, since that independence allowed her the freedom to not depend on any man. Much as he'd chafed at his late wife's over-reliance on him, he wouldn't mind Maggie leaning on him a bit more. But he'd have to be content with being the friend she chose to consult, if and when she needed him.

And keep his desire for her a subject only of his dreams.

Walking into the stable, they located Russell and spent half an hour consulting about the purchase of a phaeton. If the head coachman looked dubious about a female driving such a vehicle, he knew better than to voice his scepticism.

As they left the stables and proceeded into the garden, a curious mood seemed to come over Maggie. Seeming suddenly tense and watchful, rather than take the allée that led straight to the front entry, she clutched his sleeve and steered him onto one of the side paths. Before he could question her, she leaned up, pulled him close and kissed him.

He managed to avoid succumbing to the immediate, intense desire to embrace her. But rogue that he was, he did clutch her shoulders and hold her against him as she kissed him—and this time, he kissed her back. The delight of feeling her sweet curves against his body was as powerful as the desire throbbing in his blood.

Her kisses were more expert now, as if she'd already learned the contours of his mouth and just the place to caress him that gave him maximum pleasure, setting off ripples of delight that vibrated down his arms and torso all the way to his toes.

He wanted to go on kissing her for ever, but even in the greenery of the garden they were not truly hidden, for a servant walking to the stables or a tradesman searching for the kitchen entrance might at any moment stumble upon them. He imagined the Comeryn servants were discreet, but one couldn't count on them being able to keep from sharing with some 'confidante' the delicious news that the daughter of the house had been kissing a man in the garden—after which, the gossip would swiftly spread through the household and beyond.

So, reluctantly, he broke off the kiss, her sigh of regret mirroring his own. He wished he might at least hold her close while their unsteady breathing slowed, but that would be as damaging, were they discovered, as continuing to kiss her. The most he dared was to linger beside her for a few more minutes.

'Not that I'm complaining, but I thought you promised no more kissing,' he said at last.

'Admit it, Lady Laura's news this time was even more shocking than her father's financial reverses. Yes, it was taking a risk, but some things I simply must taste. I know we can't share more than kisses, but if we are careful…oh, so careful…can't we at least share those?' she asked, her tone pleading.

He hated to deny her—and himself—but he knew he must refuse, even though every fibre of his being craved her touch. He longed for so much more, but how could he justify to his conscience indulging his desires when doing so put her independence at risk? When honour reproved him by pointing out even kissing was a privilege that was supposed to be reserved for marriage. A marriage she didn't want, something he wouldn't want either of them forced into.

'You mustn't think I don't desire it as much as you, but even kissing is taking unfair advantage.'

She made a dismissive gesture with her hand. 'How can it be "taking advantage" when it's what I want, too? Must your sense of honour be that strict?'

Julian shrugged. 'I can't help the standards bred into me. Besides, I don't think we could ever be careful enough. Sooner or later, someone would see us and set tongues wagging. Society would pronounce you'd been compromised, and you know what that would mean. Unless you've changed your mind about marriage?'

She sighed. 'If I were ever to marry, you would be the only gentleman I'd consider. But…no, I cannot face the possibilities involved in wedlock. Not yet, anyway. Well, we should get inside before anyone discovers us.' She turned to walk back to the house.

It took him a moment to set off after her, his mind arrested by the implications of her last comments. Did her 'not yet' mean she *might* contemplate marriage sometime in future?

He'd never thought he would consider it himself. But he was beginning to think he might have been wrong. That he might not only consider that possibility, if marriage meant making Maggie his, he might even embrace the idea.

Wedding a woman who showed every sign of being just the sort of companion he'd long been seeking, who had expressed on several occasions her distaste for the very idea of romantic love, and was so independent that he'd prefer her to be more rather than less reliant on him…one whom he knew would thrillingly satisfy all his sensual desires… might be more attractive a prospect than he'd ever before imagined.

In the late morning a week later, Julian took a hackney to Portman Square. Earlier that day, Lady Margaret had sent a note asking if he might stand in for Miss Hasterling, who at the last minute had been tasked to assist her sister. Maggie and her friend had arranged to meet an estate agent to look at properties on behalf Lady Laura, who was unable to view all the available houses in the limited time before her wedding.

It would all be very proper, she assured him in the note. In addition to the agent, her maid Anna would accompany them and they would travel in the Comeryn landau with her coachman on the box. She'd appreciate his expertise, she added, since, though she knew her friend's tastes, he was better acquainted with London and would be able to advise on the suitability of the locations and their pricing.

Happy for any excuse to spend time with Maggie, still Julian had shaken his head in bemusement at her once again proposing an activity so different from the usual Society outing.

After dismissing the hackney, he trotted up the entry stairs. Viscering escorted him to the parlour, where Lady Comeryn waited with her daughter.

'I'm so relieved you were able to offer your assistance, Lord Atherton,' the Countess told him. 'Had you been unable to step in, I would have had to accompany Maggie, and I'm afraid I'd be no help at all. I've so seldom been in London the last two decades, I know little about the desirability of various areas of the city and nothing whatever about rents.'

'Are you sure you don't wish to accompany us?' Julian asked. 'There will be plenty of room in the landau.'

'I'd rather not. Maggie, curious girl, takes an interest in almost everything, but tromping through buildings, some of which will doubtless be dusty or unsuitable or both, doesn't appeal to me at all.'

'Besides which, two of Mama's friends are coming for tea. She'd hate to miss out on the…*information* they will be eager to share,' Maggie said with a grin.

Meaning 'gossip,' he assumed as the Countess blushed. 'Go on with you, then,' she said, waving a hand at them. 'Anna awaits you in the entry.'

The maid met them with Lady Margaret's pelisse, while the carriage arrived as they descended the entry stairs. Conscious of the maid's presence, Julian kept a respectable distance between himself and Lady Margaret on the bench opposite. Though from the impatient tapping of her foot and the tension in her body, Julian suspected Maggie had something she wanted to discuss that she didn't want the maid to overhear, they chatted only of suitable neighbourhoods and current rental rates during the transit to the first property.

A property they didn't even bother entering, for when they climbed out, Julian discovered that the building was located near Hans Place, almost into Kensington. 'This won't be suitable,' he announced. 'With Mr Rochdale working in the City, it would be much too far to travel.'

The estate agent raised his eyebrows. 'I understood the property was being rented by a marquess's daughter and her new husband.'

'A marquess's daughter whose husband is a banker,' Lady Margaret said. 'If you find that objectionable, we can consult another estate agent.'

'That won't be necessary, my lady,' the man said quickly. 'I have several other sites to show you, further west towards St James's Park and Westminster.'

'Those locations sound more suitable,' Julian said.

As Julian handed Maggie back into the carriage—the most physical contact he was likely to have with her on this excursion, so he made every second of it count—she murmured, 'Goodness, there really wouldn't be any hope for Laura and Rochdale in Society, when even the estate agent disapproves of the match.'

'Ton employees are often even more exclusionary than their masters,' he agreed.

They found the next townhouse more suitable. An older structure of brick, the front elevation facing the street was three windows wide, with a handsome entry door set under a stone Roman arch a few steps up from street level. To the left of the front entry, a spacious parlour overlooked the street, with a dining room and a morning room behind that gave on to a neat garden. The first floor boasted two reception rooms and a library, and the bedchambers on floor above were commodious.

Walking through them, Maggie on his arm, Julian couldn't help daydreaming about the two of them going together to choose a place they might rendezvous… Imagining a bedchamber like this one, where they could freely touch, kiss, embrace without worrying about being discovered.

A place where he could initiate Maggie into all the delights of lovemaking her ardent kisses promised she would find as exquisitely pleasurable as he knew he would. How eagerly he could envision slowly, reverently removing the layers of clothing concealing her body, until she lay naked before him and he could worship her with hands and lips...

Such forbidden imaginings produced a predicable wave of heat. While Maggie made a minute visual inspection of the chamber, Julian walked over to stand by the window. Desire still heated his blood, but he was also filled with an intense, bittersweet longing different from anything he'd ever experienced—passion expanded by a yearning for a connection beyond just the physical.

He shook his head at his foolishness. He shouldn't allow himself even to imagine such things. He couldn't take Maggie as a lover. It wouldn't just ruin her and destroy his honour, it would put her at risk. Lovemaking would inevitably lead to pregnancy, and giving birth, as Sarah Anne's experience proved, was a dangerous business. Nor had Maggie ever expressed the overwhelming desire for children that drove his late wife to plead for him, if he cared for her at all, to continue their physical relations, even after she barely survived the complications she'd suffered after the birth of their second son. Conflicted, torn, unable to give her the intensity of devotion she craved, knowing he could at least grant her that, he'd agreed. That concession had provided him another precious son but led to her death.

Besides, despite his desire for Maggie, even if the affair didn't place her in physical danger, he couldn't reconcile with his honour conducting an affair that would ruin her and destroy any chance for her to wed, should she ever change her mind about marriage.

An immediate protest rose up from deep within at the thought of her married to anyone else. A sacrilege, to imagine any other man claiming the privilege of touching her!

'These rooms seem suitable,' Maggie said, jolting him out of his thoughts. 'We should go inspect the kitchens.'

Relieved to have his unsettling thoughts interrupted, Julian joined her, the maid and the estate agent in descending to the basement level. Once there, Maggie invited Anna's observations, the maid being more familiar with the requirements the staff below stairs needed to carry out their tasks.

When the maid took the agent off to inspect the scullery, Maggie turned to Julian.

His senses still agitated from his passionate imagining in the bedchambers, Julian put himself on alert. 'Not going to surprise me with kissing, are you?'

She chuckled. 'Much as I'd like to, it wouldn't be wise, with Anna and the agent liable to pop back in at any moment. I'd rather use this bit of privacy to confide a concern that's troubling me. If I may?'

So he'd been right about her underlying agitation during their carriage ride. 'Of course. How can I help?'

'What do you know of Lord Stratham? You did see him at the ball last night?'

'Stratham?' he repeated, thrown off balance by the unexpected enquiry. Recovering, he said, 'I did…which is unusual. Though his father, Lord Markham, recently re-entered Society after finishing a year of mourning for his late wife, his son seldom attends Society events.'

Julian didn't add that the baron was usually found dancing attendance on the beauty rumoured to be his *chère amie*, dashing widow Lady Evans, who moved in government circles and preferred political dinners to balls.

'It seems Eliza helped Lord Markham avoid some awkward situation with Lady Arbutnot. I don't know the particulars, but can well imagine one would be grateful not to be caught in embarrassing circumstances in front of her!'

Julian nodded. 'One of the most malicious gossips in Society.'

'Indeed. Apparently, Markham didn't mention the incident to his son, who has now started dogging Miss Hasterling's steps whenever his father approaches her. Though he's not accused her directly, Eliza thinks he believes she's *dangling* after Lord Markham! Is Stratham as arrogant and puffed up with his own consequence as that makes him sound?'

After considering the question, Julian said, 'I don't know him that well. He seems pleasant enough, not noticeably high in the instep. Though one never knows how a man would act if he felt someone were trying to take advantage of a kinsman. I do know Lord Markham was very attached to his late wife and was devastated by her death. Perhaps his son feels it is too soon for his father to be receiving attention from unmarried females.'

'Lord Markham seems congenial, but possessing such high rank, he's rather above Eliza's touch. Still, it is as presumptuous of Stratham to make judgements about Eliza's behaviour as it is for him to question his father's! If Markham does favour Eliza, that's his business. It's not for his son to interfere.'

Julian laughed. 'Are you going to hunt Stratham down at the next ball and tell him that?'

'I just might. But if you feel he is not normally dictatorial and high-handed, I'll give him the benefit of the doubt for a while longer. But I'll not allow him to patronise or intimidate my friend!'

'Is she intimidated?'

Lady Margaret frowned. 'Not intimidated, exactly. She seems…disturbed by him. I'm hoping to interest her in Fullridge or Garthorpe, who each showed their sterling worth by continuing to pay their respects to Lady Laura even after it was believed she'd lost her dowry. Eliza is to perform at

Lady Chiverton's musicale two nights from now and told me Lord Markham asked her to perform a duet with him. Though reluctant to be put on display, she couldn't think of a polite way to refuse.' Maggie sighed. 'Dear girl, she's *hopeless* at coming up with a little white lie to avoid situations she'd rather not be in. In any event, I promised to attend the musicale and support her. I wondered if you'd consider attending, too.'

'Are you going to be matching her up with Fullridge or Garthorpe?'

Maggie's face coloured. 'Mr Fullridge will be there.'

Julian blew out a breath. 'You know my opinion of helping with your schemes.'

'Yes, but we could play a duet later, too. We've not played together yet this Season. I'm not as talented as Eliza, who will likely do some complicated Beethoven piece, but we could perform an air and sing together. I very much enjoyed performing with you last Season.'

Julian frowned, considering. 'I enjoyed performing with you, too. Very well, I'll arrange to attend—but as usual, I'll come later, so you may complete your matchmaking activities before I arrive.'

'Thank you, best of friends,' she said, squeezing his arm. 'I think this house may do, don't you? You said the rent was reasonable, and the distance to his bank not excessive?'

'Yes, on both accounts.'

'I had an ulterior motive when I volunteered to help Laura look at property.' When Julian gave her a quizzical look, she continued, 'I agreed to live at Comeryn House so as not to cause a scandal that would embarrass my mother or impede my ability to help my friends. But with Mama re-established and once my friends are settled, I still plan to find a place of my own. Sooner or later, Comeryn will come to town and I'd rather not deal with him ever again. Mama could live with me, or not, as she chooses.'

'You don't intend to live alone, surely!' Julian said, appalled. 'It wouldn't just be scandalous, it isn't safe.'

Maggie waved a dismissive hand. 'Widows live alone. I'd have staff, after all. It's unlikely some housebreaker is going to murder me in my bed some night.' She laughed. 'I told Eliza if she ends the Season unwed—annoyed as I might be at her for rejecting my candidates—we could live together. Two eccentric spinsters setting Society on its ear! But that's not really what she wants, so I must make best efforts to find her a husband to give her the home and family she's always dreamed of. If necessary, I could turn up some worthy widow or spinster to be my companion and satisfy Society's demand for propriety. But if I manage to travel as I hope I will, I won't be in London all the time anyway.'

Julian found the idea of Lady Margaret travelling in foreign places far away from him as disturbing now as it had been the first time she'd mentioned the possibility. Pushing away the disconcerting thought, he said, 'Are you sure you want to end up an eccentric spinster?'

'Maybe. If, like Laura, I eventually decide to abandon Society, what difference will it make what anyone says? If I'm willing to be exiled, living on my own might offer opportunities for…all sorts of adventures.'

She gazed up at him then, the message in her eyes sending a sharp jolt through him. Did this house hunting make her think—as it had him—about finding a place they could be together, far away from Society's prying eyes?

The intense emotion that had overcome him in the bedchamber flooded back. His mind going blank, he couldn't seem to find the words to reply, only gazing at her with the same intense longing he saw mirrored in her eyes. With a little sigh, she put a hand on his arm, rose up on tiptoes and leaned towards him…

Before their lips could touch, Julian heard the maid's voice extolling the merits of servants' hall, and stepped back, just before the girl entered the kitchen.

Julian shook his head, well aware of the danger they'd just skirted. The maid's voice had sounded unusually loud, he belatedly realised. Had the girl sensed her mistress's attraction to him and sounded a warning before leading the estate agent into the kitchen? If so, he could only be grateful.

Though her face flushed, Maggie recovered quickly. 'You find the area below stairs acceptable, Anna?'

'Indeed, my lady. I think Lady Laura's staff would find it a fine place to work.'

'Then I believe we've seen enough, Mr Gooding,' Maggie said to the agent. 'I'll give my report to Lady Laura. She or Mr Rochdale will contact you if they decide to move forward with the property.'

Taking care not to touch her, Julian followed Lady Margaret out. After the estate agent departed, Julian helped Maggie and her maid into the Comeryn carriage and climbed in after them.

'I appreciate you taking the time to assist me today,' Maggie said as the carriage set off. 'Might I call on you again, if the need arises?'

To inspect other properties she might take for her own, he wondered? 'Of course.'

The presence of the maid meant no private conversation was possible on the journey back, which was just as well. Julian's mind was still cluttered with a jumble of conflicting thoughts and emotions. A deep, instinctive passion for her that seemed only to be strengthening. An unanticipated desire for a closeness on some nebulous, deeper level beyond the mere companionship he'd always thought was what he wanted. The disturbing thought of her travelling far away; the even more troubling idea of her potentially marrying another man.

And strongest of all, the temptation of becoming her lover, the possibility she'd seemed to hint at in stating that taking a house of her own offered 'opportunities for adventure,' clashing with the impossibility of reconciling with his conscience either ruining her or subjecting her to the risks of childbirth.

Arriving at Portman Square, he helped her down, trying to shut down the thoughts he'd by no means resolved. She asked him to stay for tea, but he declined, still too agitated and knowing she would sense it, then want to know what was disturbing him. Not fully understanding it himself, he certainly didn't want to try to explain.

He couldn't reveal he was so unsettled because he now burned to be more than just a friend to her. And could see no path to resolving that dilemma.

Chapter Twelve

Two nights later, Maggie sat beside the Countess at Lady Chiverton's musicale, Eliza Hasterling on her other side, next to Mr Fullridge. While the latest performer entertained guests with some lively ballads, she kept looking towards the door, waiting for Atherton to appear.

She should be used to his late arrivals by now. Since she'd began her matchmaking efforts, he had come late to every entertainment they both attended. But she was always impatient to see him.

Her mind drifted to their last several encounters. While touring the house for Lady Laura, she'd all but spelled out she would like her own residence so she could make him her lover.

She gave a rueful laugh. Heated imaging was all that intention would ever be, probably. She hadn't even been able to coax him into allowing her to kiss him when circumstances were favourable. It was unlikely she'd ever be able to seduce him into an affair that would violate his standards of honour, even if she had a discreet location in which to conduct it.

It wouldn't be safe to do so, anyway. Much as she desired him, she couldn't shame her mother with the scandal of bearing an of out-of-wedlock child. Nor could she bear visiting the stigma of illegitimacy on some poor innocent babe. Even if she could convince Atherton, she wouldn't attempt to do so unless there were some reliable way to prevent conception. Though maybe there might be...

She'd overheard a tantalising bit of conversation while in the ladies' withdrawing room at the last ball she'd attended. Two young matrons, both having provided their spouses with the requisite heirs, were carrying on a low-voiced conversation about their desire to avoid ruining their figures with any further pregnancies. With Maggie loitering as close as she dared, straining her ears, she heard one say she was looking for a way to purchase certain 'supplies' from an apothecary, a product she'd been told was kept in good supply at the best brothels to ensure the activities of their high-class courtesans were not curtailed by unwanted 'consequences.'

Once her friends were settled, if desires continued to bedevil her, she might try to discover the name of one of London's best fancy houses and pay a visit to the madame. If she could be reasonably sure of being protected, and had a place of her own, she could plan a campaign so irresistible that she could seduce Atherton out of honour, doubts and into her bed. Where she might enjoy the delights of passion, with him being for that space of time hers alone.

What bliss, to savour complete union with him without being forced into marriage! Though marriage might eventually be a choice. Would she ever choose it?

Only a few weeks ago, she would have answered with an emphatic negative. Her answer was still no...but her refusal was no longer quite as vehement. When she contemplated sharing life with someone as amusing, interesting, intelligent and passionate as Julian Randall, marriage began to look...somewhat more appealing.

Sharing *too* much with him might risk her coming to care

for him too deeply, though. A vision recurred of her mother's face, bereft as Comeryn swept past her without a word.

She never wanted to become one of those poor females who hung on every word dropped from a gentleman's lips or grew all aflutter when he smiled at her. Or even worse, found her happiness dependent on how much and how pleasant was the time he spent with her.

Much safer to continue remaining just friends.

Though remaining friends would never satisfy one's very intense longing.

Would she dare pursue more?

She sighed, irresolute. Fortunately, she didn't have to answer that question now. Whatever she decided to do, she'd have to wait until after Eliza was settled.

As the soprano finished to enthusiastic applause, the gentleman she'd been awaiting finally walked through the door, just as their hostess announced there would be an interlude before the next performer began. As the guests rose and milled about, Maggie waved to catch the Earl's attention. With the Countess chatting with some friends and Eliza borne off to the refreshment room by Mr Fullridge, Maggie was left free to talk with Atherton.

'I'm so glad you are here at last!' she said, returning a curtsey to his bow.

'Were you missing me that much?' he asked, a twinkle in his eye.

'Wretch,' she said, batting his arm with her fan. 'Not to swell your vanity too much but yes, I have been waiting for you.'

His teasing smile faded. 'Then I'm doubly glad to have arrived,' he murmured, taking her hand and kissing it.

Rather than immediately letting go, he held on, staring down at her. Her fingers tingled, igniting that now familiar melting sensation in her belly. She looked up to meet his gaze, struck anew by the richness and depth of his green eyes, their hue like that of a verdant forest, a place of calm and refuge. A refuge, like in his arms, where she might find shelter?

Someone moved behind them—their hostess, Maggie realised, who'd halted and was eyeing them curiously. Quickly Maggie withdrew her hand.

'Has the evening been a success thus far? Miss Hasterling seemed happy with Fullridge's escort,' Atherton observed. 'You must be pleased by that. She survived her performance with Lord Markham?'

'She did. She played first by herself, Fullridge turning the pages. Then played with Lord Markham, which was fine. But as Fullridge returned to claim her, *Stratham* pressed her into playing a duet with him. I was never so annoyed. Mr Fullridge was not best pleased to be dismissed like a lackey by Stratham, either.'

Atherton chuckled. 'I imagine he was not.'

'Although, as even I must admit, Stratham is almost as talented as Eliza. They performed a Beethoven piece together, and it was exceptional.'

'I imagine Mr Fullridge was not pleased by that, either.'

'No. I suppose Fullridge having a little competition is not a bad thing, if it encourages him to try harder to win Eliza's regard. Fortunately, Markham and Stratham left shortly after. Eliza did seem…discomposed at first by having to accompany Stratham, but once she begins playing, she becomes totally absorbed in the music.'

'She becomes totally absorbed in something she feels passionate about? As does another lady I might mention.'

'Very well, I suppose I do become somewhat…single-minded when I'm sketching,' Maggie admitted.

'Or when you are pushing your friends towards matrimonial candidates?' Atherton added, lifting his brow.

'Not too hard!' she protested, a little annoyed. 'I didn't try to intercept Stratham, even though I could see that Eliza would rather not have played with him. And I have nothing against Lord Markham, who seems genuinely engaging. Still, I admit I was happy to see him and his annoying son depart, leaving the field open again for Mr Fullridge.' She paused. 'I haven't prodded Eliza about her feelings for any of them…yet.'

'I sincerely hope you *won't* "prod" her!'

'She hasn't much time left to make a decision! You know I only want the best for her.'

'That's as may be, but I'd still urge you to let her arrive at a decision on her own. It could only distress her if you try to push her before she's ready. It might even cause a breach between you. *You* wouldn't want to be prematurely forced into making such a life-changing choice, would you? One only knows one's feelings when one knows them.'

She swung her gaze to his, struck to silence by an observation that cut a little too close to home.

Before she could decide whether that comment was meant for him or her or them both, he said, 'Rather than brangle, why don't we find Lady Chiverton and volunteer to perform?'

It would be a relief to forget all her anxieties about Eliza, Fullridge, Markham and Stratham and just lose herself in the joy of performing music. To say nothing of putting out of mind her own unsettled thoughts of what she meant to do, eventually, about her inconvenient passion for Julian Randall.

She nodded. 'Very well. What have you in mind to play?'

Atherton named several popular ballads, to which both

she and then their hostess readily agreed. Once the audience settled back into their seats, they chose their first song and began to play.

Dismissing all her other concerns, Maggie simply revelled in Atherton's nearness beside her on the bench, their hands working in unison to produce the tune while his bass provided a counterpoint to her soprano.

From the smile he gave her as they finished their first selection and began the next, Atherton was enjoying himself as much as she was. They played and sang a second ballad, then with the urging of the audience launched into a third, which Maggie proclaimed must be their final piece so that other guests would have the opportunity to display their talents.

He'd suggested 'Robin Adair', and as they sang together Maggie wondered suddenly if he'd chosen that song because the lyrics resonated as deeply in him as they now did in her.

> *What made th'assembly shine?*
> *Robin Adair!*
> *What made the ball so fine?*
> *Robin Adair!*

And at the end:

> *Yes, he I loved so well*
> *Still in my heart shall dwell*
> *Ah! I can ne'er forget*
> *Robin Adair*

She realised anew that when she wasn't preoccupied with promoting her plans for her friends, it was Atherton's presence that made balls and routs and musicales so enjoyable. That he'd come to occupy a central place in her life as the dearest of friends, someone she looked for to ride and dance and play cards with, to express her ideas to without having to ask herself first if he would consider them appropriate for a lady. She could ask his advice and depend on receiving a blunt, honest assessment—whether she always liked the truth as he saw it or not.

He made her an excellent partner in so many things. Best of all, unlike her father and the rest of Society, he didn't try to imprison her in the narrow box of marriage, children and household management into which everyone else seemed to believe all females belonged. He allowed her to free her mind, expand her horizons, even encouraged her to go and do things the rest of the ton would not consider 'proper' for a well-bred maiden.

And underneath all the rest beat the constant throb of her deep attraction to him and the desire he could arouse so readily with just a touch.

Did he have similar feelings about her? And if so, where might their relationship be headed?

The question both excited and alarmed her. Retreating from pressing herself for an answer, as they finished the piece to the applause of their audience, she told herself she'd worry about that on some other day. For now, she would simply enjoy his company and the guilty thrill of the passion he stirred.

She must not have conquered the unease those reflections produced as successfully as she imagined, for as Atherton escorted her from the piano bench he murmured, 'Are you angry with me? Upset in some way?'

'No, not at all.' Both unwilling and unable to try to explain her tangled thoughts, especially not here in the midst of a crowd, she fell back on, 'It's just…temptation continues, you know.'

He gave her rueful smile. 'Indeed, I do. And if anything, becomes harder to resist. Which is why music is so liberating. Something we can share in the full glare of an audience with no qualms.'

'Though what one desires most and cannot share is always lurking there, in the back of one's consciousness.'

'True as well. Despite that, we should concentrate on the possible. What are your plans for the rest of the evening?'

Was his abrupt change of subject a rebuke? A warning not to entertain fanciful dreams of a future that would never be realised?'

That should teach her not to envision passionate trysts. Trying not to feel chastened, she said, 'Mama is looking weary. After checking with Eliza and Fullridge, we'll take our leave. When will we see you again?'

'I meant to tell you earlier, I'm heading out tomorrow to see the boys at their school. It is near Eton College, where they will go when they are older, so we'll spend the night in Windsor and return to London the day after. I'll probably take them to Astley's first, then to see the Tower.'

She laughed, diverted from her disgruntlement. 'They'll want to see dungeons, imagining prisoners in chains.'

'Ned will probably ask Stephen, who's our history scholar, to recite every gory detail of the few executions that have taken place there. I've also written to one of the Fellows I know for permission to take them to the Zoological Gardens in Regent's Park. We will visit that and the British Museum on alternate days, depending on the weather. Are you still game to join us?'

'Did you think I would have second thoughts and cry off?' she rallied, feeling a little better at knowing he valued her friendship enough to want her to join his excursion with his beloved sons.

'Intrepid Lady Margaret? I think you can handle anything my boys come up with.'

'I expect I can. Let me know which day you've chosen and the time and I'll make sure I'm ready.'

'I see your mother—shall I take you to her?' At Maggie's nod, he walked her over.

'I enjoyed your lovely duets with my daughter,' the Countess said after greeting him. 'You make a fine pair—' she stopped and held up a hand. 'But I'm not matchmaking, Maggie, I promise. Only observing that you are well-matched as performers, the music you create is a delight to listen to.'

'Thank you, Mama. Matchmaking is only for others, and I shall direct it,' Maggie said tartly.

'Whether those others like it or not,' Atherton murmured.

'How are things progressing with Miss Hasterling and Mr Fullridge?' the Countess asked, glancing over to where Eliza sat conversing with that gentleman.

Frowning at Atherton, who rolled his eyes at the question, Maggie said, 'Well, I think. And better if certain arrogant individuals would cease upsetting her.'

The Countess sighed. 'Referring to Lord Markham or Lord Stratham?'

'I think Stratham disturbs her the most. Which is hardly surprising, since he spends most of his time glaring at her disapprovingly.'

'I'll let you ladies continue your discussion and take my leave,' Atherton interjected.

Knowing Atherton wouldn't want to listen to her telling her mother how her plans for Eliza were proceeding, Maggie couldn't begrudge him his desire to depart, especially after he'd honoured his promise to come support her tonight.

'A safe journey to see your boys. I'll look forward to meeting them.'

He bowed to them both. 'Countess, Lady Margaret, I'll bid you goodnight.'

Maggie's gaze followed him as he walked away. How gatherings always seemed duller after he left them, Maggie thought, with the inevitable dip in her spirits as he exited the room. But she would see him again soon. And have the added entertainment of meeting his sons. Would they be very like him? she wondered.

She turned to see her mother's thoughtful gaze fixed on her and, to her annoyance, felt herself flush. Thankfully, the Countess made no comment about it, saying mildly, 'I'm glad your plans for Miss Hasterling seem to be progressing well. Though I am weary. Are you ready to leave?'

'Let me fetch Eliza and I'll be ready.'

Maggie felt her mother's gaze follow her. Did she suspect her daughter's strong attraction to Atherton? Maggie sighed. Probably she did. Mama knew her too well, and was concerned about her welfare, too.

Fortunately, unlike so many matrons with unmarried daughters, her mother had never tried to push or even mention a desire for her daughter to wed.

After living through a union with Comeryn, the Countess would probably understand her daughter's reluctance ever to marry at all.

Although, seeing her partiality for Atherton, who possessed so many positive qualities, Maggie imagined that she might hope that her daughter, if she chose anyone, would choose to wed him.

As long as she didn't suspect Maggie's intention to explore the possibility of a less formal and more carnal arrangement. Even with the distaste for marriage the Countess couldn't help but feel, she'd be shocked at that alternative.

Chapter Thirteen

Five days later, Julian arrived at Portman Square with his three sons to collect Lady Margaret for the promised outing to the Zoological Gardens in Regent's Park. Leaving the rambunctious boys in the vehicle, Julian trotted up the entry steps, eager to see Maggie and hoping that his sons, once let loose to roam the gardens, wouldn't prove too rowdy for her, even though they'd been warned to be on their best behaviour.

He'd never introduced the boys to an unrelated lady before, always keeping close to himself alone this dearly beloved part of his life. But with Maggie now claiming so much of his time and attention, he wanted to show them off to her—and her to them.

If they were to end up long-time companions…or more, establishing good relations between them was essential. He didn't think Maggie had spent much time around children, which made him half-excited, half-concerned about how the meeting would go.

As he was shown in by Viscering, Julian saw the lady herself descending the stairs, already garbed in pelisse and bonnet, carrying her satchel.

'I didn't want to keep you waiting,' she said as she halted beside him. 'I'm sure your boys are impatient to view the marvels at the gardens. I did bring my sketching supplies in case they slow down long enough for me to draw some scenes.'

His heart leaping as she smiled at him, Julian felt a smile curve his own lips, his misgivings fading as he remembered their outings to docks and banking establishments. Touring the gardens with his sons and this adventuresome, adaptable lady was going to be pure pleasure.

'The boys are rather energetic, so I can't guarantee they will be still long enough for you to do much sketching. But I did promise them we'd buy buns to feed the bears. They'll certainly tarry long enough to do that.'

Maggie laughed as she handed him her satchel. 'That should make for a wonderful sketch.'

'I must warn you, excited by the prospect of this expedition, the lads may be a trifle…boisterous.'

'So I would expect. I was often boisterous myself growing up. Sometimes I still can be,' she added, giving him a heated look that set him thinking about kisses on terraces and garden paths.

Shaking his mind free, he led her to the landau—where his sons, too restless to sit still, had scrambled out and were awaiting them on pavement. It did allow the boys, he acknowledged ruefully, to make proper bows to her curtsey.

'Lady Margaret, allow me to present my eldest, Stephen, Viscount Randall, the Honourable Mark and the Honourable Edward Randall. Boys, Lady Margaret d'Aubignon.'

'Pleased to meet you, gentlemen,' Maggie said, while Stephen spoke for the boys, saying, 'Honoured to meet you, my lady.'

Formal greetings complete, boys tumbled back into the vehicle, Julian helping Maggie up at a slower pace. But as they were seating themselves, Maggie said, 'Atherton, why don't we let the boys have the forward-facing seats. You and I know London well, but seeing it for first time, it would be easier if they were not facing backwards.'

Touched that she'd consider them, he said, 'That's thoughtful of you, but a lady always rides facing forward.'

'Pish-tosh, we don't need to stand on ceremony. Do we, boys?' she asked, giving them a wink. 'You know you'd rather see what is coming rather than what we left behind, wouldn't you?'

Julian smothered a laugh as they all looked at him hopefully while Stephen said, 'We wouldn't want to inconvenience you, Lady Margaret.'

'I'd not be inconvenienced at all. Sometimes I prefer to look back at where I've been rather than only where I'm allowed to go,' she replied, her wry tone telling Julian she wasn't referring only to this transit to Regent's Park. 'You will permit it, won't you, Atherton?'

'You'll make me appear an ogre if I do not. Very well,' he conceded, then chuckled.

'What's so amusing?' Maggie murmured as they shuffled around, shifting seats.

'I was just thinking what Lady Arbutnot would say if she saw us riding with the children facing forward and the adults opposite.'

'Probably nothing, as she'd faint dead away at witnessing such a breach of propriety,' Maggie said.

'Have you been to the Zoological Gardens before, Lady Margaret?' Stephen asked.

'As matter of fact, I have not. I'm very much looking forward to it, especially as I understand they just received some new residents—giraffes! Great beasts with long, tall necks.'

'I want to see lions and bears,' Edward, the youngest, announced. 'Something fierce that roars.'

'As I believe giraffes don't make much sound, you may find them disappointing,' Maggie said, exchanging a smile with Julian.

'Bears are fierce,' Mark said. 'Papa says we'll be able to feed them. The keeper ties buns on a long pole, and one holds it over the bars of the cage for them to bite at.'

'That sounds exciting. What are you most interested to see, Lord Randall?' Maggie asked.

'The elephant, which is quite a huge beast. Although I'm interested in all the animals. Papa had the foresight to obtain a map and guidebook for us, so we shall be able to identify all the creatures,' Stephen said.

'Which are identified by both their French and botanical names, giving you boys a chance to practise your Latin,' Atherton said, eliciting a groan from Mark that made Maggie laugh.

'Since you've studied the map and exhibits, we'll let you be our guide,' Julian told his oldest son.

It being a fairly short transit from Portman Square to Regent's Park, they soon reached their destination, the landau travelling down the Outer Circle and into the grounds themselves. The boys quickly alighted, Ned practically jumping up and down with excitement. Julian handed the guidebook to Stephen before helping Maggie down and fetching her satchel of supplies.

Thus began a brisk walk from one exhibit to the next, the boys exclaiming over birds in the aviary, the aquatic birds in their pond, the fields with zebra and ibexes, and the lions— which did roar—in their enclosure. Climbing the overlook, they laughed at the monkeys on their poles and exclaimed over the swift chimpanzees, which ran along the bars of their enclosure after the boys, making their high-pitched squealing noises.

In addition to the large collection of birds and animals, Maggie expressed her appreciation for the unexpectedly fine decorative plant borders that had been added between the meadows and wooded sections to embellish the zoological buildings, some fanciful like the Gothic structure topped with a clock tower that housed the dromedaries and the Tuscan barn, complete, the guidebook said, with a heating system inside, for the newly arrived giraffes.

After admiring said giraffes, which even Ned admitted were impressive beasts despite their lack of a fierce voice, they went to the bear pit, where buns were obtained from the keeper, who assisted the boys to feed the animals.

Maggie took out her sketchpad and did several quick drawings of each boy, chuckling at their shrieks of laughter and alarm. 'You must let me have those,' Julian said, watching over her shoulder.

'Not these. Knowing the boys won't be still for long, I'm doing them so quickly they are very rough. But I promise I'll prepare more finished ones later. As a memento of this excursion. Sons are an investment far more precious than docks.'

Pleased at her recognising that and encouraged that she and the boys seemed to be getting on so well, Julian pressed her hand. 'Thank you,' he murmured.

'For what?'

'Appreciating them. Which makes my enjoyment today complete.'

'How could anyone not appreciate them? They are delightful—like their father.'

Strong emotion stirred deep inside him. If she found him and his sons delightful, did that not augur well for the long-term companionship he felt now more than ever he wanted with her? Maybe he had found the one woman who could be independent enough and compatible enough to marry… eventually.

Given her views on the institution, she was a long way

from viewing with favour so binding a commitment. Still, today had him thinking about the possibilities...

The bear feeding complete, Julian helped her store away her sketchbook, then strolled with her as the boys ran ahead, curious and commenting on everything.

'How was your visit with your sons?' she asked.

'Very successful. I met with the boys' tutors to check on their progress—all good. We had a fine meal together at the inn to celebrate Stephen's birthday.'

'Which is the same as his late mother's, isn't it?'

'Yes. That's the main reason I wanted to visit them when I did. Ned and Mark don't remember Sarah Anne, but Stephen does, which makes his birthday a bittersweet occasion. I wanted to try to make the day a happy one for him.'

'I'm sure he appreciated your kindness.'

'He did eat a large share of cake, so I know he appreciated that at least.'

'Are the boys enjoying London?'

'They loved Astley's and have begged me to visit it again before I take them back to school. Ned told me he wants to become a performer there when he grows up.'

Maggie laughed. 'Hopefully he will outgrow that ambition before he's old enough to act on it.'

'Indeed. They liked the Panorama, too, but I think they enjoy just as much simply riding ponies in the park or being driven around the city in the landau. The scenery is so much different from the rural fastness of Randall's Roost or their cloistered school.'

'You love having them with you, don't you?'

'It certainly makes life more dynamic. They are interested in everything, never still, full of curiosity and unexpected questions. Much like a lady I know. When do we lose that sense of wonder, so we no longer see the marvellous in the things around us?'

'When we become too preoccupied with the busyness of life. One doesn't worry about food or clothing or shelter as a child—someone else takes care of it. How much longer can you keep them?'

'I should take them back the day after tomorrow. I don't like holding them out too long—they would have too much to catch up on. I have to admit, though, the house is going to seem terribly quiet and empty once they've gone.'

She must have heard the sadness in his tone, for she pressed his hand. 'I'll just have to keep you too occupied to notice.'

'I'm always happy for you to keep me occupied.'

Her smile turned sultry. 'Would that I could keep you occupied in a manner designed to make you forget…everything.'

His mind went immediately to kissing, which she must have known it would. Shaking a finger at her reprovingly, he said, 'As you know how to do all too well. But you shouldn't tease, making me remember it.'

She sighed. 'Remembering teases me, too.'

The boys ran back to report on the latest curiosity, ending their private chat. As they continued their rounds of the park, Julian noted how easily and naturally Maggie interacted with his sons. At last, Ned announcing he was starving, they agreed to tear themselves away from the fascinating displays. Julian's proposal that they stop at Gunter's for ices was met with a cheer of enthusiasm from his offspring.

They loaded up in the landau, the boys gallantly insisting on Maggie having the forward-looking seat. As the carriage rolled along into Mayfair, they chattered about their favourite animals and how envious their mates at school would be upon hearing about their adventures.

After reaching Gunter's, Julian escorted the group in. Recommending his sons try the pineapple ice for which the establishment was famed, he ordered it for everyone, along with tea for the adults. Conversation languished once their treats arrived, his sons tucking in at once.

'We don't get anything like this at school,' Stephen said after the first few bites. 'Thank you, Papa, for bringing us here.'

'I don't get anything like it at home, either,' Julian said. 'It's a treat for all of us.'

'It's the best thing I ever tasted,' Ned declared. 'Maybe the best thing we've done in London. Although feeding the bears was awfully nice, too.'

Silence fell again while the boys finished their ices. Pushing back his empty bowl, Ned said, 'Are you going to marry Papa, Lady Margaret?'

Maggie choked on her tea, Julian felt his face flush and Stephen hissed, 'You don't ask a lady a question like that!'

'Why not? The boys at school all have mothers. I'd like one, too, and I like Lady Margaret. She wasn't afraid when the lions roared, and she told me she had a bug collection when she was growing up.'

While Julian debated whether it would be better to apologise and prolong the discussion or let it pass—and deal with his youngest son later, Stephen said stiffly, 'We had a mother.'

While Julian gave a tiny shake of head to her, whispering 'Sorry!', Lady Margaret said calmly, 'Indeed you did. A lovely mother, and no one could take her place. Your Papa and I are just good friends. He makes a capital companion, doesn't he?'

'He does,' Mark said. 'He treated us to the most wonderful meal at the inn in Windsor and here in London, he's taken us to see the horses at Tattersalls and the performers at Astley's. And he always goes fishing and riding with us when we're at the Roost.'

'Papa is happier when he spends time with you, Lady Margaret,' Ned persisted. 'His face isn't so sad, and he smiles a lot. I think—'

'Can you take us riding in the park again before we go back to school?' Stephen interrupted, giving Ned a sharp look that warned him he'd said enough.

Undaunted, Ned stuck his tongue out at his older brother. 'It's true, though. Mark told me he noticed it, too.'

Equal parts embarrassed and exasperated, Julian said, 'I think we're finished here. Boys, leave your cups and bowls on the table and go out to the carriage.'

Stephen hopped up at once, grabbing his little brother none too gently by the elbow while Mark followed close behind.

His face still hot, Julian said, 'I am truly sorry about that.'

To his relief, Maggie laughed. 'No harm done. I'm flattered that your son considers me worthy of inclusion in your family. Who knew how impressive a bug collection could be?'

'Don't forget standing by bravely in the face of a roaring lion,' Julian said as he led her out, grateful that she was passing the comment off so lightly.

'Oh, yes, intrepidity when confronted with wild beasts is definitely an asset. Your sons are a charming lot, Atherton. You must be proud of them.'

'I am. Ned in particular could learn a bit more discretion, but they are good boys.'

She chuckled. 'How misguided of him to consider me potentially a mother! I've never considered myself at all maternal. I'll leave that to Marcella and settle for being a doting aunt.'

She might not think so, but after observing her with his sons, he was more inclined to share Ned's view, a conclusion that had excitement and anticipation building within him. Though he mustn't let his thoughts run too far ahead. They'd need to continue their association a while longer before he could think about something more.

'You've done a fine job with your mother. Watching out for her, defending her from your father, always looking to create the happiest situation for her. Traits that would make you a good mother.'

'Well, maybe. Mama's such a dear, she deserves all the love and protection one can give her.' She gave a short laugh. 'She certainly doesn't get any from her spouse.'

So much for favourable thoughts about matrimony. Letting her comment pass, Julian said, 'Thank you for accompanying us and being so indulgent.'

'I've enjoyed it! Strolling around the extensive grounds, watching all the animals, reminded me of growing up, when I used to wander around the countryside with Crispin and James.'

'Of course. You grew up knowing how to deal with grubby boys.'

'I was as grubby as they were,' she said with a chuckle. 'I certainly never had anything in common with my starched-up, impeccable sister, Elizabeth! Boyish and unmaidenly, she called me. A true daughter of Comeryn, she looked down at me with as much disdain as he did.'

By that time, they'd exited the establishment and walked over to the landau, where the boys had already taken the backward-facing seats. After the carriage set off, Stephen jabbed Ned with his elbow, giving him a significant look.

'Stephen says I embarrassed you and must beg your pardon,' Ned said. 'If I did, I am sorry. I didn't mean to.'

'I was…taken aback,' Maggie said. 'But I also must thank you for the compliment. It's quite high praise to be told I was worthy of associating with such fine young men. And thank you, Lord Randall, for wanting to be sure I felt comfortable. Now, before we get back to Portman Square, you must each tell me which were your favourite parts of performances at Astley's.'

Thus diverted, the rest of transit passed in the boys' enthusiastic reminiscences of trick riding, clown's jokes and the smoke and noise of simulated battle scenes.

A short time later, the landau pulled up at Portman Square, Julian walking Maggie up to the front entry.

'You're to take the boys back to school day after tomorrow? You will return in time for the dinner we're giving for Eliza, I trust.'

'I promised, didn't I?'

'Good, for I'm holding you to it.' She paused on threshold, looking up at him thoughtfully. 'Does it make you happy to be with me?'

A little embarrassed again, Julian thought of evading the question. But if they were ever to become as close as he now hoped they might, he must begin easing her towards it. 'It does. Very happy.'

Maggie's face lit, sending a glow of relief and warmth through him. 'I'm glad. Well, you mustn't keep the boys waiting. Call on us when you get back.'

'I'll do that.'

Julian wished he could press her hand, or even better kiss her, but with his curious boys and now the butler looking on, settled for a bow.

As the landau headed back to St James Square, boys chattering, Julian thought about their excursion—and her.

With his boys approving of her—Ned even ready to recruit her as their mother, the rascal!—he could confidently continue towards whatever the future held for the two of them. A wave of emotion gripped him at the vision of having a complete family, a happy family, a family not marred by the disappointment, guilt and unfulfilled expectations that had soured his former union.

He was almost sure he wanted to have her company, and hers only, in his life permanently. But it was still premature to suggest formalising their companionship into marriage. He'd need to settle his own doubts—and do a lot of convincing to counter hers.

He did have one compelling argument in his arsenal of persuasion, he thought with a grin. Marriage would allow her to indulge in all the kissing she desired, and much more.

Initially he'd felt it wouldn't be fair to think of marriage when he wasn't able to offer that intensity of romantic love such a special lady deserved. But she'd been adamant that she didn't want to experience that sort of love; she might not want to receive it either. After living with a needy, clinging wife, he could appreciate that preference.

Not that what he felt for her was tepid or trivial; with a trace of lingering guilt, he acknowledged he already felt for her a much deeper fondness than he had for his late wife. They were surely more compatible, sharing a multitude of interests. How wonderful it would be to face the future with a partner as enthusiastic about its innovations and changes as he was!

Excited as he was to consider the possibilities, he knew they couldn't fully explore their own relationship until she saw her friends fully settled. But after…he couldn't wait to see where their shared interests and potent desire might take them.

Chapter Fourteen

In the evening a week later, Maggie prepared to leave her chamber, her maid having finished putting the final touches to her gown and coiffeur for the dinner party she and the Countess were giving tonight to help Eliza and Mr Fullridge become better acquainted. Nervousness and excitement flared in her belly with her hopes the meeting would go well—and at the prospect of seeing Atherton again.

Though only a few days had passed since their excursion to the Zoological Gardens, she'd missed conferring with him, soliciting his observations on what was happening and hearing his advice, even when he disagreed with her. She was eager to report to him what had happened at the two balls she'd attended while he was visiting with his sons—entertainments that, as echoed in the lyrics of 'Robin Adair', hadn't been nearly as enjoyable without him to partner her.

Then there had been Lady Laura's wedding to Mr Rochdale, a small affair with just immediate friends and family that she, her mother and Eliza had attended yesterday.

Which had prompted her to mull over again what his son Ned had asked. She briefly considered that Atherton might have mentioned the idea of remarrying to his children, but quickly dismissed it. The Earl was too obviously taken aback and embarrassed to have discussed anything beforehand with the boys.

She'd enjoyed seeing another view of Atherton's caring side. Surrounded by ton gentlemen most often notable— like her father—for ignoring their offspring, she admired his evident love and care for his sons. She'd enjoyed rambling with and teasing his boys, activities that reminded her of her happy childhood roaming Montwell Glen with her brothers. She wouldn't know what to do with a fussy girl child in a starched pinafore, but she could cast a rod, skip a rock or catch frogs happily.

For a moment, she had a vision of herself in that family picture. But remaining close to such appealing youngsters would make caring too much for all of them an even greater risk, raising such alarm she immediately dismissed the pleasant scene. Still, if she were to see Julian over the long term, she'd enjoy occasionally spending time with his sons.

Was he even interested in remarrying? Though he didn't share her distaste for the institution itself, from what he'd revealed about the difficulty of his first marriage, she could understand why he'd felt no inclination to replace the wife he'd lost over six years ago. He'd apparently been satisfied with a series of dalliances, though she'd heard no rumours that he'd found another *chère amie*. Of course, she'd been keeping him rather busy since her return to London.

The idea of him making love to another woman was so distasteful, she immediately pushed it from her mind. But it was unreasonable to expect so virile and vital a man to remain celibate indefinitely.

She'd grown to depend on his escort, his advice, even his scolding and looked forward to seeing him almost daily. A close partnership that would probably cease if he set up a new mistress.

But once Eliza was settled, if Maggie could arrange matters satisfactorily, she might make a bid to replace Mrs Barkley. Add lovers to friendship, and surely he would be hers for a good long time.

But she wouldn't start strategising about that—yet. There was too much to figure out, too many conflicting thoughts and emotions to sort through, and her first priority must remain getting Eliza settled.

Putting all other considerations out of mind, she descended the last stair and went to meet her mother in the salon.

Several hours later, the meal finished and the party adjourned to the parlour, Maggie took a seat on the sofa while Atherton fetched them tea, watching Eliza who was accompanying Mr Fullridge.

Maggie smiled as Atherton handed her a cup and seated himself beside her. 'Thank you for tea—and for your help at dinner in keeping the conversation flowing.'

'Mr Fullridge held his own, but Miss Hasterling had little to say.'

'She can be rather shy, but she seems to be doing better now.' Maggie inclined her head towards the two sitting together, chatting.

Atherton shook a finger at her. 'When I promised to attend, *you* promised that after getting them together, you would let the two of them decide the pace of their relationship. If they chose to have one at all.'

She sighed. 'So I did. It is…hard. I want so much for this to work out for Eliza.'

'Let me divert you from your worries, then. You mentioned that Lady Laura jumped into the parson's mousetrap with her banker yesterday? Did all go well?'

A clever ploy, for she was diverted, as he'd known she would be. 'Very well. They held the ceremony in the parlour in Mount Street, her father giving her away, the vicar from our parish church performing the rites, then had a small reception. Besides Mama, Eliza and me, Mr Rochdale's sister and their parents attended and Mr Ecclesley, a close friend of the groom.'

'Did the couple appear happy?'

'Disgustingly besotted,' she confirmed with a grin. 'She told us she intends to work with her husband on investments, by the way.' Maggie laughed. 'I shall have to ask for their advice so I may increase my holdings. Since I might wish to rent a house myself in the not-too-distant future. After Eliza is settled.'

She thought of hinting again the main reason for which she'd want her own house, but decided, with guests milling around them, it wasn't the time or place.

'Has observing the marital happiness of your friend and your brother softened your harsh view of wedlock?'

She shrugged. 'Perhaps. A little. It's still a terrible risk for a woman, though I'll be the first to admit most females believe marriage their only lot in life. Which is part of my problem. I resist having anyone dictate what my lot in life should be. I want to make my own choice.'

'You don't think Lady Laura made her own choice?'

'She did,' Maggie admitted. 'I only hope and pray it will bring her all the joy she deserves.'

'But you're not convinced yet marriage could ever be for you.'

She gave him a sharp look. Was he asking her out of idle interest—or did he have a particular reason? Could it be important to *him* to know the answer?

The possibility that it might be was intriguing, exciting…but also alarming.

'My stance might be softening somewhat, but I'm not prepared to entertain the idea for myself…not yet. There's a wide world to explore! After our trip to the docks, I'm more than ever excited about the possibilities.'

'Ah, yes. Paris, the Orient, India?'

'Paris for sure. Perhaps India, if James will take me back after he comes home on his next leave.'

As they were finishing tea, her mother stood, announcing to the guests, 'Miss Hasterling has agreed to play for us. I promise, you are in for a treat.'

'Are you willing to take the keyboard after?' Atherton asked.

'You're in the mood to play?'

'When with you, I'm always in the mood to play.'

The heated look he gave her sent a wash of warmth through her, reviving again the desire to kiss him. She wished there were a moonlit terrace they could slip out to—but could she lure him to come with her? When she'd last asked him about kissing, he had firmly pronounced it too dangerous.

But after just making that comment…did he still feel that way?

She wasn't sure how or when, but soon she would put that question to the test. Unfortunately, not tonight.

She had to content herself with sitting beside him on the sofa, his comment sparking an intense consciousness of his nearness, something even the spell of Eliza's music could not entirely mask. Since she couldn't lure him away for kissing, by the time her friend finished playing, she was glad to take the keyboard and occupy her hands and mind with something else.

That frustrated need eased as they played together, performing with him tonight as enjoyable as it had been at the musicale. How pleasant it would be, spending evenings like this, playing for their own amusement and that of their friends.

Even better, if playing of one sort led to playing of another. If, after the guests departed and the music room candles were snuffed, she might lead him to a bedchamber and let him show her all the delights of love she hungered to experience at his hands and lips...

Sighing, she dragged her mind back to the music.

After they finished playing, the party began breaking up. Having bid goodbye to the other guests, Maggie asked Atherton to linger for a final glass of wine while her mother shared one with her friends.

'Now, the evening wasn't too much of a trial, was it?'

'The dinner was excellent.' As she raised her eyebrows at him, he chuckled. 'And yes, the rest of it was not too much of an imposition. But now I want to claim my reward.'

'Ah—the drawings. I do have them finished. Shall I get them for you?'

'Give them to me when I call next, when we have time to sit down, review them together and remember the outing. I don't want to just take them and go.'

'Very well, I'll have them ready then. For now—I know you don't want to become involved, but will you answer if I ask how you thought Eliza and Mr Fullridge did together?'

Atherton gave her a reproving look, but after a moment said, 'Since I agreed to be "obliging", I'll answer—this time. Fullridge seems to be a kind, intelligent, responsible gentleman and I think he's attracted to Miss Hasterling. He seemed more engaged than the lady, who appeared... distracted.'

Maggie frowned, having noted the same thing. 'She's shy

with strangers, so perhaps it will just require a little longer for her to feel comfortable around him. Still… I do worry that Eliza would never marry just for security. She would have to feel a great deal of affection for the gentleman, as well as respect him. Fullridge is older and more sensible, probably willing to settle for respect and companionship.'

'Just because a gentleman is older, he's no less desirous of being admired and valued.'

Atherton's tone seemed so sharp, Maggie looked up at him. 'I imagine we all wish to be admired and valued.'

'Could you allow someone to admire and value you?'

She might not want marriage, but she knew that answer. 'I would very much like to be…admired and valued. In every way.' Reaching over, she pressed his hand, all the contact she dared with her mother and her friends sitting nearby.

The other guests were rising to take their leave. Rising as well, Atherton took her hand and kissed it. 'I'll keep that in mind and bid you goodnight.'

She walked him to the parlour door. 'I'll see you at the Knightly-King ball next week?'

'Yes. I'd invite you to ride in the interim, but I must make a quick trip into Kent. You must save me some dances so we can chat.'

'With pleasure.'

She watched as he walked down the stairs, trying not to let her spirits sink at the news that she wouldn't see him again for a whole week.

Did he want to 'admire and value' her? Was he hinting that he desired the intimacies she craved—or something more?

Her mother came to give her a hug. 'I think that went well. I'm for my bed. Goodnight, darling.'

After bidding her mother goodnight, Maggie walked up to own bedchamber, where Anna helped her into her night rail and brushed out her hair. Once again, though, she bypassed the bed and took a chair by the hearth, too restless to sleep.

She was grateful for Atherton's assistance tonight. Despite his oft-expressed disapproval of her matchmaking plans, he'd participated as fully as she could have wished, displaying a deft hand at keeping the conversation flowing, posing questions that allowed Fullridge to reveal more about himself and even drawing out the too often monosyllabic Eliza. After tonight, she must add 'skilled conversationalist' to the list of his talents.

Her smile at that realisation faded as she considered the implications of their veiled interchanges. Did he hint of marriage? Could he be coaxed into an affair? Or would he prefer to remain merely good friends?

She wasn't sure friendship would be enough. But pushing for more risked pushing him away, and the thought of losing his companionship was intolerable. She didn't want to consider what her life would become without him to tease, entertain, challenge and arouse her.

That realisation almost as frightening as the spectre of marriage, she pushed away the thought, blew out her candle and went to bed.

Chapter Fifteen

$\sim\!\!\sim\!\!\sim\!\!\sim$

A t the Knightley-King ball a week later, Maggie waited anxiously with the Countess while her mother chatted with friends, watching Miss Hasterling dance with Fullridge. With Eliza having asked to leave the ball after this set, she worried that she might not see Atherton at all before she must escort her friend home. Not only was she eager to see him after a week apart, she wanted his advice on what to do about the vexing problem of Lord Stratham.

To her relief, soon after the dance began, she spied his tall form enter the ballroom. He scanned the room to find her, then gave her a nod before walking over to greet his hostess. Eager to salvage as much time as she could with him, Maggie hurried over to claim him the minute he finished exchanging pleasantries.

He raised his eyebrows upon realising she'd come to fetch him. 'So impatient for my company you've come to carry me off? I'm flattered.'

'Don't preen too much,' she said tartly. 'I promised Miss Hasterling we would leave after this dance, and I badly need your opinion.' Relenting a bit, she admitted, 'And I have very much missed your company. A week seemed… a long time.'

His smile softened. 'For me, too,' he murmured, pressing the hand she'd laid on his arm. His gaze lowered to her mouth, making her wonder if he'd thought, as she had upon seeing him, that greeting with a kiss would have been his preference, had they not been in a crowded ballroom.

Breaking the gaze, he led her back near her mother, far enough away that they could talk under cover of the music without being overheard. 'What concerns you so greatly? Miss Hasterling and Mr Fullridge are dancing together. I should think you'd be pleased.'

'And so I am. Except...' She blew out an exasperated breath. 'Stratham was here earlier. He literally swept Eliza away for a waltz while we were chatting with Fullridge, as if he had every right to take precedence! Honestly, I wanted to trip him.'

Atherton chuckled. 'You think doing him an injury would take him out of the running?'

'If only! Bad enough that she ended the dance looking far too starry-eyed, which Fullridge had to have noticed. Then...the *incident* happened.'

'Incident? It couldn't have been as shocking as the public renunciation of an engagement made by a certain young lady at a ball last Season,' he said, obviously trying to tease her out of her agitation.

'It wasn't that dramatic,' she said drily, appreciating his effort but too upset to be so easily soothed. 'When we returned from the refreshment room, Stratham was dancing with Lady Evans.'

Atherton's eyes widened. 'That is a surprise. Her appearances are normally limited to soirees and dinners with the political set.'

Maggie nodded, her unease deepening. 'Indeed. So why did she show up, dance with Stratham and leave immediately after? I suspect she came hunting for him, which must mean his attendance has been less faithful of late. Which leads me to wonder if she and Stratham quarrelled and he has been paying attention to Eliza to arouse her jealousy and lure her back.'

Atherton shrugged. 'It's possible, I suppose. Though Stratham has been at her beck and call for years, he might have finally tired of chasing her.'

'I don't care what games those two play as long as they do not entangle Eliza in them! Now,' she continued, knowing if criticism was to come, this point would bring it on, 'you may think I said too much, but when Eliza asked me who Stratham was dancing with, I didn't just identify her, I warned Eliza that the two had been *chère amies* for ever. I told her I hoped she wasn't developing a *tendre* for a man who has been dangling after another lady for years. She assured me she was not, but as she suddenly claimed a headache and asked to leave immediately after, I'm afraid she *is* developing feelings for him. Which cannot but end in disaster! But I love her too dearly to look at this objectively. If you had a young, vulnerable sister, you would have done the same, wouldn't you?'

Atherton gave her a rueful look. 'True, if I had an innocent sister, I'd be concerned about her receiving particular attention from Stratham, given his long relationship with Lady Evans.'

'Have you heard anything about him breaking things off with her? Not that I'd want him to pursue Eliza, even if he has.'

'No, but I haven't visited my club since returning to London.'

'Will you tell me if you do hear anything?'

Looking troubled, Atherton did not immediately reply. Suddenly realising the dance was in its final figures and she would have to leave soon, she said, 'Please! I understand your dislike of investigating, but I truly do feel the need to protect her. How awful if she is falling under his spell, and he is only toying with her to reignite Lady Evans' interest!'

'I thought in your opinion it would be even worse if his intentions were serious.'

Maggie shuddered. 'You're right, that would be worse. But I can't steer her if I don't know what is going on. Surely you agree it is acceptable to protect an innocent from being deceived into having her heart broken!'

'I agree that innocents should be protected, but it isn't your job is to "steer" Miss Hasterling into a relationship you feel is better. That should be her decision and hers alone.'

'But to make a sensible decision, she needs to know all the facts. Including some we have no other way of discovering.'

'I suppose I can keep an ear tuned,' he said with a sigh and shook his head. 'How you have a way of drawing me ever more deeply into your scheming, despite my continuing opposition to it! Maybe you are bringing *me* under a spell.'

Her heart stuttered. 'Would it be so awful if I were?'

He looked deeply into her eyes, his expression intent. 'No,' he said quietly at last. 'It might be sublime, if it were for the right reason.'

Before she could decide whether to ask what he might think the 'right' reason would be, the dance ended.

'You'll be leaving now with Miss Hasterling?'

'Yes, I'm afraid so. Mama is hosting another dinner soon for Eliza and Fullridge—I hope you'll have information for me before then. When I spoke with Fullridge earlier, I tried to delicately enquire—'

As Atheron made a choking sound, Maggie rapped him with her fan. 'I *was* delicate! I needed to know if he was still interested even after witnessing her...preoccupation with Stratham tonight. I would have cancelled the dinner if he'd said he preferred to bow out. Fortunately, he seemed undeterred.'

When Atherton said nothing, keeping his lips pressed firmly together, Maggie sighed. 'I know you don't approve, but I just want Eliza to be settled, safe and happy. Unfortunately, I must postpone the dance and the card game I'd been counting on partnering with you tonight. Promise me I can claim it at the next function we attend.'

He nodded. 'Once I get estate matters settled, shall we ride again?'

Maggie felt herself flush. 'What a terrible friend I am! I never even enquired if your visit to the estate went well.'

He grinned. 'Belated concern is better than none. There were some disputes among the tenants over the refurbishing of the cottages. Applying some soothing words and bit of diplomacy, I was able to resolve them. Now I must see that the necessary materials are ordered.'

'I expect you are good at diplomacy. You certainly managed conversation at dinner the other night with aplomb.'

He made her a little bow. 'So glad I was pleasing.'

'I can think of another way you could be even more... pleasing.' She looked up, her gaze focused on his lips so he could be in no doubt about what she meant.

He groaned. 'Minx. You'll frustrate us both, pursuing that line of thought.'

'In a ballroom in full view of everyone, perhaps. But later, in the park? By the way, rather than ride, could we take your phaeton? I'd like to try it before ordering one for myself.'

'Please do let me give you some instruction and see how you manage it before you go about ordering one. I'd like to make sure you can drive it without overturning and breaking your neck—or running amok and mowing down all the pedestrians in the park.'

'I'm insulted you have so low an opinion of my skill! I may not have driven a phaeton, but I can manage a gig or a curricle quite well, thank you very much.'

'Very well, we'll take my phaeton,' he conceded, smiling. 'Is the day after tomorrow good for you?'

'I'll consult my diary and let you know if it isn't. Otherwise, shall I call for you at eight, so we might ride before the park fills with visitors?'

'Perfect. By then, you will have visited your club and have news for me, if there is any.'

Atherton gave an elaborate sigh. 'Yes, I suppose.'

She pressed his hand. 'I am very grateful.' She gave him a mischievous smile. 'I only wish I dared show you just how grateful.'

At that moment, Maggie noted Fullridge walking Eliza off the dance floor. 'I shall have to leave now. Will you be staying?'

'I'll go myself after I exchange greetings with some acquaintances.'

'Because the ball won't be very interesting without me to bedevil you?' she dared ask.

He smiled. 'Something like that,' he said, then walked her over to her mother.

'Lord Atherton, lovely to see you!' the Countess said. 'I wish we had time to chat, but I'm afraid we're about to leave. You must come for tea this week, then, and for dinner soon. I'll be having another small gathering of friends in a week or so.'

'With Miss Hasterling and Mr Fullridge?' Atherton said drily. 'So Lady Margaret was telling me.' Eliza and Mr

Fullridge having just reached them, Atherton turned to greet the newcomers.

'I'm sorry, I have a slight headache,' Eliza told him. 'Now you've arrived, I'm sure Lady Margaret would prefer to stay longer.' Turning to Maggie, she added, 'Truly, I don't mind taking a hackney, if you want to remain.'

'Nonsense, I'll not allow you go alone in a hackney this time of night,' Maggie said. 'I'll meet Lord Atherton again soon, so I'm perfectly ready to leave now. Mama?'

'Yes, my dear. Come along, Miss Hasterling. Let's get you home and get a cold compress for that head.'

Under cover of the exchange of farewells, Atherton murmured, 'I'll let you know about the drive.'

'Make it soon,' Maggie said, daring to press his hand again before putting a protective arm around Eliza and leading her out.

She would have liked to stay and have a dance with Atherton—especially if it were a waltz. Where she might feel the warmth of his hands on her body, breathe in the scent of his shaving soap…and dream about greater intimacies. Intimacies for which she increasingly longed. For which, she was increasingly convinced, once Eliza was settled, she must scheme to make happen.

At least she had the drive of his phaeton to look forward to. And maybe there'd be a leafy glade in the park where she could persuade him into another kiss.

Julian watched Lady Comeryn's party walk out, his brow furrowed. Much as he disliked taking any part in Maggie's matchmaking plans, she'd struck home when she pointed out if he had an innocent sister to whom Lord Stratham was paying attention, he would definitely want to know the status of the liaison between the baron and his long-time paramour. No more than Maggie would he want a girl he cared about to become entangled with a man who was toying with her affections to make a mistress jealous—or so amoral about women he could court a maiden with marriage in mind while continuing to carry on with a lover.

He felt a renewed irritation that preoccupation with Eliza Hasterling's problems continued to distress Maggie. And seeing her distressed increased that still-surprising desire to lift burdens from her shoulders and solve any problems that caused a frown to mar her lovely face.

With a grimace, he concluded that meant he would have to make more 'discreet enquiries' at his club. Fortunately, he enjoyed the company of garrulous old Colonel Millhousen, whose chief occupation since his retirement was playing cards at the club and keeping abreast of all the latest Society happenings. If there were any murmurings about Stratham and Lady Evans, Millhousen would surely have heard them.

His thoughts shifted to more pleasant imaginings— Maggie's continued veiled insinuations about ways she might 'please' him, which were surely references to more of the kissing he'd been denying her. Should he continue to deny her, since the lady so persistently indicated that she wanted more?

Since she *was* so persistent—and so deliciously responsive when he did kiss her—that might be the path to softening her resistance to a more permanent relationship in which he could fully satisfy those sensual cravings.

His body stirred and his lips curved into smile at envisioning so pleasurable an outcome.

After all, he told his conscience, it was one thing to kiss an innocent with no care for her reputation. Quite another if he envisioned it could eventually end, as he was increasingly certain it might, with an offer of marriage those kisses could persuade her into accepting…

But not, knowing his strongly resistant Maggie, anytime soon, he concluded with a sigh.

If he wanted to win the ultimate prize, he'd have to be patient and bring her along slowly to the idea of becoming more than friends. Give her time to enjoy the independence she'd suffered so much to gain. He knew instinctively if he pushed too hard or too soon for something permanent, she would retreat. Like coaxing one of the Zoological Society's wild creatures to eat from one's hand, he would have to proceed cautiously until he won her trust, lest he scare her away—or get bitten by rejection.

But the reward, a lifetime with the woman he was coming to believe he didn't want to live without, would be well worth the effort.

Spying a group of Oxford friends entering the card room, Julian walked after them. He wouldn't mind distracting himself from the desire Maggie always aroused with a few hands of cards.

He'd see her again in just a couple of days, giving her a driving lesson in the park.

And maybe figure out how to indulge them both with a kiss.

Chapter Sixteen

Two days later, Julian manoeuvred his phaeton through the busy morning streets to Portman Square, his tiger perched behind. He'd already planned that, after giving Maggie instructions on handling the vehicle, then supervising her attempts to drive, he'd have Henry walk the team while he invited her to stroll along the most deserted pathway he could find. Where, behind an obligingly massive tree, he'd give her the kiss for which she'd been hinting.

His blood heated and his body hardened as he recalled the contours of her lips, the taste of her mouth, the sensual brush of her tongue. If she responded as eagerly as she had before, this time he'd let himself bind her against him so he might feel the whole length of her generous curves along his body while he kissed her, the swell of her breasts, the round of her belly. He intended to go on kissing her until the approach of some potential observer forced him to stop.

But he *would* stop, knowing discretion was imperative. He might be able to use passion to persuade Maggie to start envisioning something permanent between them. But it would be disastrous if their intimacy was discovered too soon.

She'd already told him she instinctively resisted being forced into acting according to Society's norms. Even if she were slowly becoming more amenable to the idea of marriage, being compromised and faced with Society's demand that they marry immediately would almost certainly cause her to reject him.

So he must be exceedingly careful. The pathway he chose would have to be secluded, the tree effectively broad, and he must retain enough presence of mind to break the kiss at the first sound of anyone approaching. Unless he could be sure of keeping his head, he couldn't let himself kiss her at all.

And he was already too fired with anticipation to abandon the idea now.

A few minutes later, he pulled up the team in front of her townhouse, tossed the reins to Henry and paced up the steps. He'd barely exchanged greetings with Viscering when Maggie came tripping down the stairs.

'I was watching for you from the front window,' she announced, giving him a beaming smile.

She wore a deep green habit of military cut whose bodice moulded to her curves and a dashing shako that set off her dark auburn hair and brought out jade highlights in her hazel eyes. Already aroused by thoughts of kissing her, his breath caught and he froze, simply admiring her.

'Like it?' She twirled for his inspection.

'You look enchanting.'

'Hopefully enchanting enough to beguile you into letting me have a nice long drive of your phaeton. I was so excited, I awoke at dawn and have been waiting impatiently ever since.'

As had Julian. Though the kiss he intended to give her *after* the drive inspired most of his impatience. Would she be impatient for it too, if she knew what he'd planned?

He hoped so. It would be a humiliating check to his aspirations if the kiss ended with a quick slap rather than her enthusiastic participation.

After they set off, Julian forced himself to concentrate on driving, trying not to be distracted by her presence—the rose scent wrapping around his head, the warmth of her body on the seat beside him.

It was good practice, he told himself. He'd have to retain some powers of observation if he were going to allow himself to kiss her later.

The park was mostly deserted, as he'd hoped for conducting a lesson in driving a vehicle as tricky as a phaeton. The need to concentrate on driving would also help him rein in his desire. It would be as disastrous as being discovered kissing her if some lack of attention to detail while instructing her ended with her overturning the carriage.

Once inside the park, he pulled up the team. 'As you've already driven a curricle and a gig, you probably know the basic principles. Your hands being smaller than mine, I expect you prefer a two-handed grip on the reins, so I'll demonstrate that. Hold the whip lightly, though you shouldn't need it for this pair, as they are well accustomed to pulling a phaeton. Keep your elbows and hands close to your body and make sure the reins are taut but not too taut—you want to feel horses' mouths.'

She nodded. 'Higgins was very particular about that when he was teaching me to drive. One can injure the horse's mouth with an improper grip as easily as if using the wrong bit.'

'Exactly. Start them off with a walk—once you have the feel of that, go to a slow trot. The pace might seem too tame for a spirited lady like you, but it's best to get a good feel for the way the horses respond before ordering them faster.'

'Their paces so are beautifully matched, it will be a pleasure to drive them.' She gave him a saucy look. 'At least I'm allowed *that* pleasure.'

'Perhaps it won't be the only one,' he replied, smiling as her eyes widened when she caught his meaning. Was she recalling her wish that they might share a kiss in the park?

'Then I shall be doubly attentive, that this lesson concludes quickly—' As if suddenly recalling the tiger on his perch behind them, she continued in a barely audible murmur, 'So we might proceed to…other pleasures.'

'That is my intent,' he murmured back, his pulse speeding at the thought.

Julian proceeded to drive the team several circuits along the north carriage drive, gradually increasing speed from a walk to a slow trot to a hard trot back down to a walk, then showing her how to back the team. 'You could order them to a canter, but I wouldn't unless some emergency required it,' he told her as he brought the equipage once again to a halt.

She nodded. 'Such a fast pace is much too hard on the horses, as well as being dangerous in a vehicle this unstable. Don't worry, I'll save galloping for when I'm on horseback. Sitting so high, it's exhilarating even at a trot. May I take the reins now?'

As he handed them to her, she caught his fingers and stroked them, smiling as she looked up at him. Swallowing hard, his pulse again racing, he felt the throb of arousal through the whole of his body. Then she took the reins from his hand, focused her attention on the horses and gave them the office to start.

Julian sat back, working to steady his erratic breathing. She affected him so strongly with a simple touch, how thrilling it would be to feel those caressing fingers all over his body…if he ever had the right to possess her completely.

Prying his mind free of that beguiling thought, he fixed his attention on observing her as she carefully practised handling the reins. 'It's not so much different from a curricle, other than in the balance,' she observed. 'I can appreciate how easily the carriage could be overturned.'

After Maggie made several circuits on her own at various speeds, she looked over. 'Are you ready to pronounce me competent?'

'For driving in a park empty of traffic. You'll need much more practice before taking the vehicle on a crowded carriage way during the Promenade Hour, much less a city street.'

She wrinkled her nose at his caution. 'But you're confident enough in my abilities to give Russell your endorsement for my ordering a phaeton?'

'If you promise to get to know the horses and their paces and practise driving in the deserted park. Better yet, bring me along to observe while you get used to it.'

After she nodded agreement, he said, 'I think it's time to let the team rest. Shall I hand you down?' he asked, conscious of a dull thrum of anticipation in his blood.

She looked up, her intense gaze meeting his. 'I'm ready for the stroll I suggested.'

So she did remember her comment. Feeling his body heat, he helped her out of the vehicle, instructed Henry to walk the team along the verge and turned to Maggie, offering his arm. 'Shall we?'

The park was still mostly deserted; a few nursemaids strolled with charges in prams, one or two riders trotted by, but he saw no other carriages. He led her off the carriage way, back along the grass verge flanked with tall plane, lime and oak trees until he found one with a suitably broad trunk. After walking her behind it, he paused, gazing in every direction.

No nursemaid or walkers in sight. He waited until the single rider passed them and trotted into the far distance, then turned to Maggie.

Looking up at him, heat and anticipation in her gaze, she murmured, 'Am I given permission, finally?'

'With all my heart.'

'At last,' she said, going up on tiptoe, pulling his head down and kissing him.

He let her trace his lips, then opened to her, exquisite sensation coursing through his body when she stroked his tongue with hers. Wrapping his arms around her, he pulled her close, nestling her against him.

She didn't slap him and pull away—but leaned eagerly into his embrace.

The feel of her breasts against his chest increasing his arousal, he had to restrain himself from sliding his hands down to cup her bottom and pull her against his hardness. He contented himself with stroking her back with one hand while clasping her to him with the other as he met her exploring tongue with his own, deepening the kiss.

It was glorious, wonderful, both gentle and incredibly sensual. In addition to the heady pleasure illuminating his senses, he felt a deeper, even more powerful sweet exultation of spirit, as if his heart literally ached with tenderness.

But knowing how great the stakes were—that discovery could ruin all he now hoped for even more ardently—he kept a small portion of his brain alert while the rest of his mind was lost in the pleasure coursing through him.

As the sound of distant hoofbeats registered in that small sentient part, he ended the kiss, gently released her, then took her limp hand and placed it back on his arm before starting to walk her back to the carriage way.

She halted, perforce halting him, and looked up. Her lips

rosy from his touch were so beguiling it was all he could do, despite the rider bearing down on them, to keep from kissing her again.

'That was…wonderful. Please tell me we will be able to do that again—often.'

He chuckled. 'You've convinced me it's foolish to refrain. We'll do it again as often as it's safe.'

'Then I will pray for safety.'

'I want you to be safe,' he murmured soberly. 'I want you to have the future you envision embarking on once your friend is settled. The ability to realise all your dreams. Your happiness is incredibly important to me, you know.'

She nodded, a glimmer of tears in her eyes. 'I appreciate your understanding more than you can imagine. And your happiness means a great deal to me, too.'

'Then we are well-matched,' he said, heartened by her reply. How could he not be ecstatic at the delight of kissing her! It made him all the more impatient to move on to further intimacy…

But he still must move slowly, he cautioned himself. He sensed her softening to him, but he knew she was not ready yet for the level of commitment he envisioned. Earning her complete trust and confidence would take more time.

'Henry's bringing back the team. Shall we return you home? As we go, you can practise driving again if we take the long way around. Go west by Kensington Gardens, then down Rotten Row.'

'I'd love to.'

The carriage arriving, Julian helped her up, his hands lingering on her waist. She slipped her hand in his when he released her, squeezing his fingers.

'You've offered me one final pleasure—driving another

circuit of the park. Which will make this day perfect when it's hardly begun.'

Julian could agree with that assessment. Nothing could make the day brighter than feeling he was making progress in deepening their intimacy, giving him renewed hope of winning her in the end.

With more kisses to speed them on the way.

She let conversation lapse as she set the carriage in motion, focusing on driving, with an expression of such fierce concentration on her face that he had to smile.

His Maggie. She tackled everything with passion—sketching, driving, kissing.

Ah, how he appreciated the kissing.

They'd turned onto Rotten Row, headed towards the junction where the carriage way approached closest to the edge of the Serpentine, when she gave an exclamation and pulled up the team.

'What's wrong?' Julian asked, looking around for some hazard or obstacle, but seeing nothing.

'Over there,' she murmured, angling with her chin. 'Walking by the Serpentine. Isn't that Eliza—with Lord Stratham?'

Gazing in the direction she indicated, Julian spotted a group of people, including the two she'd mentioned.

'I believe so. Looks like Lords Landsdowne, Carlisle and Althorp with them, with their ladies.'

Maggie frowned. 'Cabinet ministers and their wives are rather elevated company for Eliza. I can't imagine why she is here with them—and *him*.'

'There's a tiger walking a vehicle there with Stratham's crest on the door,' he observed. 'Apparently your friend enjoyed a drive to the park this morning as well.'

'She'd better not have been kissing Stratham,' Maggie

muttered, setting the team in motion again. 'I'd rather she not see me. I'll speak to her later, when I can do so privately. Which reminds me, did you learn anything about Stratham and Lady Evans at your club?'

Maggie had gone tense and troubled, the mood of ease and intimacy destroyed. Annoyed anew that Miss Hasterling's romantic intrigues were affecting their own, Julian said brusquely, 'My informant says Stratham has broken with Lady Evans and she is not happy about it.'

'But what does that mean for Eliza? I don't like either possibility—Stratham singling out Eliza to make Lady Evans jealous, or Stratham pursuing her in earnest. I must talk with her as soon as possible, certainly before our dinner with Fullridge next week. You will come, won't you? I'm doubly in need of your support now.'

In his disgruntlement at having their outing spoiled, Julian was even less inclined to assist in her schemes. But he was never able to turn down her rare requests for help. 'If you need me, of course I'll be there.'

She gave him a quick glance. 'Reluctantly, I know. But it means much to know I can count on you, especially in a matter that distresses me.'

'You know I'd do anything I could to alleviate your distress.'

'My dear Atherton,' she murmured, then turned her attention back to the horses.

It was testament to the intensity of her worry that when asked to relinquish the reins when they reached the park gate, she handed them over without protest. Then remained silent and brooding during the transit back to Portman Square.

Julian handed her down, still frustrated that the glimpse of Miss Hasterling and Lord Stratham had spoiled the warm afterglow of the kiss, arresting his progress in drawing her to him. After promising again to meet at a ball in two days' time, he left her with a bow. Wishing he could have left her with a farewell kiss.

Maybe he ought to abandon his scruples and take a more active role in her schemes to marry off Miss Hasterling, Julian thought as he walked back to his phaeton. The sooner her friend was settled, the sooner he'd have Maggie to himself, free to explore just how far affection and passion might take them.

Chapter Seventeen

Two nights later, Maggie walked with her mother into the ballroom at Montrose House, absently greeting her hostess before following in the Countess's wake to the chairs at the edge of the ballroom. Giddy with anticipation at seeing Atherton again, the sole thought in her mind was discovering whether the townhouse boasted a torchlit terrace off the ballroom where she might meet him later. Ever since that thrilling, bone-melting interlude in the park, all she'd been able to think about was that *kiss*—and how much she wanted to kiss him again.

So mesmerised had she been, reliving over and over the feel of his hardness pressed against her, the taste of his mouth, the incredible sensations that flooded her body as his tongue tangled with hers, even her need to question Eliza about Stratham had lost its urgency.

She'd returned after the drive and written to Eliza asking to call. But when her friend returned a note requesting that they postpone their chat until the Montrose Ball, as she was needed to tend her sister's children, Maggie accepted the delay without protest.

The Maggie of before the kisses wouldn't have been fobbed off so easily. She'd probably have ignored the rebuff and invited herself to share the children's activity, determined to draw her friend away for a private talk.

Instead of interrogating Eliza, she'd been thinking seriously about how to facilitate beginning the affair with Atherton her keenly awakened senses now demanded.

She'd definitely need a house of her own and had begun to make a list of areas to consider: something on a safe street, but not so fashionable that she would likely encounter other members of the ton while coming and going.

She'd also need to investigate an effective means to prevent an unwanted child. She'd decided against trying to pry information about the ton's most exclusive brothels from Crispin; even her broad-minded brother would probably balk at helping her locate a suitable establishment. Nor could an unmarried lady of quality stroll into an apothecary's shop and boldly request the devices she'd overheard the matrons discussing.

Instead, she'd enlisted her maid Anna's help, as a servant could travel to places and make enquiries without attracting the attention that would be given an unmarried lady of quality. Her enterprising maid assured her she'd be happy to find a madame for Maggie to consult as well as discover a source where she could obtain the suitable materials.

So, once Eliza was settled, she would be ready to move on to her next project: seducing Julian Randall.

She couldn't wait to experience the wonder of having him possess her completely.

After greeting her mother's friends, Maggie slipped to the edge of the room, noting with disappointment that the ballroom did not have an adjoining terrace. Her senses, heated to a state of heady anticipation at the possibility of kissing him, settled to a disappointed simmer.

With the possibility of stealing another kiss ruled out for tonight, and knowing Atherton wouldn't appear at the ball until later, the urgency of her need to talk with Eliza resurfaced. Having glanced around to find a suitable alcove where they might have a private chat, she waited impatiently for her friend, turning down several invitations to dance in the interim. Fortunately, Atherton's protective stance had freed her from further annoyance by persistent fortune-hunters, so the several gentlemen who requested her hand took her refusal with good grace and bowed themselves away.

Finally, she spied Eliza's sister, Lady Dunbarton, entering the ballroom. Maggie prepared to hurry to her friend, but Eliza didn't follow her sister in. Frowning, she waited, speculating that some acquaintance had detained her in the hallway.

After several more minutes elapsed without Miss Hasterling appearing, Maggie excused herself to her mother and headed across the ballroom to Lady Dunbarton.

'Lady Margaret, good evening,' Eliza's sister said as Maggie halted beside her. 'How lovely you look.'

'And you, ma'am. I've been anxious to speak with Eliza—did she not accompany you?'

Lady Dunbarton frowned. 'She did not. Indeed, she has been laid up in her bed since yesterday evening. I didn't think anything of it when she returned from the ball several nights ago pleading a headache, for she seemed perfectly fine the next day. Though she assured me when I visited her this afternoon that it was only a return of a headache and would pass, I admit I am…concerned. It's highly unusual for her not to leave her chamber.'

Maggie felt her anxiety increase as well. 'How odd. Eliza is never ill.'

'No, she isn't, which is why I'm worried. If she's not herself by tomorrow, I will insist she allow me to call a physician. My oldest son had a trifling malady last week.

Though she doesn't usually succumb to anything the children suffer, perhaps she contracted it as well.'

'I shall call on her tomorrow.'

Lady Dunbarton shook her head. 'Wait another day. If it's the same thing that Andrew had, it took him three days to fully recover. Whatever it is, I shouldn't want you to contract it, too.'

'I'm disappointed to miss her tonight! I was looking forward to having a good chat between dances. You will give her my best, won't you, and tell her I will call soon?'

Lady Dunbarton nodded. 'I will. Do stop by in three days' time. I know she will be anxious to see you.'

After an exchange of curtseys, Maggie walked back across the ballroom, thoughtful. She was as concerned as Eliza's sister at her friend's sudden indisposition. Having grown up one of the eldest in a large family, Eliza had long ago weathered most of illnesses common to children and often served as the family nurse. Maggie couldn't recall the last time Eliza had sickened with anything.

Pushing away her anxiety and concern, she told herself there was nothing she could do about her second disappointment of the night. Not only would there be no kissing Atherton on the terrace, she'd have to wait several more days before she could quiz Eliza about her trip to the park with Lord Stratham.

Eliza was usually quite practical and down-to-earth. Maggie hoped the flattering attentions of the handsome baron hadn't dazzled her friend into ignoring his longstanding liaison with one of London's most beautiful women.

Distracted and impatient for Atherton's arrival, Maggie returned to where her mother sat chatting with the other matrons, occasionally agreeing to dance with one of the gentlemen she'd known since her debut Season. Finally, late in the evening, she spied the Earl entering the ballroom.

A dizzying excitement filled her as she waited for him to spot her. When he did, the smile he gave her warmed her to her toes as she relived that kiss in the park, momentarily distracted from her worry about Eliza.

He walked over, still smiling, to greet her mother and friends before turning to Maggie.

'Ready for a dance?'

'I'd hoped for something else,' she murmured. 'Alas, this ballroom does not boast a terrace.'

Atherton chuckled. 'Anxious for another drive in the park?'

'I do need to practise with your phaeton before ordering one of my own.'

'That would be prudent,' he agreed, her amusement fading as he studied her face. 'But you seem disturbed. Has something else happened to upset you?'

'Escort me for a glass of wine and I'll tell you about it.'

Atherton bowed, offering Maggie his arm. 'As you command, my lady.' As they walked off, he murmured, 'How can I help?'

Maggie felt a wave of affection and gratitude that Atherton seemed so attuned to her mood and so willing to support her. As their physical entanglement had deepened, so too had their emotional relationship, progressing from the light-hearted teasing of last Season to this deeper, closer connection. Not even with Crispin had she ever felt so in tune with another person, or so supported.

Regardless of whether she achieved her sensual ambitions, she knew she must always keep Atherton in her life. An image of Mrs Barkley's beautiful face flashed before her, causing a momentary chill. How long would she be able to monopolise the attention of such a compelling, dynamic man?

It made her almost physically sick to think of him with another woman—treating her with the tender concern he was showing her tonight. Kissing her as he had kissed Maggie in Hyde Park…

How could she ever bear to lose that?

'What is it?' he repeated, frowning. 'You look suddenly more distressed.'

Pushing aside that alarming, unexpected fear, she refocused on the worry of the moment. 'I am…concerned. But it may be over nothing.'

He walked her to a table in the refreshment room and procured her a glass of wine. Handing it over, he said, 'Tell me.'

'You'll recall we saw Miss Hasterling with Lord Stratham when we drove in the park the other day.' She held up a hand to forestall him commenting. 'Yes, I'd prefer her to fix her interest with Fullridge or someone else more suitable, but I wouldn't stand against her if she truly favours him…despite my severe misgivings!'

'Which I'm sure you've shared with her,' Atherton said drily.

'I certainly intend to! When a friend's lifelong happiness is at stake, it's no time for being timid.'

'I'll refrain from comment on that. What did she reply when you mentioned your concern?'

'That's just it. I haven't been able to yet. I intended to call the day after we saw her in the park, but she put me off. I was supposed to see her tonight, but her sister told me she's been ill, declining to leave her chamber for two days now. Eliza has the hardiest constitution of anyone I know. She's never ill! Even her sister is concerned. Lady Dunbarton asked me to give her another few days to recover, and I'll honour that request, of course, but I'm still…uneasy.'

'You fear she is suffering some serious malady?'

Maggie shook head. 'I don't know. I suppose it's possible, but something…just doesn't seem right.'

'You're probably worrying over nothing. You told me Miss Hasterling often tends her sister's children. As I well know, a child can sicken with something at the drop of hat and quickly pass it along.'

'Perhaps. Strange as it is to say, I almost hope she *is* ill! It's just… I fear there may be something else wrong. Something connected to Lord Stratham.'

'You think he may have snubbed or rejected her?'

Maggie frowned. 'If he did dismiss her after paying her such particular attention, it could well have overset her. I might be overreacting to what is only a trifling illness from which she'll soon recover. But… I still have this uncomfortable feeling I can't seem to shake.'

'I wish I might distract you by enticing you with…something that affects you even more strongly. But there'll be no opportunity for that here.'

'You can't regret the impossibility more than I do,' she replied feelingly.

'Come now, finish your wine. There's nothing more you can do tonight to solve the riddle. Why not assuage your frustration by trouncing some poor unsuspecting player at whist? I'd be happy to assist.'

Maggie blew out a sigh. 'With no moonlit balconies to which we could retreat, it may be the only distraction available.'

'Come along, then.' He tipped up her chin with one finger and despite her anxiety she felt a thrill run through her body. 'Let's head for the card room and cheer you by emptying some hapless opponent's purse.'

'Kissing would be better,' she muttered, setting down her wine glass. 'But I suppose annihilating an opponent will have to do.' Laying her hand on the arm Atherton offered, she let him lead her to the card room.

Three days later, Julian was reviewing account books when his butler brought in a note. Recognising his name written in Maggie's hand, he set aside the ledger. They were to meet tomorrow night at a ball; he wondered what could have prompted this unexpected message. Breaking the seal, he unfolded the note and swiftly scanned it.

> *My dear Atherton,*
> *It's been more than three days, and I am still not able to see Miss Hasterling. I've called twice and been turned away both times. I can't imagine Eliza refusing to see me, even if ill!*
>
> *Her sister said she declined to let her call a physician and that she seems no worse—but no better—than when she first revealed she was indisposed.*
>
> *During my last call this morning, Lady Dunbarton confessed that even she suspects Eliza's withdrawal may stem not from illness, but from some reversal in the matter of suitors. I know how great your distaste is for involving yourself in this matter, but I have no other means of investigating.*
>
> *Please, if you care for my state of mind, could you visit your club, make another discreet enquiry to see if there are any rumours about her involving either Mr Fullridge or Lord Stratham, and call afterwards to let me know what you discover?*

*If you can find it within you to indulge me in this,
I will be in your debt for ever.*

Julian dropped the note on his desk, sighing. On the one hand, he truly did have a 'great distaste' for sticking his nose into the personal—especially romantic—affairs of other individuals, which seemed to him both a breach of decorum and an invasion of privacy. On the other hand, he knew from Maggie's behaviour at the Montrose ball that she was genuinely worried about her friend. Even winning a hefty sum from several opponents had scarcely cheered her.

He glanced at the mantel clock; there was still time to go to his club for a light luncheon. Colonel Millhousen would almost certainly be there, holding court at the card table, ready to share a story about his days in India and report the latest gossip.

'I'll go, but this is the last time,' he muttered to the note on his desk.

Ah, Maggie, he thought as he rose and headed to his chamber to change into appropriate garb for a visit to his club and then a call at Portman Square. *The things I'll do to end your quest and move you on to focusing all that passion on us.*

Several hours later, Julian presented himself in Portman Square. As Viscering announced him, he found Maggie pacing the salon, garbed in pelisse, bonnet in hand, her maid Anna seated by the window working on some stitchery.

She flew to him, dropping a curtsey to his bow. 'Lord Atherton, how good of you to call. I've been pining for a walk in the garden. Won't you accompany me?'

The better to converse without being overheard, he

knew, as her maid would follow at a discreet distance. 'I'd be delighted to escort you.'

They spoke of inconsequential things as they descended the stairs and walked outside. Once they'd paced down the first allée, the maid dropping behind, she said, 'Did you visit your club? Have you discovered anything? I do hope so! I would have disguised myself as a page and gone on my own, but I wasn't sure how to gain admittance—or how to discover the information I sought if I just lurked in corners, unable to direct the conversation.'

'Thank heavens you did not,' Julian said, appalled. 'You'd almost certainly been found out. The resulting scandal would have dwarfed even your public refusal of Tolleridge last Season!'

'Maybe I'd not have been discovered,' she replied, a mischievous look momentarily lightening her worried expression. 'I have had much practice wearing breeches, you'll remember.'

'It's one thing to gallop over a country estate with no one to observe you,' he retorted. 'Quite another to masquerade as a boy in the midst of a group of gentlemen.'

'Oh, pish-tosh, no one takes any notice of servants. I'd have been invisible.'

Julian just looked at her, noting the graceful, hip-swaying walk. 'Perhaps. Unless you did happen to catch someone's attention as you sauntered by. No man would take you for a page or waiter then.'

'Well, I thought better of it, so no harm done. Did you discover anything? Was Fullridge dismissed? Did Stratham cause a scene with her?'

'I had a long chat with Colonel Millhousen and learned more about London scandals than I ever wished to. But he made no mention of Miss Hasterling, Fullridge or Stratham.

If something other than illness is causing her malaise, it either wasn't connected with those gentlemen or occurred so privately that no one else was privy to the incident.' He made her an exaggerated bow. 'So, I've done your bidding, Madame. I hope you are properly appreciative.'

She took his hand, looking up earnestly. 'I am, truly. I have kept my word to not involve you—mostly—haven't I? I wouldn't have asked again if I weren't so worried about her.'

As always, her distress softened his disgruntlement. 'I don't like to see you so worried.'

'I'm not sure what to do now. I'm relieved nothing public is being bandied about…but that doesn't convince me nothing happened. *Something* must be causing Eliza to behave in such an uncharacteristic manner.'

'I don't see what else you can do. There's certainly nothing else I'm prepared to do! Besides, it appears not even her own sister is privy to the reason for her withdrawal, if it is in fact not illness.'

'I shall have to call again. I may just have to invade her bedchamber, if there is no other way to confront her.'

'I really wouldn't advise that,' Julian protested. 'She deserves some privacy, even from well-meaning friends. You can't force her to confide in you.'

'How can I help her if don't know what is troubling her?'

'How can you not respect her feelings? It must be a very sensitive matter if she does not want to share it even with her closest friend.'

'I'll just have to figure out some way to persuade her. I know I can, if I can just *see* her!'

'Can you not leave the poor girl alone?' Julian asked, exasperated by her persistence. 'Heavens! Sometimes you are so intent on forcing things your own way, you remind me of your father.'

He regretted the rash words the instant they left his lips, for she stopped short, recoiling as if he'd slapped her. 'You— you think I'm acting…like *Comeryn*?'

'Sorry! I didn't really mean it like that,' he cried, watching with dismay as she almost visibly retreated from him. 'I know you're just concerned, wanting the best for those you love.'

'If you didn't mean it, you wouldn't have said it,' she muttered.

For a moment, they both stood silent, he trying to figure a way out of the hole he'd just dug himself. Then abruptly, she began pacing back towards the house. 'Thank you for making enquiries at your club. I know it went much against the grain and I do appreciate it. I won't ask again.'

'I'll always do what I can to relieve your anxiety. You know that, don't you?'

He reached for her hand. She snatched it away. In a few more accelerated paces, they reached the stairs at the front entry. 'Obviously, I need to do some reflecting. I think you'd better go now.'

'I'm so sorry, Maggie. I didn't mean to hurt you.'

She gave him a fleeting smile that didn't reach her eyes. 'Thank you for calling, Lord Atherton. I'll give your respects to my mother.'

It was a clear dismissal. Julian fumbled for words, but having so obviously upset her, he couldn't think of anything to say that might redeem himself. Of course he didn't think her as self-absorbed and uncaring as her father, but he couldn't honestly deny he did feel she had intervened in her friend's affairs far more than he thought justified.

Maybe it was better to leave now and come back later to apologise when she was not so upset and angry.

Gritting his teeth, he bowed. 'I'm ever your servant,

Lady Margaret.' With no other choice, he watched her walk up the stairs and disappear back into the house.

Julian cursed his stupidity all the way back to St James Square. *How to woo a lady, Atherton*, he told himself acidly. Want to win her heart? Why, just liken her to the father she detests! True, he'd been exasperated at her persistence, but he shouldn't have let his impatience lead him into blurting out something so hurtful.

Surely he hadn't alienated her completely. They'd grown much closer over the last few weeks. She wouldn't condemn him for a few ill-chosen words. Would she?

A cold sickness settled in the pit of his stomach at the thought of what the future would be like if she did.

He pulled his mind back from the abyss of dismay. He should give her more credit. She might be strong-willed, strong-minded and intent on achieving her aims, but she was intelligent and fair. She knew how much he valued and admired her. Didn't she?

But she did detest and revile her father. To be compared to him would be a punishing blow, especially as, though he'd apologised, he hadn't completely withdrawn his accusation of her being too manipulative.

He shook his head. He hoped the matter of Miss Hasterling would be resolved speedily, alleviating Maggie's concern. In the meantime, he needed to come up with an apology abject enough to recover from that disastrous conversation.

Chapter Eighteen

Dismissing her maid at the entry door, Maggie ran upstairs to her bedchamber, trying to stem the tears that threatened. Retreating to a chair by the hearth, she flung off her pelisse, tore off her bonnet and started pacing the room.

Atherton's accusation touched her on the quick—but it was terribly unfair! Just his overreaction based on his continued objection to being involved in her plans.

Her mind flashed to the memory of her mother at dinner after being harangued by her father, the Countess white-faced and shaking, unable to take another bite as she waited for her husband to finish his meal and leave the table. She recalled her progression from fury to disbelief to an uncertainty edged with fear when she returned from London last Season, was marched into her chamber by her father, the door slammed behind her—and locked from the outside. Leaving her helpless, not knowing how long she would be incarcerated and under what conditions. Knowing with Crispin out of touch and mother unable to countermand her father, no one could assist her.

Why should Atherton not resist intervening? As a man, he couldn't truly appreciate how vulnerable Eliza was, how vulnerable under the law *every* woman was. Like all Englishmen, *his* life and welfare were not completely dependent on who and whether he married.

Maggie just wanted Eliza *safe*, and she wouldn't be unless she had the funds and independence to support herself.

But when she thought of Eliza's lukewarm reaction to the type of marriage Maggie had been championing, her anger faded.

Was she like her father, always pushing people to do what she wanted? She had been leading Eliza rather forcefully to consider Fullridge or some other rich, older commoner, even though her friend insisted she was not as concerned about fortune as she was to wed a gentleman whom she could love and respect, who could give her children.

Probably not a wealthy widower content with the sons he already had, who merely wanted an agreeable companion.

Recalling all the occasions when she'd led Laura and Eliza into dancing and conversing and dining with the prospects she'd put forward, she realised maybe she *had* been pushing too hard, just as Atherton accused.

As anger dissipated, remorse set in. It was horrifying to think she'd acted anything like Comeryn. But she could see how her persistence in trying to marry off her friends to gentlemen *she* thought most suitable might give Atherton that impression.

Might even her *friends* think that of her? Could Eliza be refusing to see her because she feared Maggie would try to force her to make the choice Maggie thought best, one she didn't want? That she'd behave as if she were some superior being who alone possessed the answer to happiness and security, to the point of not listening to or respecting Eliza's feelings?

That *would* make her just like her father, she thought, a sick feeling in the pit of her stomach.

Well, she could change. Maybe Atherton was right about the way forward after all. She'd introduced Eliza to Fullridge and others. Maybe she should back away completely and let her friend make her own choice, without offering any more advice or persuasion.

Very well; she'd not call on Eliza again until her friend invited her. She'd not seek out Fullridge to query him about his intentions or steer any more candidates towards Eliza.

What was she to do with her time, then?

Once Eliza was settled, she had planned to move on to attempting to seduce Atherton. Though he might well no longer want to be enticed by so 'managing' a female, she'd already set in motion a scheme to learn how she might conduct an affair without the risk of conceiving a child.

To conduct such an affair, she'd also need a house of her own. She'd make plans to contact the estate agent again and see what was available.

Safe in a place of her own where Atherton was just a visitor, she could explore the bliss of passion with him… but with limitations. There'd be no long, cosy snuggles in the bedchamber, the expectation of seeing his smile over the breakfast table every morning, watching him read the papers while she sipped her tea, looking forward to playing duets or cards of an evening before returning to that bedchamber.

No chance to become as besotted as her mother had been, losing control of her heart and her life. Something she wasn't willing to risk—even for this man who'd become so dear to her.

So, she'd leave Eliza to her own devices and move forward, the next step her scandalous consultation, then a visit to the estate agent.

The knowledge she'd gain would be enlightening—

whether or not she would ever get the opportunity to use it, she thought, battered by a wave of anguish at the idea of perhaps having alienated Atherton for ever.

Early the following morning, a heavily veiled Maggie walked with her maid several streets away from her home to engage a hackney to take her to an address near Covent Garden which, Anna had discovered, housed one of London's most select brothels.

She didn't know much about how business was conducted there, but assumed most activity would occur in the evenings. Visiting in early morning, she'd be less likely to experience an embarrassing encounter with any gentlemen clients whose identities she'd rather not know, and the working girls would be taking their rest. The owner might be as well, but she would chance that.

She wasn't sure she would be admitted, but she figured curiosity alone might persuade the madame to receive her.

She sat silent during the drive, excitement warring with trepidation at what she might find. She'd heard tales of country maids coming to the city seeking employment being lured away from posting inns by procurers and virtually imprisoned in houses of ill repute. But the most select establishments were unlikely to traffic in unwilling girls, particularly not one accompanied by her maid and obviously well-born enough to have family who could make trouble for a business that abducted her.

Instead, within she might discover the means to allow her to unlock all the secrets of passion for which she yearned.

If Atherton were still susceptible to her. Pushing back the fear of having lost him, a dread that now constantly hovered at the edge of her thoughts, she refocused her mind on the interview ahead.

The hackney pulled up before a well-kept townhouse that looked like any on the prosperous streets of Mayfair. Maggie proceeded to the front door and knocked, Anna following.

The individual who answered wore the usual garb of a butler, though his size and bulk indicated he might have had a prior occupation as a prize fighter. 'I'd like to call on Madame Desirée,' she said, proud her voice didn't wobble as she handed the man her card.

He glanced at it, looked her up and down, then at the maid in her wake. 'This way, ma'am,' he said, ushering her into a nearby salon. 'Wait here. I'll see if Madame can receive you.'

The anteroom was as tastefully furnished as a salon in any respectable home. Elegant, well-chosen furniture, subtle silk wall hangings adorned with handsome landscape paintings, a fire burning on the hearth, the only hint of the activities taking place within the subtle carving of naked cherubs on the marble mantle.

The woman who entered a moment later would not look out of place in a duke's drawing room. Tall, dark-haired, her statuesque figure tastefully displayed in a stylish gown, and no trace on her handsome face of the rouge and lip paint Maggie half expected.

Maggie realised the proprietress was inspecting her as closely as she was her hostess. After making a graceful curtsey, the woman said in a voice with no trace of a lower-class accent, 'Lady Margaret, I'm Desirée Challen. With what can I help you?'

If her establishment catered to the highest in the land, Maggie supposed it was to be expected that the house would be furnished and its ladies dressed and behaved in a manner to which such gentlemen were accustomed.

Returning the curtsey, Maggie said, 'Thank you for receiving me. I wanted to make enquiries about…a situation I think you have expertise on which to advise me.'

Madame Desirée lifted her eyebrows but made no comment. 'Billings, bring us tea? Your maid can wait in the kitchen if you like.' She gave a slight smile. 'No harm will come to her, I assure you.'

'I wouldn't have chosen your establishment if I'd felt there would be any danger,' Maggie said. She nodded to Anna, who followed the burly butler from the room.

'What information do you seek? If you want to enquire whether a certain gentleman is entertained here, I must warn you that I don't divulge any information about our clients.'

'I'm not enquiring about a client. More about the…process.' She faltered a moment, but having come this far, told herself to soldier on. 'There's a gentleman with whom I'd like to establish an…intimate connection, but I don't wish to find myself with child. I've been informed that you are likely to have expertise in ways of preventing that.'

Thankfully, the madame didn't enquire about the particulars of her situation. After regarding her coolly, she said, 'No method is completely foolproof. Short of abstinence. Which I imagine you've already discounted, since you are here.'

'But there are means which are fairly sure, certainly.'

Madame Desirée nodded. 'Successful in most cases— but not all. I advise you, should you choose to proceed with this, that you have a plan in place if protection should fail. Making sure your husband could just as easily be the father, perhaps? Men have the luxury of not worrying about such outcomes, but the consequences for females are much graver.'

There would always be a risk, Maggie realised. After her rocky parting from Atherton, she wasn't even sure she'd ever need the information. But she was determined to gather it.

'I understand. Consequences for most things in life are graver for females than for men.'

'Indeed.' The butler having returned with refreshments, Madame said, 'While we have tea, I'll have Billings fetch some of what you seek.'

Madame murmured some instructions to her henchman before turning to pour Maggie a cup. The servant returned a moment later and handed the item to his employer.

Despite her desire to know everything about passion, Maggie felt a blush warm her face as her hostess held out the French sheath. 'I'm told it's reasonably comfortable, but some men resist wearing one. I recommend having your gentleman don it before you begin your interlude, while heightened desire makes him eager to accommodate you.'

As they sipped tea, Madame went on to describe how to prepare the sheath and how best to apply and remove it. As she listened, nodding her understanding, Maggie felt a sense of detachment at how bizarre this was, a lady of her background conducting such a conversation, in such a place!

She was still amazed and somewhat proud of herself for having the sheer nerve to go through with it. What a splendid accomplishment to venture so far out of what was comfortable and familiar, a reassurance that she could become a woman with the courage and spirit to explore more of the world outside the small, protected corner in which she had always lived.

Madame Desirée was advising her where and how to obtain the best quality of sheaths when there was a commotion at the door. A young girl in a maid's uniform burst in, followed by a scowling Billings. 'Sorry, Madame, I told her you was occupied but she darted past me.'

Madame motioned to him to let the girl alone. 'What is it you want, child?'

Her bravado seemed to desert her then and tears filled her eyes. 'Don't have much choice what to do now. Can't never go home, but…but I can't stand to go back there and suffer *him*.'

'Is you employer abusing you?' Madame guessed, a tremor of anger in her tone.

'Yes, ma'am. When I arrived from Yorkshire a week ago, a lady at the posting inn told me the household was needing another maid. Seemed right as rain when I first arrived, the other staff a little standoffish, maybe, but I thought nothing of it, me being new and all. Then, two nights ago, I was sent upstairs to deliver a bottle of wine to the Master. He took it—then pulled me into his room and despite me fighting him, he…had his way with me. He summoned me again last night, for more of the same. None of the other servants would intervene, just stared at me when I asked for help, like they thought I asked for it. But I never did, I swear! Then I figured, if this is to be my life, I want to have a choice about it. I ran away this morning, asked around and people said this was one of the best houses. If you don't want me for work, I can clean for you. I'm a hard worker, ma'am.'

'Do you want the life, child?' the madame asked gently.

The girl wiped tears away. 'Not really,' she admitted. 'But what else is there for me now?'

'The best courtesans don't merely endure, they take pains

to do their job well. They flirt with and entertain gentlemen—tease, flatter and satisfy them however they wish. Could you do that? My ladies might not have had much choice about pursuing the life, but they are not forced to stay here.'

The girl's face paled. 'Maybe I'd be better as a maid. I'd even work in the scullery.'

Maggie waved a hand at Madame Desirée. 'If I might?'

When the woman nodded, Maggie turned to the girl. 'What did you hope to do in London?'

'I'm right good at cleaning and mending and I can sew anything. I'd hoped to work my way up to being a lady's maid, maybe even a housekeeper someday.' Her eager expression faded. 'Not possible any longer.'

'Maybe it is. My name is Lady Margaret D'Aubignon, and I know a lady who runs a school for young women who have no family or resources. After training them to become shop girls, lady's maids or housekeepers, she finds them employment. A very respectable lady and a very respectable school, I promise you.'

The girl's eyes brightened. 'True as true, ma'am?'

Maggie crossed her heart. 'True as true. Would you like me to take you there?'

The girl looked to the madame, who shrugged. 'I don't need another maid, child. If you'd prefer to remain in a… different sort of service, I'd recommend you accept this lady's offer.'

The girl looked back to Maggie. 'I'd be ever so grateful.'

'Then it's settled.' Maggie stood and curtseyed to Madame Desirée. 'Thank you for your frank advice. I very much appreciate it.'

'You are welcome, Lady Margaret,' the madame said, rising to return Maggie's curtsey. 'If you'll wait here, I'll have Billings fetch your maid and summon you a hackney.'

She paused. 'I admire a woman who takes charge of her life. Few have the courage to do so, even if they have the means and opportunity. I wish you joy of your gentleman.'

She walked towards the door, halting on the threshold to look back at Maggie. 'And it goes without saying, I've never met you and you were never here.'

As Madame disappeared, Maggie turned to the maid. 'May I know your name?'

'Faith Hardwick, Lady Margaret. Where…where are you taking me?'

'To Dean Street, where Mrs Ellie Lattimar runs her school. In addition to classrooms, there's a sleeping dormitory and dining room, with a housekeeper and a cook as well as the teachers. Mrs Lattimar was once forced to become mistress to a titled gentleman. When the man died and her servitude ended, she vowed to use the house he'd left her and the resources she'd earned to help other girls escape a similar fate. She's wed to a respectable gentleman now but continues the work she thinks so important. I'm sure she would help you, too.'

Faith's eyes teared again. 'Sounds like Heaven, ma'am.'

'Have you things you need to fetch from the house where you were employed?'

The girl shook her head violently. 'What I'm wearing will be enough. I'd rather walk down the street naked than ever enter that house again. Unless I could creep in to strangle Lord Tolleridge in his sleep.'

Maggie had been listening sympathetically, but at the name straightened with a start. 'Who did you say?'

'Lord Tolleridge. You…know him?'

Her lips set in a grim line, Maggie nodded. 'We are acquainted. I'd heard rumours that he abused young girls, but they were never confirmed. I'd be delighted to help you escape him.'

A knock sounded, the butler stepping in to announce, 'Your hackney is here, Lady Margaret.'

Maggie turned to the maid. 'Shall we go?'

The girl seized Maggie's hand. 'I shall never forget your kindness, ma'am.'

'You are quite welcome.'

Maggie escorted the girl into the hallway where Anna awaited them, giving fervent thanks to God and Lord Atherton that *she'd* managed to escape Tolleridge.

Later that afternoon, with Faith settled at Mrs Lattimar's school, proclaiming her everlasting gratitude, Maggie returned home. She was sitting before the hearth in her chamber, contemplating in what area she might wish to start investigating properties to let, when Viscering knocked to tell her Lord Atherton had called.

She felt a flutter in her belly at the knowledge of intimate matters she now possessed. Though she wasn't sure yet what she was going to do with it. Before doing anything, she must still wait for Eliza to be settled and find that suitable house.

Not to mention, procure the necessary supplies.

But that was putting the phaeton before the horse. First, she needed to see if her arrogant management of her friends' affairs had given Atherton a permanent disgust of her.

Trying to quell the dismay that possibility evoked, she told herself if he intended to end their association, he wouldn't be calling on her.

She'd find out soon enough. Rejecting the craven desire to delay a bit before facing him, she asked Viscering to inform the Earl that she would join him shortly and rang for Anna to help her into her most flattering afternoon gown.

Despite her misgivings, her spirits rose and warmth expanded in her heart when she walked into the parlour and Atherton rose to greet her. It seemed he had dressed with care, too, for he sported a more formal cravat than the casual knot he usually wore and the expertly cut coat showing off his broad shoulders looked brand new. A prickling awareness raced down her spine and desire spiralled in her stomach as she gazed at his handsome face.

The faint smile he offered further relieved her apprehension. Releasing the breath she hadn't realised she'd been holding, she smiled back, only belatedly noticing the enormous bouquet laid on the table in front of him. Her spirits rebounded even further. If he intended to break with her, he wouldn't have brought her flowers—would he?

'Lady Margaret, thank you for receiving me,' he said, making a deep bow.

She curtsied, then indicated the sofa. 'Won't you have a seat? Viscering, bring tea, please, and have Mrs Johnson put the flowers in a vase. Thank you for the bouquet, Atherton— these are lovely.'

Carrying the wrapped blooms, the butler bowed himself out, while her maid settled on the window seat, occupying herself with some sewing. Maggie took a place on the sofa beside Atherton, acutely conscious of his nearness, the familiar scent of his shaving soap wafting to her and her heart flooding with enormous relief that he was here, sitting beside her.

'I hoped you hadn't—' he began while she said, 'I'm glad that—'

'I'm usually a believer in "ladies first", but in this instance, I ask you to let me speak.'

When she nodded, he continued, 'First, let me offer my sincere apologies for my maladroit statement yesterday. I was completely out of line and inaccurate to boot. I hope you believe that I know you are nothing like your father. If you are forceful about directing your friends to some particular action or person, you do so only out of a fervent desire for their well-being. Not because you feel entitled to order others about or believe the world should conform itself to your wishes.'

She smiled. 'So I realised when I looked more closely at your choice of flowers. Lily-of-the-valley for humility, ivy for affection and fidelity, white carnations and daisies for innocence and pure love.'

'I was careful to consult the florist. There are geranium leaves in there, too—an admission of folly.'

She laughed, her relief that their friendship—and maybe more—was intact making her a little giddy. 'I accept your apology. And offer one of my own. Your accusation was… painful to hear, but it did prompt some honest reflection. I was forced to concede that you were right. Regardless of the purity of my motives, I *have* been too dictatorial in trying to force my friends to accept a type of suitor and a style of marriage that, as events prove, did not appeal to Lady Laura. I fear it doesn't appeal to Miss Hasterling either. I feel terrible that they might think I've cavalierly disregarded their feelings! So I've vowed to take your advice and do no more meddling.'

Atherton's eyes widened. 'Truly?'

Maggie nodded. 'As you've pointed out, I've introduced Eliza to Fullridge and given them several opportunities to become better acquainted. What happens now should be up to them. Nor will I try to find Eliza any other suitors.'

Atherton made a show of looking around the room. 'Where is Lady Margaret and what have you done with her?' Before she could reprove him, he took her hand and kissed it. 'First, I'm humbly thankful that you've forgiven me. I know how hurtful my comment was, and I deeply regret that. Second, I enthusiastically approve this new resolution about Miss Hasterling.'

'I cannot stop being anxious about her, but I accept that it's not my place to direct her actions.' Maggie sighed. 'Much as I'd like to!'

'Maybe you can now focus on what would bring you… the most pleasure.'

The warmth in his eyes sparked the always smouldering desire in her, while her joy at removing the burden of discord between them made her as light as if she were floating. 'I shall still delay implementing my own plans until she is safely settled. But I have been laying the groundwork for something I hope will…delight us both.'

He clasped her hand, his thumb stroking hers from wrist to fingertip, setting off little eddies of pleasure. 'I've plans in that regard, too.'

'Would that I'd thought to have us stroll in the garden, and I'd provide an example,' she murmured, conscious of the maid across the room.

'Were it not pelting down rain, I'd suggest we do so after tea. But I fear we will have to wait for a drier opportunity.'

'I suppose,' she said regretfully after rapidly envisioning and then discarding excuses to take that walk despite the weather. Even faithful Anna would balk at being dragged out for a drenching. 'How very disappointing.'

Viscering returned then with the tea tray, a maid following him to place the vase of flowers on the table beside it. After pouring for herself and Atherton, Maggie said, 'I'm so glad you called so we could make things right between us again. The idea of being estranged from you was intolerable.'

Atherton shuddered. 'The only thing worse was knowing I'd hurt you. I never want to do anything but make you happy and bring you pleasure.'

Recalling the knowledge she'd just gained to take that pleasure to ultimate fulfilment momentarily distracted her. Before her mind could veer off into heated imagining, she jerked those thoughts to a halt. There wouldn't even be kissing today; best not to fantasise about more until she was sure she could make it happen.

'I'm glad you called for another reason. I want to redouble my thanks for you shielding me from the misery of ending up wed to Tolleridge. We've all heard whispers and rumours of his predilection for young girls. This morning, I received proof of it.'

'Proof?' he echoed. 'In what way?'

Certain he would not approve of how she'd happened to meet Faith, Maggie said only, 'I came upon a maid, scarcely older than child and fresh from the country, induced by a lady she met at a posting inn to apply for a position at Tolleridge's house. After she'd been there a week, he started abusing her. I encountered her, frantic, after she'd fled the house and took her to Ellie Lattimar's school. She'll be safe there and taken care of if there are any…consequences from his ravishment.'

Fortunately, the news about Tolleridge was shocking enough that Atherton didn't enquire more particularly into how she'd encountered the maid. 'You say a woman at the posting inn directed the girl to Tolleridge's employ?' he asked after a moment, frowning. 'As I imagine you've guessed, there are, regrettably, professional establishments who cater to men who prefer young girls. But this seems to indicate Tolleridge employs a procuress to work for him personally. The contemptible blackguard!'

'Could he not be prosecuted for…something?'

Looking grim, Atherton pondered her question before shaking his head. 'I wish there were a way, but probably there isn't. If one could locate the procuress, she'd doubtless deny working for him. None of the servants in his house would uphold the story—if they were not needful of keeping their positions, they would have already left his employ. Tolleridge would probably claim he never met the girl. The master of the house having his way with a maid is all too common an event, sadly.'

'Since only powerless females are being abused, no man with the authority to change anything is concerned about it,' Maggie said bitterly.

'That's unfair! No true gentleman would countenance such abuse. But unless Tolleridge actually kidnaps a girl, he's not breaking any law. The maid entered his house voluntarily and all the servants would probably swear she submitted to him willingly, only complaining when she became dissatisfied with her treatment or was dismissed.'

'That's at least one girl he can't abuse any longer. I'm proud I was able to stop him.'

'I wouldn't bandy it about. Tolleridge will probably be infuriated when he discovers he's been robbed of his prey. I wouldn't want him to find out you had a hand in it.'

Maggie shrugged. 'There's not much he can do to me. It's no longer in his power to wed me and he's not daft enough to try to abduct me and exact revenge.'

'Be careful, regardless. Take a stout footman with you as

well as your maid if you venture anywhere. You're welcome to my escort to any entertainment you plan to attend.'

Maggie pressed his hand. 'Mama has asked me to accompany her to several dinners with her friends the next few days, but I plan to make it to Lady Harding's ball. Shall I meet you there?'

'I shall look forward to it.'

'I understand their ballroom gives on to a very fine terrace.'

'My anticipation just doubled,' Atherton said, grinning at her.

Chapter Nineteen

As it turned out, Maggie had another reason almost as compelling as the anticipation of kissing him again to be eager to see Atherton at the Harding ball. After waiting impatiently for him to pay his respects to the hostess, when he reached her, she said, 'Tonight is another occasion upon which I have interesting news to share.'

'Good news this time, I take it,' Atherton said as he walked with her to an adjacent salon where several sofas and groupings of chairs invited guests to linger and chat.

As they settled in chairs near the window, farthest from the other guests, Maggie said, 'Good news, yes, and information that vindicates your advice to me. Miss Hasterling finally asked me to call—and informed me she is engaged. To Lord Stratham.'

Atherton blinked, clearly surprised. 'That is…unexpected. Had you any notion things had progressed that far between them?'

'None. As I came to suspect after your rebuke, Eliza had kept from me almost all the details about her meetings with Stratham. Which, it turns out, were far more numerous than I could have imagined! He *had* broken with Lady Evans, who did appear at the Knightly-King ball to try to entice her former paramour. When whatever inducement she offered didn't bring him back, she devised a plot to destroy his relationship with Eliza. She called on her—'

'She actually called on the girl Stratham was seeing. The audacity of the woman.'

'Indeed. As I was saying, she called on Eliza to inform her she and Stratham were back together, then told her he was to visit her that very night, and invited Eliza to witness it, if she didn't believe her. On the excuse of granting her one parting chat, she'd persuaded Stratham to make that call. Eliza saw him enter her house and assumed Lady Evans had told her the truth—despite Stratham having implied he intended to offer for Eliza. Distraught that she'd fallen for a man who was incapable of fidelity, she shut herself away. Fortunately, at length Stratham insisted on seeing her and they were able to untangle the conspiracy. And so, she's agreed to marry him.'

'That's a tale fit for a Gothic novel!' Atherton exclaimed. 'But all's well that ends well—again. You are happy for her, aren't you?'

'I'm done with trying to guide friends into situations I feel offer them the best chance of happiness and security. It's just as well, since they both ignored my advice and chose quite different solutions.'

'Credit them with the intelligence to know what's best for them and their gentlemen with the intelligence to know the ladies should be valued for the lovely and exceptional women they are.'

'What's this I hear about lovely and exceptional women?'

Maggie looked up to find Mrs Barkley smiling down at them. The unpleasant pang she felt was mirrored in the face of Lord Atherton, who nonetheless rose politely and bowed in greeting. 'Mrs Barkley.'

'Would you mind terribly if I steal your escort for a

dance, Lady Margaret? In honour of our long friendship?'
She sent a look of appeal to Atherton.

Maggie had heard the lady had moved on to several other
admirers; as far as she knew, the woman had not sought
out Atherton at any of last few entertainments they'd all
attended. In any event, whether Mrs Barkley was still interested in reviving their former relationship or not, there
was hardly a polite way for Atherton to refuse.

'I'll claim a dance later,' Maggie said, easing the awkward
moment. 'I must check on my mother anyway.'

She could tell Atherton was irritated, but he said, 'Until
later, Lady Margaret.' Giving the other woman a hostile
look she appeared not to notice, he offered his arm.

Shaking her head in sympathy, Maggie watched them
walk out.

Maggie returned to the ballroom and was easing her way
past the waltzing couples towards her mother when another
matron, also not dancing in the set, tried to squeeze by her.
Swerving to avoid an imminent collision, the other woman
stumbled against her.

'Oh, excuse me, Lady Margaret!' the woman cried.

'No apologies necessary,' Maggie said, offering a steadying hand to help the matron regain her balance.

Not until she started to move away and felt the fabric
pull did she realise the lady had stepped onto her train. She
looked down to find the lace ruffle torn.

The lady, whom she thought she recognised as one of
Lady Bellingame's friends, put her hands to her cheeks with
an expression of dismay. 'I'm so sorry! I must have caught
your hem with my heel. How clumsy of me! Let me send
one of Lady Harding's maids to attend you in the ladies'
withdrawing room.'

Viewing the torn flounce with exasperation, Maggie said, 'Very well. Please do send up that maid.'

'At once, Lady Margaret,' the woman said. 'Again, my apologies.'

Careful not to trip on the trailing hem, Maggie climbed the stairs to the room their hostess had set aside for the use of her female guests. She took a seat, greeting the various ladies who filtered in after the dance finished. As the minutes passed, impatient and wondering when the promised maid might appear, she wished she'd brought a needle and thread in her reticule. By now she could have made the repairs herself. As faint strains of music indicated the next dance beginning, the other ladies hurried out, leaving her alone in the room.

Finally, the door opened, but instead of a maid, Lord Atherton came rushing in.

'Are you all right? How can I help?'

Surprised to see him, she gasped, 'What are you doing here?'

'Mrs Jessup told me she saw you in great distress and suggested I see if I could assist. She told me you'd be waiting upstairs in the second anteroom to the right.'

Maggie laughed. 'I'm always happy to see you, but I'm not in that much distress. Just the small matter of a torn hem. I don't think you'd be much help with that.'

Atherton chuckled. 'You'd be surprised. As a widower with three active sons, I've developed a few seamstress skills.'

He took her by the shoulder and turned her around to inspect the damaged hem. 'Hmm, better wait for the maid. I'm handier at simple trouser hems than lace and ruffles.'

'That said, better for you to leave. This room was designated as the ladies' withdrawing room, you know.'

He started. 'Heavens no, I didn't! And I thought there'd be a maid with you,' he added, as if just noticing there wasn't. 'I'd better scamper.'

Before he could move, the door opened, two matrons walking in. They both stopped short, their eyes widening as they took in Maggie with her torn lace and Atherton standing behind her with his hand on her shoulder. Then they hastily hurried back out, shutting the door behind them.

With an oath, Atherton released her. 'Let me go and see if I can control the damage,' he said, striding out after them.

Everything had happened so quickly, not until he left did Maggie wonder first why Mrs Jessup would have thought she was 'in great distress,' and second why the woman would have asked Atherton to help her—and sent him to this precise location.

Suspicion had begun to harden when Lady Bellingame walked in, a triumphant smile on her lips. 'Well, well. So bad breeding does tell in the end, doesn't it?'

'Would I be correct in assuming that you arranged this little scenario?' Maggie asked, trying to restrain a growing anger. 'Had your friend step on my hem and send me here to wait, then had Mrs Jessup induce Lord Atherton to look here for me? Both particular friends of yours, aren't they?'

'Indeed. But Lady Wentworth and Mrs Armstrong are not. And they saw enough to ensure everyone will soon know just what sort of strumpet you are. My poor brother was telling me again just last night that he still hardly dares show his face at any entertainment this Season, so mortified he remains at the scandal you caused him. How he wished you might know what it feels like to be scorned and humiliated, though he knew such a thing was impossible. That poor, dear man, who took such tender care of me all the years I was growing up! It made me furious to see him so cast down.'

Tolleridge was telling me again last night...

Had he somehow discovered her part in rescuing the maid and used his sister to exact his revenge? Was he that clever?

While her mind raced to make sense of it, Lady Bellingame continued, 'I assured him that it was entirely possible for you to be humiliated. And how easy it was to arrange! You claim you never want to marry, but now you'll have to wed Atherton—if he'll have you—or be completely ruined. And even if you do persuade him to marry you, everyone will know he did so only because he was forced into it. Somehow you emerged after jilting Tolleridge with your reputation intact. Well, you won't this time!'

Turning on her heel, Lady Bellingame left the room.

Shocked, furious, aghast, Maggie stood frozen. How was she to extricate them both from this dilemma?

The rest of the ball passed in a nightmarish haze. The maid did appear, finally, to repair her hem. And as she'd feared, when she returned to the ballroom, an audible hush fell over the room, followed by a tidal wave of murmuring. A number of ladies turned their backs on her as she walked by, several others refusing to meet her gaze.

Worst of all was the hurt and anxiety in her mother's eyes. Lady Comeryn hurried over to meet her and clasped her hand. 'I don't believe a word of it, and neither will anyone who knows you.'

'Unfortunately, what you heard was probably true,' Maggie said bluntly. 'We cannot discuss it here.'

'You want to go home?'

She shrugged. 'As I expect I'll be given the cut direct by

most of the ladies and receive lascivious leers from many of the gentlemen, we might as well.'

At that moment, Atherton appeared at her side, his expression grim. 'You ladies mentioned being ready to leave,' he said, holding out an arm. 'May I escort you?'

Feeling tears threaten, Maggie was on the point of refusing, wanting to brazen it out without involving him, but her mother whispered urgently, 'Please, Maggie?'

Reluctantly, she nodded and placed her hand on Atherton's arm while he offered the other to her mother and walked them out of the ballroom. Thus showing the assembled guests that he did not intend to abandon her.

'I already tried—and failed—to stop the gossip,' he murmured in her ear. 'We can't accomplish anything useful tonight.'

She let him lead them down the stairs and stand guard while their carriage was brought round. 'Ride with me tomorrow?' he asked as they waited. 'We'll sort this out.'

Much as she felt an urgent need to do something immediately, Maggie knew she should take time to figure out the best response. 'I'd like to start by strangling Lady Bellingame, but I suppose that's out of the question.'

'Sadly, yes. I'll see you tomorrow morning?'

'Tomorrow,' she agreed.

Her mother pressed Atherton's hand and whispered her thanks as he helped her into the carriage. 'Get some sleep,' he murmured to Maggie as he handed her in. 'Things will look better in the morning.'

Then he shut the door and waved for the coachman to depart.

Maggie hoped in the morning light circumstances might look brighter. But she expected a long night of serious reflection ahead and little sleep before morning.

Chapter Twenty

A good while before he could reasonably expect Maggie to be up and ready, Julian arrived at Portman Square for the promised ride, too agitated and worried to stay away. He'd not followed his own advice to sleep soundly, tossing and turning as he tried to figure out the best response to their dilemma. For despite his optimistic parting words, he was by no means sure there would be a happy outcome to the predicament in which they found themselves.

As he tooled his mount around the square, delaying until he thought it late enough to present himself, he reflected that it wasn't the inevitable outcome of the situation that angered him—after all, even before the disaster at the ball, he'd all but decided to propose to Maggie—but the uncomfortable circumstances that would force their union.

He wished now that he'd been more forthcoming about his intentions. Yes, he'd hinted at his growing desire to marry, but never clearly spelled it out, so that she might well have interpreted his comments as a desire for further intimacy rather than a formal and permanent union.

Of course, he'd not mentioned anything because he was nearly certain that a premature proposal would have been refused. Having his hand forced meant he wouldn't now be able to allow her to revel in her independence, while he worked towards dissipating her reluctance to wed and nurturing her affection and the passion they shared into trusting him enough to allow him to share her future.

How would she react to the box they'd been trapped in? Her barely restrained fury last night didn't bode well. To his consternation, in her anger she'd nearly declined the gesture of support he offered, needing her mother's urging to accept it.

The worst possible way to begin a marriage would be with Maggie angry and resentful at having been forced into it. How would he be able to resurrect the easy comradery they'd shared, when every minute she would be regretting the independence that had been stolen from her?

Just thinking of that possibility made *him* wish to strangle Lady Bellingame.

He'd just finished his second circuit of the square when Maggie surprised him by appearing at her front door. 'Meet me at the stables,' she called before disappearing back inside.

Anxiety swirling in his gut, Julian guided his mount towards the mews.

He found her mounted and ready, and with her groom Higgins trailing, they rode in silence to Hyde Park, a pale dawn sun showing promise of a clear warm day to come. Would it be clear and warm for him? Or soon clouded over by her anger, resentment and grief?

'Shall we have a gallop first?' she asked after they'd entered the park. 'I could use something fast and wild and free.'

His heart sinking at those unpromising words, Julian said, 'Of course. After you.'

She dug in her heels, setting her gelding off in a flash. He urged his mount after hers, the horse having difficulty keeping up, so brutal a pace she set. But, fast as Midnight was, Julian knew her mount couldn't sustain such speed for long. And no matter how upset she was, Maggie was too good a horsewoman to push the horse beyond his limit.

At length the horses slowed. Still silent, Maggie signalled her mount to a walk, Julian bringing his horse alongside. After a few moments, she pulled up and abruptly dismounted, holding out the reins to her groom, who trotted up to take them.

'Walk with me?' she asked Julian.

'Of course.' Jumping from his own saddle, he handed off his reins and caught up with her as she set off at a spanking pace.

'It was Tolleridge, you know,' she said at last. 'His sister arranged the debacle, but the night after Faith's rescue, he suddenly urged her to find a way to embarrass me. He must have found out I'd intervened to help his maid escape him.'

'How could he have known that?'

She shrugged. 'Obviously, he had a procuress on payroll who trolled the posting inns, looking for new victims. He might well have had someone else on staff to monitor the girls who were lured in. To prevent their escape at first, then turn them off when he was done with them. I can't believe Faith was the first maid he debauched, nor is it reasonable that no one else in his household knew what was going on. Perhaps they followed her and saw me taking her to Mrs Lattimar's. His revenge, to induce the sister who never liked me to trap me in an even bigger scandal than the one of our repudiated engagement.'

'How ever she got the idea, Lady Bellingame cast a wide net with her scheme,' he informed her. 'After you left last night, I tracked down Mrs Barkley. After some pointed questioning, I induced her to admit that Lady Bellingame had recruited her to distract me, promising her she'd devised a plan that would discredit you so thoroughly that I would repudiate you—and leave the field open for her. Something I swiftly assured her would never happen, so she'd tarnished her honour to ruin an innocent for no good purpose.'

She turned to face him, steely resolve in her eyes. 'Fortunately, I have no intention of letting this ploy succeed. Eliza will be settled by her own choice with a man not associated with me. I'm very sorry for the embarrassment it will cause Mama, but her position is well established and she will weather this, once I am no longer around to remind the gossips.'

'"No longer around"?' he echoed, confused. 'Maggie, surely you see that, unfortunate as the situation is, we must marry. Otherwise, your reputation—and mine—will be ruined.'

She shrugged. 'As I once told you, a female who doesn't care about marriage has no need of a reputation. It will be an advantage, actually, that no one in Society will take notice of me any longer. I had already planned to look for my own house—this situation just accelerates that process. And once I have a place of my own…' She looked up at him, her certitude wavering a bit. 'I'm hoping that you will be happy to…visit me.'

He stared at her for a moment. 'Are you saying…you don't want to marry me, but you'll take me as your lover?'

Her face flushing a bit, she nodded. 'I want to experience passion—not just kissing, but everything that follows. I want it with you, Julian. I *yearn* for it. I… I hope you want me, too.'

'I do want you,' he said roughly, anxiety, confusion and dismay making it hard to think clearly. 'But we can experience all that you crave—more easily and permanently— once you become my wife.'

She sighed and shook her head. 'As I told you before, if I were tempted to marry, you would be the first, the only man I would consider. But even were I ready to give up my independence—which I am not—I would never marry because some venal man or rule-bound Society tried to compel me!'

It was just as he feared—though she might be softening towards making a commitment to him, being pushed to conform to Society's rules virtually guaranteed she would fight back.

'What if we weren't forced? What if I ask you to marry me because I want to? Because I've discovered you are the perfect companion with whom I want to share my life?' he asked, for the first time fully revealing his intentions.

Her eyes widened with shock, and something that looked like joy lit her face. Then it faded and she looked away. 'It's good of you to try to dress up your offer in promises of commitment, rather than simply acknowledge that Society's rules require our marriage. But you've long maintained that you have no desire to remarry.'

'I admit that was true—until recently. As you already know, my previous marriage was…stifling. My wife's almost slavish devotion, her constant efforts to try to win a corresponding depth of feeling from me became like an iron weight bearing down on my chest, an obligation I didn't want and couldn't meet. But you're nothing like her—so independent, so insistent on standing on your own, hardly ever letting anyone share your burdens, much less shoulder them. Talented, intelligent, challenging, deeply desirable—how could I not help wanting to be with you? We've become the best of companions. We could become even better lovers. You know I would never hem you in or restrain you. Why should we not make our harmony permanent?'

She stared at him, uncertain, as if she were weighing whether or not to believe him. As he read in her eyes how she wavered, hope filled him that he might win her after all. 'Marry me, Maggie. Not because you have to. Because you want to. You do care for me, don't you?'

He held his breath, pinning her gaze with the intensity of his own.

Some emotion curiously like fear crossing her face, she looked away. And he knew he'd lost her.

'I do care for you, but I can't marry you, Julian. Oh, I know you're not my father, but I've only just begun to experience what it means to be *free*. Can't you appreciate that and be part of that freedom…as my lover? If you want me as much as I want you, come to me, once I have a house for us.'

Much as he did want her, Julian knew in that moment that a mere physical relationship wouldn't be enough. He wanted more than furtive interludes, hiding from everyone he knew. He wanted a bond he could announce from the rooftops and proudly display to the world.

Desolation beginning to trickle through him, he offered his one last argument.

'I can't be just your lover. For one, I wouldn't want to risk getting you with child out of wedlock. And it's not only your reputation ruined if we don't marry. It affects my honour, too.'

She waved her hand. 'Gossips will say you had a lucky escape.'

'Those who know your character will say I'm a cad who compromised a lady of quality and refused to marry her. You know few in Society will truly believe that under the circumstances, you were offered marriage and refused it, despite your previous insistence on not wanting to wed. I've lived my whole life maintaining a sterling character that reflects well on my family and heritage. If my name is tarnished, the dishonour will pass on to my sons. How can I leave them such a legacy?'

'You would force us into marriage to save your sons embarrassment?'

'I would wed you because I want to marry you,' he said, trying one more time to reach her.

Suddenly she picked up the pace, and he had to accelerate to catch up. After striding along silently for a while, she said, 'Very well, I won't take a house in London. I can see how…awkward that would be for you, especially with your sons growing up surrounded by classmates who would be sure to tease them about the scandal. I've always wanted to travel. I should leave quickly, so there isn't time to arrange things with James to come to India, but I could go to Paris. With me no longer in England, Society would soon forget about the scandal and your life could return to normal.'

His life become *normal*…without her? Having her leave was an even bleaker prospect than having her remain in London unmarried and ruined.

'Please!' She held up a hand when he would have spoken again. 'Let's not argue any more. If you cannot reconcile it with your honour to have an affair with me, I accept that. But neither will I be forced into marriage, not by Society, not by you. I'm sorry I can't resolve this to your satisfaction. We'd better go back now. I have a great number of plans to make, and quickly. The sooner I leave London, the better for Mama and—and everyone.'

'Not for me,' he said quietly, not sure she heard him as she paced over and motioned for the groom to give her a leg up.

She was right. He couldn't force her. He didn't want to force her. He'd hoped so badly that she'd choose him. The agony of it was, he was almost certain that given enough time, if Lady Bellingame's scheme hadn't forced his hand, he might have persuaded her the joy of sharing a life with him would be worth whatever limits marriage might place on her freedom.

Surely she didn't fear he would try to control her as her father had done…if that had been fear he'd seen on her face.

But he couldn't keep her in London if she were determined to leave.

Heartsick and, for the moment, out of arguments, he mounted his gelding and rode after her.

Two days later, Maggie stood in her chamber, directing Anna which gowns to pack into chests for transport to France. With the advice of several individuals who'd recently returned from Paris, she'd written ahead for accommodations and hoped to leave within the week. She'd purchased every guidebook Hatchard's possessed, studying plans of the city and contemplating where to reside once she arrived in the capital. She wasn't sure how long she might tarry while she sketched its monuments and boulevards and visited the most fashionable modistes. Perhaps she'd remain at the hotel, but she might well let a townhouse. On the Left Bank, perhaps, near the Jardin de Luxembourg.

Maybe she would travel on afterward to Greece or Italy. Visit and sketch ruins like those that had inspired the beautiful temple Sir John Sloane had constructed on the exterior of the Bank of England. The one Atherton had taken her to see.

Atherton. The spirits she'd determinedly been trying to raise sank again. The excitement and anticipation she'd always felt when imagining travelling to foreign places had vanished at knowing that she wouldn't be able to share the experience with him, not even by letter.

She knew without his having to confirm it that her leaving England would end any chance of continuing a relationship between them. As she'd been doing ever since their ride in the park, she pushed the pain and regret of losing him away.

She'd been so close, within a breath of accepting his proposal. Until she looked into his eyes as he asked if she *cared* for him—and realised in that blazing instant that she didn't just enjoy his company and desire him. She wanted him, all of him, always. Despite all her caution, all her vows to resist the emotion, she'd fallen in love with him.

The horror and fear engulfing her at that realisation had made her want to flee from the park as fast as her horse could carry her.

So she was doing the next best thing—fleeing England. Surely if she stayed away long enough, pursued her other interests with enough determination, she would eventually carve out of her heart this ravening beast of emotion that roared at her to return to him, love him, turn her life over to him.

True, he'd assured her he wanted to marry her. She knew he desired her. But knowing her heart would be overflowing with a need to be with him, to occupy his thoughts and monopolise his time—a compulsion nearly as extreme as that which his unlamented late wife had tormented him—how soon would that willingness be extinguished by her need?

He didn't feel himself capable of love and never wanted to receive it from a woman again. She couldn't burden him with hers.

Bad enough she herself had contracted the malady to which she'd always promised herself she'd be immune.

Now she needed to figure out how to survive succumbing to it.

She would put Julian out of her mind, until she was far away and unable to give in to the temptation to seek him out. Until the agony had eased enough to be bearable.

A knock at the door halted her pained reflections. To her surprise, a moment later her mother walked in, took one look at her and pulled her into a hug.

'Must you really go?' she asked softly.

'It will be better for all concerned, Mama. I'm…so sorry for the scandal.'

Her mother waved a hand. 'That's nothing compared to how terrible I feel. All this is my fault. If I'd managed your father better…if we had ended up being happier…you wouldn't have set your face against love and marriage as you have.'

'Oh, Mama, you mustn't blame yourself for any of this!'

'But I do. So much so that, though I have no right to ask anything of you, I ask this. Will you not wait a while longer before leaving? Atherton is a good man. I think the two of you could be happy together. Please, don't throw away that chance because my experience has led you to believe no marriage can succeed.'

'Oh, Mama, it's not just that. I'm afraid… I love him. And he doesn't love me—oh, he likes me, I know. But I've seen what happens when one partner is in love and the other isn't. I don't want to do that to him…or to me. I don't want to be forever pining for something I cannot have.'

'What you believe may be true—although seeing him with you, I can't believe he doesn't feel just as deeply for you, though he may not realise it. At least see him one more time before you leave, won't you? I'd hate for you to sacrifice what could bring you joy out of fear. You're stronger than that, Maggie, my dearest girl. Well, I've pleaded my case. I'll leave you to reflect.'

* * *

After her mother departed, Maggie returned to her prep-
arations, trying to put out of mind the temptation to see
Atherton again. As she opened her stationary drawer to
pack her supplies, on top of the stack of vellum were the
sketches of Atherton's sons she'd made during their excursion to the Zoological Gardens—another lifetime ago, it
seemed. She'd already given the finished pastel drawings
to Atherton, who'd had them framed to hang over the desk
in his library, where he could see them daily, he'd told her.

She smiled wistfully down at them. Stephen, the eldest
who so closely resembled his father. Who was so responsible about looking after his younger siblings. Mark, running
excitedly from one enclosure to the next. Ned, the feisty
youngest, enamoured of bears and creatures that roared.

She remembered how, for a brief moment, she'd envisioned being part of this family.

The smile faded as she recalled Atherton asserting that
his abandoning a woman he'd compromised would tar-
nish his family name, a disgrace that would linger to af-
fect his sons.

She looked at the sketches. Could she condemn innocent
boys to live down scandal, just because she wanted the independence and freedom to live on her own terms? Because
she was too cowardly to admit she loved their father, too
afraid to allow herself to be vulnerable to the finest man
she'd ever met? She thought herself capable of meeting the
challenge of travelling in the unknown, but couldn't face
navigating her familiar world because she couldn't be sure
what the future might hold?

Knowing she loved him, could she continue on her own
selfish course—once again trying to arrange the world to
suit her own wishes despite the desires of the people she

264 A Season with Her Forbidden Earl

loved, as her father had always done? Leave England, and be the cause of Atherton's disgrace, the origin of the stain on his name and honour? Maybe leaving his heart hurting with some of the same pain she felt?

Should she not instead stay and marry him, whether he loved her or not? Give up the struggle to be completely in control of her own life, and do what was best for him, which without question would be to safeguard his sons, his honour and his reputation.

There were no guarantees of happiness, but they did share so much. Wasn't there just as much chance of creating a joyous and fulfilling life with him as there was that the union might prove a failure? An even better chance, for Atherton was a far better man than her father. He might not love her, but he'd vowed that he wanted her always to be happy.

Maybe they could be…if she had the courage to choose that path.

She sat for a long time gazing at the sketches, irresolute. Finally, a calm resolve filled her.

If she truly loved him, she must give up her freedom for his honour. She'd deal with the suffocating trap of wedlock as best she could and face up to the cost of leaving herself vulnerable to being hurt. After all, she would be able to experience passion to the fullest, which would be no small compensation.

Pulling out a sheet of vellum, Maggie wrote Atherton requesting him to visit at his earliest convenience.

A few hours later, Viscering interrupted her nervous pacing of the salon to announce that Lord Atherton had called. 'I'll walk with him in the garden,' she told the butler.

Already garbed in her pelisse, she hurried to the mirror to tie the bonnet ribbons under her chin and followed Viscering, relieved that Atherton had answered her summons—she'd been half afraid he might refuse to see her.

'Shall I send for Anna?' the butler asked.

'No,' she replied, earning the lift of an eyebrow from Viscering, who in the way of long-time servants, probably guessed how things stood.

'May I offer congratulations, my lady?' he murmured as they reached the foyer.

'I hope so,' she replied before turning to Atherton. 'Thank you for coming so promptly,' she said, putting her hand on the arm he offered and walking out.

'Actually, I was about to call when I got your note,' he said as they descended the stairs and headed for the garden.

Surprised, she looked up at him. 'To renew your arguments?'

'No. To tell you I'd like to accompany you to Paris. As your friend, your lover—or whatever you want me to be.'

She was so shocked, she stopped short. 'Come with me to Paris? But…but what of your concern for your reputation?'

He shrugged. 'Possessing a sterling reputation would be cold compensation for not having your passion and beauty and wit in my life. And I must apologise.'

'Apologise? For what?'

'For offering you such a reasoned and unemotional proposal. I thought for years I was incapable of romantic love. Well, maybe I'm not—at least, not of the sort of *coup de foudre*, love at first sight about which poets sing. But after you'd told me you intended to leave England and I thought what it would mean if I were never to see you again, really examined what my life would be like without you, I realised—it would be unendurable. Love may have crept up on me rather than arriving in a sudden blinding light, but I know now that I love you with all the intensity and passion any poet could wish. Living without you would be a cheerless, grim existence. You shine the light of your intellect and enthusiasm over everything you touch—even if you are a bit managing at times. I know I'm not responsible for assuring your happiness—you are the sole architect of your own destiny. I want more than anything to share that destiny and help you realise your dreams. Accompany you to Paris, maybe to India. Teach you every nuance of passion, as I've dreamed of doing practically since the moment we met.'

'But…but what of the harm it will do your reputation when it's known you accompanied me without benefit of clergy? To the legacy you leave your sons?'

Atherton shrugged. 'By the time they are men grown, our shocking behaviour will be ancient history. Besides, they might think it dashing that their stodgy old father was once involved in a notorious scandal.'

'So…you'd give up everything here for me? You truly love me?'

'I do. I probably have from the first, if I'd only had wit enough to recognise it. I want you in my life, in my bed, teasing me, challenging me to expand my horizons and question my assumptions. Making me *more*. Cherishing you,' he added softly.

The tenderness in his eyes melted the last of her reserve, sending a joyous thrill bubbling up. 'Then… I will marry you. I've been holding on to old assumptions too. I don't suppose I'll ever overcome my fear about the powerlessness of a wife under law, but you are not my father. As afraid as I am to be so vulnerable, I am going to trust that the care and concern with which you've always treated me will not lessen over the years. I want you in my life and my bed, too, and I don't want you to have to sacrifice your honour to have that.'

He halted again, staring down at her. 'Does that mean…
you love me too?'

She stamped her foot. 'What do you think I'm trying to
tell you, foolish man? Yes, I l—'

Her avowal was cut off as Atherton seized her and bound
her against him, kissing her with all the passion of a man
rediscovering paradise after fearing he'd lost it for ever.

Sharing that feeling, she kissed him back with equal fer-
vour.

They clung to each other, their initial frenzy easing as
relief gave way to a slower more sensual exploration of
mouth, lips and tongue. Julian paused the kiss to trail his
lips down her neck and up again to nibble the shell of her
ear before taking her mouth again, while one hand slid from
her shoulders to caress the edge of her breast, buried under
far too many layers of pelisse, gown and shift.

At last they paused, he still holding her tight against
him, where she could feel his rapid heartbeat and the thrilling hardness of his desire pressed against the softness of
her belly.

'Marry me, Maggie?'

'I will.'

'At once?'

'Get a special licence. Since, stodgy man that you are,
I doubt I can convince you to make passionate love to me
until after our nuptials are properly recorded in the parish
register.' She sighed. 'I do hate that Lady Bellingame and
Tolleridge will feel they've forced us into this.'

'We can avoid that if you like. Leave for Paris together
with as much scandalous fanfare as you please. Wed after
we arrive there.'

'Outrage Society and confound Lady Bellingame just a
little? Don't tempt me.'

'You tempt me. Every day, every minute.'

'Do I?'

The sound he made was half-laugh, half-groan. 'You don't know how much you strain my control. How close I came to losing it on several occasions.'

'Good,' she said, pleased. 'So it would only require a bit more of a push for you to lose it entirely?'

Atherton sighed. 'I'd better take you inside and head to the Archbishop's to apply for that special licence.' He took her arm again to walk her away, then halted.

'You do mean it? You will marry me, won't you, Maggie?'

She leaned up to give him another lingering kiss. 'I will never *not* marry you, Julian Randall. Let's go begin our new life…together.'

Beaming, she tightened her grip on his arm and led him towards their future.

* * * * *

If you loved this story,
make sure to catch up with the previous books in
Julia Justiss's Least Likely to Wed miniseries

A Season of Flirtation
The Wallflower's Last Chance Season

And when you're all caught up,
why not pick up her Heirs in Waiting miniseries?

The Bluestocking Duchess
The Railway Countess
The Explorer Baroness

HARLEQUIN
Reader Service

Enjoyed your book?

Try the perfect subscription for Romance readers and get more great books like this delivered right to your door.

See why over 10+ million readers have tried Harlequin Reader Service.

Start with a Free Welcome Collection with free books and a gift—valued over $20.

Choose any series in print or ebook.
See website for details and order today:

TryReaderService.com/subscriptions